Memoir of a Martian

A Perceptions Novel

David Parker-Ross

Tairis Anders Media, LLC

COPYRIGHT

CONTENTS

ALSO BY DAVID PARKER-ROSS

All Titles Available on Audio

Perceptions – The Rise of Jenna Plural
Jenna Plural Wants You
That Girl from Wagga
Walking in Her Shadow
Awakening of Hannah Grant
The Angel of Phobos
Memoir of a Martian (Out November 2023)
The Cult of Artemis Baily
The Rise of Artemis: The Golden Age Edition
The Amazon Chronicles
Miss Eve and the City of Men

DEDICATION

For Jason Byrne

Jason, you have become one of my dearest friends. Your constant support for my work always gets me out of a funk when I feel negative. Our lunch times at Arby's discussing our mutual interesting writing Is one of the ,ost enjoyable activities I engage in. You are a phenomenal writer and potentially one of the Greats. And now it's time for you to get it out there for the world to see.

Meanwhile, you will also be pleased to see there are a lot of appearances by your favorite character, Charlotte Kensett, in this tale.

Thanks for always being there for me, and remember, I am always here for you.

David

Author's Note

Perceptions is a series that tells tales from different characters' perspectives. Each has their own ideas, their own values, their own beliefs, and their own memories.

The characters, including the narrator, have their own perception of the events that took place at the time of the stories. They may very well have political and social opinions. Those opinions do not necessarily reflect those of this author. Indeed I have very much tried to keep my personal opinions out of the story.

The whole idea is to leave it to you, the reader, to make up your own mind on the rights and wrongs of the characters within the tales.

Memory is a fickle beast; not everyone will remember events the same way. One should not assume that the narrator is being either accurate or even truthful.

Perceptions... It's all about who you believe.

David Parker-Ross

Leesburg, VA, USA

Memoir of a Martian

By Kyla Lieberman

Introduction

I may sound like a New York girl, but I'm not. I am a Brooklyn girl, however. But that would be New Brooklyn in the Terra Maridani plateau of Mars.

I've never considered myself an American, although technically, I am, or rather was when the USA existed as a nation free from European domination. Ancestrally, my family hailed from New York several hundred years ago. It's been at least four or five generations since we moved to the Martian Colonies.

Mars was a multi-national planet with colonies from almost every country on Earth that could afford to send a ship into space. European and Alliance worked together to create a new haven on a desolate world, and soon, enough time had passed that Mars became known as 'The Second Cradle of Humanity.' When the events took place in this book, the planet's population was almost four hundred and twenty million. Of course, that would drastically change in the years that passed.

My Martian patriotism is kind of ironic, considering that my family didn't come here initially of their own free will. With a population of almost a billion, America was busting at the seams, and as resources dwindled, Martian resettlement became a solution. However, when my great-great-great... whatever ...grandparents came, Mars was not the thriving planet it is now.

It was a hard life when technology could barely keep people alive, and colonies had little resources as they struggled to develop the dead world into the expansionist dreams of the politicians back home.

Initially, the government gave great incentives for people to move there voluntarily. Large sums of money were offered, but as it turned out, at least back then, it didn't matter how much money you had. It wasn't like you could buy a lakefront property on Olympus Mons. People quickly realized this, and the volunteers stopped coming.

Soon, compulsory resettlement was introduced. A national lottery targeted the most overpopulated areas, and the City of New York was top of that list. Around fifty thousand names came up on the register every year, and that was that. You were going to Mars, like it or not.

The lottery was supposed to be extremely random. But when a series of natural disasters plunged America into a new depression, Brooklyn, NY, one of the largest Jewish communities in America, suddenly found most of its residents on one of the lists. Some thought it was no coincidence. Claims of antisemitism were made, and while I have no idea if that was the case, we, meaning my forebearers, resisted, and it got ugly for a while.

Terra Maridani was a newly constructed compound that was barely inhabitable. Life was on a par with the pioneers of the Old West, with the major differences being nobody actually wanted to be there, and you could die by breaking a window. However, a tight-knit community formed, as most colonists came from New York and were Jewish. Despite everything, they made it work over the next few centuries. Terra Maridani was renamed New Brooklyn, expanded, and became a relatively thriving extraterrestrial city.

But we never saw this as an American achievement. We saw it as our achievement. As a result, my community not only took pride in it but also in being Martians. Even now, we remain a strong Jewish community, and unlike most Martians, whose accents have started to evolve due to their multicultural nature, New Brooklyn remains distinct with its clear New York dialect.

It's not like we're some sort of Jewish state on Mars or segregating ourselves. Anyone is welcome to come here, but it's an act of human nature that like follows like, and even in days like now when people voluntarily want to take advantage of the opportunities of life on Mars, we generally attract Jewish immigrants more than other communities. I'm not a particularly religious person. I'd go as far as saying I'm an agnostic, however I do follow the traditions of my people. But that's about as far as practicing my faith goes.

I grew up in a working-class family. My father was a low-level engineer who maintained the city's dome, protecting us from instant death outside. My mother was a clerical assistant who worked for a company called Grant Industries, an Australian mega-corporation that pretty much had offices throughout the Solar System, well, at least wherever humankind was settling in a residential capacity.

I can honestly say that I knew very little about what was going on back on Earth when I was growing up. It was really no different than the knowledge Americans, Australians, or New Zealanders had about Britain, which was the origin of their countries. Sure, I knew it existed and it was where my forebearers originated, but I never really thought about it. Earth, to me, was simply that place wealthy people went on vacation. And sure, the American flag flew over government buildings and some corporations, but the nature of our origins had made us particularly unpatriotic towards the mother country.

That all changed when I was about twelve years old. The Great War across the Solar System had been going on since I was about five, and the multinational Martian colonies had negotiated their way out of participating. Mars had its own undemocratic government system, more of a cooperation than a formal government body. The cities spread out across the planet came from every country, including the new enemy.

Martians had nothing against the European Union or the Pacific Alliance, as we worked alongside them, and in the early days of the war, we were pretty much left alone. Setting us against each other would collapse the planet into a civil war requiring a response from our home countries, and they really didn't want to expend resources on what, most generally considered, dumb, hick colonial Martians.

When the war didn't come to its brief conclusion as expected, and the parent nations started running out of bodies to send out to fight, that changed. There was still no attempt to set us against each other, but both sides started calling up the eighteen to nineteen-year-olds... and then the twenty to twenty-one-year-olds, then the..... well, you can see where this is going.

Our own authorities strongly resisted the conscription, but at the time, we still strongly relied on resources imported from Earth. Come to think of it, that may have been a deliberate design. It's hard for anywhere to gain true independence if they rely on the place they want to be independent from for survival.

A new anti-war youth movement sprang up, but both sides quickly ensured it was suppressed. Media became controlled, and we could no longer receive television stations from Martian communities not part of the Pacific Alliance. Everything became "pro-American" or "anti-European", depending on which community you resided in.

To truly understand my story and my ultimate role and involvement in the rise of Jenna Plural, I'll need to take you back several years before I even met her. To the time I came to serve a country I didn't consider to have any connection with. To fight a war being raged for reasons I didn't understand and, most importantly, didn't care about.

CHAPTER ONE

GROWING UP BROOKLYN STYLE

If you were to fly towards New Brooklyn, you would rarely see a building over four or five storeys tall. Ninety-eight percent of the city is underground. The result was, we rarely saw sunlight, making us very pale. Even on the surface, Mars' lack of a magnetic field means the dome has to filter out the dangerous radioactive elements of solar energy. The only way to get a suntan was artificially.

Not to mention, when you live in a dome city, expansion is virtually impossible. You have to build annexes connected by transit tubes if you want to expand. New Brooklyn wasn't the wealthiest of communities, and we couldn't expand as much as other cities. As a result, space was at a premium, and even the most affluent member of the community didn't have much more than an apartment. Of course, even the worst communities have a wealthy elite, who held both positions of power and money and, as a result, could overcome these restrictions.

The décor in this part of town didn't look like anything on Earth. The city had been built for about four hundred thousand people, and the population now exceeded one million. Once you construct a city dome, you can't build upwards. It's not like a dome can be replaced without killing everybody in the city, or moving them out to some-place else that doesn't exist while you replace it.

So, we build down. Almost everyone lived under-ground, unless you were rich on an almost Hannah Grant scale. Yeah, that may be an exaggeration, as no one comes close to her wealth, but you get my point. Few people had wealth in New Brooklyn. To be honest, it was quite a dive. Satan's Anus, someone once called it, and the name stuck.

My family was definitely not rich. Quite the opposite. My wing of the Lieberman family lived on the seven-ty-third sublevel of the Broadway Building. There was a row of elevators, all of which went down, except for three you would have to have a key card for. The graffiti-filled lobby had a faint stench of urine permeating the area. Yeah, I didn't live in the classiest neighborhood, but it's home. We had a two-bedroom apartment. This was kind of problematic, considering I had a brother and a sister. I was the middle one, with my brother being three years older, and Samantha almost being nine years younger, due to a split condom or other unplanned 'miracle.'

The three of us kids all slept in the same room in cubicles built into the walls, with very little space between them. It never bothered us that we had to share a room because, once again, we knew no different, and everyone we knew shared a room with someone. We didn't own much be-cause, even if we could afford it, we had nowhere to store anything we didn't absolutely need. The only storage space each of us had was under half of one of the cubicles. If you want something new, you had to get rid of something.

Despite living in what Earthers would consider cramped conditions, we had very happy childhoods. The Broadway Building was completely self-contained, with shops and services available. We never needed to go to the surface, but we frequently did. My father was very insistent that we get out of the congested environment we were being raised in. The various dome filters gave everything a mud-colored hue at the surface, and the natural light that did come through had that continuously red tinge to it. Again, I didn't know any different, and never really gave much thought to it. When you go to Earth, or an Earth-type environment, you find out that, almost regardless of whatever the weather is, you need to wear sunglasses to avoid the brightness. It's only then that you realize the great difference.

Our education system followed the American standard – elementary, middle, and high school – and maintained the traditions with them, such as homecoming and prom night. As a teenager, I retained little interest in anything happening outside my little world of boys and pop music. However, when I was fifteen, my brother Aaron, turned eighteen and graduated high school. There was tension that grew within the family, but it was never discussed with me, and my brother would frequently meet with my parents to talk about things, while I was sent to my room. I wasn't a curious child and didn't try to listen, being quite content with putting on my headphones and trying to learn the lyrics to some heartbreak love song or other.

Then my brother was simply gone.

I woke up one morning and got ready for school as normal, the major difference being the stilted conversation at breakfast. We were a very chatty family, and I remember sitting there, trying to make conversation and realizing my parents were not paying attention to me, and thinking it was kind of weird. My oldest brother was no longer in school and had yet to find a job. He barely got out of bed. I hadn't seen if he was asleep in the bunk above mine. So, I thought nothing of it as I went to school that day.

When I got home that night, I found my brother was still not around. I started to ask about him.

"It's complicated, Kyla," my mother told me solemnly. "I'd rather we waited until your father got home to discuss this."

Of course, that response only piqued my curiosity, and I bombarded my mother with more questions until she got irritated and sent me to my room.

I slammed the door behind me, very annoyed. Normally my mother would not tolerate such a tantrum, yet on this occasion, she did, and that quickly ended my tantrum, as I wanted to know what was going on and why her attitude were suddenly different.

I stayed in my room until my father came home. I completed my homework with my headphones on. I didn't even hear him arrive. As he opened my bedroom door and I looked up at him, I couldn't help but notice how grey and tired he looked, as he called me out into the kitchen. I set aside my tablet and followed him out. As I sat at the table with them, they remained silent, neither looking at me nor each other until finally, my father lifted his head and spoke very quietly.

"Your brother has gone away. He received his call-up papers to join the United States Army, and he made the decision that he didn't want to go. He's gone into hiding until this all blows over."

Now, I knew we were technically an American colony, and call me dense, but I never really thought about it, and the idea of serving in the United States military had never really clicked with me. Considering how our community came into being, most of us had a negative attitude toward the motherland. Even though I knew conscription was happening, I never really cared enough to think about how it would affect us.

"Is he allowed to do that?" I inquired curiously, as we had always been raised to follow the rules, and at the time, it didn't seem like a dumb question.

"Well, not legally." My mother answered the question. "However, your brother has made a decision based on his conscience. He believes that Martians shouldn't be compelled to join this war."

"And what do you think?" I asked. I was quite confused. I was generally convinced that you could simply say no to going, and that would be the end of it. I really had no concept of the idea that refusal was considered a crime.

"He's an adult now," my father said. "It's not for us to dictate what he should or shouldn't do." As it would turn out, my parent's views on the matter were more complicated than you would have thought. While they opposed the conscription rule, they equally didn't want their children to suffer the consequences of disobeying it. As I found out, they were quite severe.

"When is he coming home?" I asked.

"We don't know, Ky." It was my mother again. "Hopefully, some sanity will return to the Solar System, and we can go about our lives, but until that happens, we don't know where he is, and therefore can't reveal to the authorities where he's gone."

"Why on Mars would you tell them anyway?"

They looked at each other. "They have ways of making you tell them."

He refused to elaborate on that. I don't recall the rest of the conversation, which was most likely about how it would affect me. I was, after all, just fifteen and a typically self-absorbed teenager.

Several days later, I learned my brother had been picked up and arrested. There was no trial, and he was instantly shipped out for service. For his attempt to avoid conscription, he was placed in the worst duty imaginable, and a few months later, we received notification that he had deserted and that should he return to Mars, we were to inform the authorities.

Family life was never quite the same again. My parents had gone from exceedingly cheerful, happy people to constantly mostly subdued. We stopped going on days out and never had another vacation. My brother wasn't stupid enough to come back, and we had no knowledge of where he was or whether he was dead or alive.

My parents grew more distant.

Mostly I was left to my own devices with little instruction, and even my parent's fastidious observation of my school grades disappeared.

No longer being parented, my sister and I went off the rails a bit. I went through a grungy phase where I stopped caring for myself, dyed my hair black, and donned black clothes to match. That was something my parents would have once put a stop to. One of their strictest values was how we appeared in our community. I was no longer the prim and proper Jewish girl my parents wanted the world to see. They no longer seemed to care, so neither did I.

Ben Rosenberg was my best friend. I'd known him since kindergarten. We went to school together, hung out together, and went through every childhood fad you could imagine.

Prior to the change in my family life, Ben had started going off the rails a bit, and I saw him less and less. However, when I developed my 'I couldn't give a fuck' attitude about everything around me, I became more interesting to him again. Likewise, I saw him as a source of letting out my growing frustration with my life. He was in a gang that called itself the silly name of "The Broadway Dragons". We even had a fancy dragon logo on our clothing. They weren't anything heavy. Petty theft, smoking jimmy, drinking beer stolen from parents, and occasionally scrapping with the neighborhood kids.

I can't honestly say why I got into shoplifting. I simply had to dump most of the stuff I stole because I couldn't take it home, as I had nowhere to put it. At least not without my mom finding it, although thinking about it, given her current state of mind, she probably wouldn't have given a shit about it. Seeing if I could get away with it was the thrill. Mostly I was the distraction to the shopkeeper while the rest of the gang devoted their time to picking out items. This worked best with male shopkeepers. Nature provided me with an overabundance of tits at an early age, and, well, men were men. A low-cut top and a sultry voice generally did the trick. Sure, there were some times that we were caught and had to make a run for it, but all in all, it killed time and was quite fun.

That, however, began to change.

The war was taking its toll. Supplies from Earth began to lessen, and the American government-imposed rationing. This was met with many a demonstration, and they were tolerated for a while, and then they weren't. That's when The US Department of Outland Security came to Mars. Like its sister organization, the Department of Homeland Security, it was basically what its name implied – ensuring the interests of the United States in its off-world colonies.

Each community got what they called a Section Chief. In our case, that was a woman known as Charlotte Kensett. You never actually heard anything from the Department of Outland Security, and to be honest, I didn't even know it existed until I came into direct contact with it.

People started to disappear. You never heard about it on the news, but people talk, and it was predominantly the most outspoken community members that disappeared. Those people who organized the protests or criticized the government. They were never seen again. This didn't actually stop the protests. It simply moved them under-ground (no pun intended).

Over time rationing was increased, and it wasn't meted out in a particularly fair manner. Ration books replaced money, and you were allocated rations based on your job, not your need. As a result, the lower-paid people got fewer rations. We even got to the stage where my family had to cut down from three meals a day to only two, and you could clearly see that I was losing weight.

That was when something happened that completely changed my life forever.

We were hanging down in one of the small recreation areas of our block. Fake grass and dim solar panels gave you the idea that you're in a park. They even dimmed the lights further to indicate the fall of night, and that's mostly when we hung out there. My parents really didn't pay attention to when I came home, so I pretty much had the freedom to stay out as long as I liked.

We met up most nights, but that night, Ben was late. I started to get worried about him. But when I started asking the others about him, all I got was jeers.

"What's going on exactly with you and Ben?" Sally asked me. She was always one to stir the shit. I looked over to her from where I sat on the back of a bench, drinking a can of beer with my feet on the seat. She was lying back on her elbows, sprawled out on the plastic grass, looking up at me with a cheeky grin.

"We're just friends, that's all," I replied snarkily.

"Yeah, yeah. Sure you are," she said sarcastically with a laugh.

I got up to get in her face, ready for a fight. She was severely pissing me off. Our unofficial leader, Curtis, put his hand out to stop me.

"Chill out, Ky; she's just fucking with you." Everyone knew he was doing Sally, and they seemed to think it was a secret.

Before anything else could be said, Ben arrived in the foulest mood I've ever seen him in.

"My dad just got put on long-term disability after that accident at the plant stop. The first thing they did was cut his rations. The accident wasn't even his fault!" He slumped down on the bench where I'd been sitting only seconds before. "Fucking Grant Industries. Fucking Americans!"

"Something's got to be done about those motherfuckers," Curtis growled. "The Ackermans on my level have six kids they can barely feed these days. If it wasn't for donations from their synagogue, they'd literally have starved to death by now. And it's not like people have leftover food that they can really donate."

"I just wish the Americans would fuck off." That was Edison, who spent most of his time whining about the Americans.

"We *are* Americans." That was Natalie. She often argued in favor of the government and seemed to believe everything she heard on the news. We tried to convince her that it was propaganda, but she would just stick her head in a hole like an ostrich. Me? I didn't really give a shit. I wasn't interested in the politics of it and didn't really care who was right or wrong. All I knew was things were getting worse, and whether that was the fault of the Americans and the Pacific Alliance or the Peons, it didn't really matter to me.

"For fucks sake, Nat!" Curtis rounded on her. "When're you gonna open your fucking eyes, girl?! Can't you see what's going on around you?"

Natalie responded indignantly. "Of course, I can see what's going on, but don't you understand it's a sacrifice we gotta make? Do you really want to live under the oppression of the European Union?"

"We're already living under oppression, you stupid bitch!" Curtis snapped back, spittle flying from his lips. "And we are not Americans. We're Martians! We owe nothing to America, or the Pacific Alliance, and we shouldn't be involved in this war. This is a matter for Earth, and correct me if I'm wrong, none of us here have anything to do with that planet."

"Of course we do! Just take a look at your ID. What does it say on the top?" She didn't wait for an answer. "United. States. Of Ammmerrrricaaa."

"We've had two referendums on independence in the last fifty years, Natalie," Ben came out of his stupor to join the attack. "Both times, it's the entire planet united, with a seventy percent turnout voting in favor of leaving the Earth-based nations and becoming our own. Each time, both the Alliance and the Union declared the referendums void. Do you think that's fair?"

"Of course. It's fair. People are stupid; even you know we couldn't survive as an independent planet. We need Earth, and we need America," Natalie retorted.

"Did you know, Natalie, that America was once in the same position as us?" Edison said softly. He rarely raised his voice for any reason. "It was part of the British Empire. Many people thought it couldn't survive without the mother country, yet here we are, hundreds of years later. And, sure, it's no longer America's heyday, but it's certainly doing fairly well as a country. You're right on one thing. We do need Earth to supply us, but that's called trade. Just like America trades with other members of the Pacific Alliance, and even with the European Union before this war."

Natalie stood up and glared at each of us in turn. "You do know that even talking secession is a crime?" she said coldly.

Curtis smirked, but there was no humor in it. "And with those words, you proved our point. On Earth, they have something called the First Amendment, which protects their right to say what they want. However, the Supreme Court of your most beloved country has ruled it only applies within the fifty-two states and not to us or any other colony in the Solar System. It's been hundreds of years since we came here, and we're no longer part of them. I'm a Martian, and I'm damn proud of it."

Natalie, red in the face, glared once more at each of us, then turned on her heel, heading off. "You should be careful, guys," I said softly as I watched her go, and all eyes turned towards me. "She's so passionate, it wouldn't surprise me if she turned you in for what you were saying."

Curtis snorted. "Bullshit! She's one of us." But even as he said the words, I could see his eyes didn't have the same confidence as they did.

Chapter Two

Ration Raiders

The number of families turning to the synagogue for help grew, as things became more scarce and rations were cut yet again. It was getting so bad, that people didn't even have enough food to spare even a small portion, because the synagogue community program could only stretch so far. Tensions were beginning to rise. People were getting edgy, and words of insurrection started being bandied about.

But nothing happened.

Then everything happened, at least for me.

Curtis came up with the idea. Apparently, Sally's mother had got herself a job working in the Department of Community Services. She was just a cleaner, but her job involved entering the offices before anyone else did. This meant she had a key card to get into the place. It didn't take much to convince Sally to steal that card.

"It's where they store the ration cards that get issued. Literally, we can walk through the front door, take them, and be gone," Curtis told us one evening in the park.

I was really up for it. My 'don't give a shit' attitude about everything was at its peak.

Ben, however, had a different attitude. "You know if we get caught, we'll do time."

Curtis shrugged that off. "We're a couple of years away from being shipped out to fight in their bloody war. Your family is starving. What've you got to lose?"

Ben couldn't find an answer to that and reluctantly agreed.

So it was that we took the elevators up to the surface. Of course, we didn't include Natalie. We refused to tell her about this for any reason. As it was, she'd been hanging out with us less and less lately.

So basically, me, Ben, Curtis, Edison, and Sally found ourselves standing outside the offices of the Department of Community Services at around two o'clock in the morning.

I'd never been out on the surface this late at night, and there was an eerie twilight around us. Now we were actually here, this didn't seem like such a great idea, and I almost chickened out. However, when Curtis told me, "Ky, you keep a lookout,", I concluded that it couldn't be too bad.

I sat down on the curb of the road, as Sally stepped up and swiped her mother's card against the door. There was the loud clunk of the bolts automatically being thrown back, and one by one, they stepped in as I casually looked up and down the road. No one was about, and I pulled out half a spliff I had left in my jacket and lit it. I started to relax as the cannabis started to seep through my veins with that calming euphoria. I got so relaxed that I actually pulled out my phone and started reading something, only occasionally glancing up and down the road.

I don't know how long they were in there, but it wasn't longer than it took me to finish the weed. I can't remember what I was reading, but it was certainly interesting enough as I forgot to look up and down the road. Not that that would've helped. Because I wasn't looking up.

I heard it before I saw it. Police drones are incredibly quiet and can sneak up on you, and that's exactly what this one did. When the slight hum reached my ears, I instantly saw it coming over the top of a three-story building across the road. The drone turned around and headed in my direction. I jumped up and ran to the door, banging on it hard. "Flying pig," I shouted out, using the euphemism for a police drone or any aerial-based cop, for that matter. Sally was first out the door, but the drone had already put on its flashing blue lights, indicating that it would be sending out an alert to the more flesh and blood variety of police officers.

Curtis came next, shouting out, "Split up!"

I needed no more incentive than that, and I broke into a run, not thinking about direction before I realized I was heading away from Broadway. I kept looking over my shoulder and saw that no one else had come in the same direction as me and that I was alone. Perhaps if I'd been paying more attention to where I was going than where I'd been, the next event would never have happened.

As I went to turn the corner, I looked one last time over my shoulder, but as I rounded it, I suddenly felt large, rough hands grab me by the shoulders. When my head spun round to look at who it was, I found myself looking straight up into the visor of one of Brooklyn's finest.

"Hey, Missy, calm yourself down there. What's the hurry?"

Thinking back on it, it was clear that he didn't know I was involved with what he was heading towards to investigate, but at the time, I just panicked. I slapped his arms away from me and ran in the opposite direction. I'm fairly fit, but I'm not "cop fit", and he was young and in his prime. I could hear him shouting at me to stop. Then suddenly, my whole world lit up as I felt electricity run through my body, and I collapsed onto the floor, jerking slightly until the sensation faded. He'd shot me in the back with some sort of taser. Before I knew it, I felt my hands roughly pulled behind my back and cuffs fastened to my wrists. I tried to struggle, but he simply planted a knee into the base of my spine, and, turning my head to one side, he held my head down onto the road. Shouting at me to knock it off, I did. I just lay there and accepted my fate. After all, that could hardly be the worst thing in my life right now. Oh, how wrong I was.

The first charges against me before I arrived at the police station were public intoxication, and the use of a prohibited substance. Marijuana in itself wasn't illegal. However, in an oxygen-controlled environment, any unauthorized flames were, and the fact it was lit, was the crime I had apparently committed. Public intoxication was bullshit. The weed had hardly taken effect before I'd gone on the run, but that, soon, would be the least of my problems.

I was booked, fingerprinted, DNA taken, retina scanned, and photographed. All the shit that you usually have to go through when arrested.

I kept looking for the others to be brought in, as I could see the reception from where they were putting me through the booking process. But no one else appeared. Had they escaped?

I was shoved into one of the interrogation rooms and cuffed to the side of the table. I sat there for about thirty minutes. I don't know if this was intended to intimidate me, but when you've stopped caring about everything, it doesn't exactly work. Eventually, a portly little cop in plain clothes came in. He sat down and paused as he looked at me, and I returned a look of disdain.

"It's really not looking good for you, Kyla," he said, like he was my disappointed parent or something. "Are you aware that you won't increase the number of rations out there by stealing ration cards? You're stealing from hungry people."

"Why not you just print more ration books?" I replied snarkily.

"If only it was that easy. Rationing is enforced because of the lack of supply. Those ration books can't be replaced, because there aren't the rations to replace them with, if the stolen ones are used."

"The rich get more of them, so maybe if you reduce theirs, it'll make up for it," I said defiantly.

"Do you think that's really how it will happen?" He snorted.

"All I know is people in my block don't have enough to eat, and we're just trying to address that."

"You don't come across to me, as someone who's stupid, Kyla. You're aware that the ration cards are individually numbered, and the moment they're used, the police will be alerted. They're pretty much useless to you."

"To be honest, never thought about it, don't care. Just seemed like a fun thing to do at the time," I shrugged.

"Do you have any concept that what you participated in today could get you thirty years to life in prison? And that that sentence will be carried out on Earth?"

My eyes widened with disbelief as I looked back at him. "They were just ration books, for fucks sake! It's not like we committed murder."

"Such crime destabilizes the community, and in the time of war, that is tantamount to treason."

I had no idea what tantamount meant, but it didn't sound good. "We were just messing around. Nothing was meant by it," I said stoically.

He sat back in his chair and studied me carefully before saying, "Look, Kyla, let me do you a little favor. The first of your little gang to work with me gets the best deal here. Work with me, and we can get the penalty severely reduced."

"What do you mean?" I asked suspiciously.

"Give me the names of your conspirators, and it'll go a lot easier for you."

I could not help but grin. "You don't have them, do you?"

"Not yet, but we will. You could just help save us a lot of time and trouble by giving us the names now."

"Go fuck yourself, pig," I said, flipping him the bird with my free hand.

He wasn't even slightly fazed by my offensive behavior, but said in a much colder tone, "You know, by rights, I should turn this over to the Department of Outland Security."

If this was supposed to be a threat, it was wasted on me, because I didn't really know much about Outland Security, so I simply replied, "Aren't you supposed to offer me a lawyer or something?"

This seemed to completely shut him up, and I had no idea at the time that asking for a lawyer meant he could no longer continue questioning me.

"Very disappointing, Kyla, very disappointing indeed."

Without another word, he got up and left, and I was left sitting there for probably about forty-five minutes this time. Eventually, two uniformed officers came in, uncuffed me from the table, and re-cuffed my hands behind my back. I was led through the police station and out the back door. A small gray car sat in the police car park just outside the door. I was led over to it and put into the back seat. A young man in a dark suit talked to the two cops and signed paperwork, before climbing into the driver's seat.

"Who are you, and where are you taking me?"

"Agent Mills, Department of Outland Security," he said quite pleasantly.

"I was supposed to get a lawyer," I replied sulkily.

"Sorry, miss, I don't know anything about that. I was just asked to pick you up and take you to the Section House. I really don't know anything else."

I sat the rest of the journey in silence until I was eventually taken into the large government building, and the process of booking me was repeated, although this time, the equipment they used looked shinier and more high-tech. Once again, I was placed in a room. It was much larger. and only had two chairs facing each other. The walls were gleaming white, as was the floor and ceiling, and there was literally nothing else to be seen. Even the door was barely visible, being white on its white background. After about ten minutes, it became a bit hard on the eyes.

I sat there deep in thought. I didn't know what I faced ahead, and for the first time in over a year, I actually started to care about what would happen to me. Then, the door opened. A woman, in what appeared to be an expensive business suit, with beautiful yet-cold features, stepped in. She looked like she was some sort of executive board member, but two things stood out about her. The first, was the clip-clop, clip-clop of her heels upon the floor. I looked down and saw that she wore what looked like a very expensive pair of three-inch pumps. The other, was the large, thick-rimmed dark blue glasses she wore. No one wears glasses on Mars. Imperfections in eyes were easily fixed. Even my eyes were replaced, due to a childhood accident, which I'll tell you more about later. There was no summer sun, so shades weren't required. So really, there were only fashion glasses, but these, although stylish, were not being worn for vanity. "Good morning, Miss Lieberman. How are you?"

I tilted my head to one side, as if this was the dumbest question I'd ever been asked. "Well, I've certainly had better days, but none quite as interesting as today. How about you?"

She smiled as she sat opposite me, crossed her long legs, and folded her arms gently upon her lap. "It's good that you can maintain such a light attitude considering the trouble you're in, Miss Lieberman." She had an accent I was unfamiliar with, but it would turn out to be an upper-class British one.

"Well, I'm not entirely sure what trouble I'm in," I replied sulkily. "I'll freely admit I was involved in what I consider to be petty theft. I'm also just a kid, so I'm not too worried about what trouble I'm in, despite what the cop back at the station said."

"Do you really think it was that petty?" she asked, her tone still light and friendly.

"Well, like the cop pointed out, it wasn't like we could use 'em. The whole thing was pretty stupid."

"Well, while you're absolutely correct that it was stupid, it's still a felony federal crime, and there are consequences to it."

"I'm no lawyer, but like I said, I'm a kid, and no harm was actually done. I'll probably get a slap on the wrist and be told not to be a naughty girl. Maybe a few months of community service, but I really don't believe I'm gonna go to prison for it."

"On the contrary, Miss Lieberman. You've undermined the war effort. Rationing is not in place here out of some form of punishment or anti-Martian sentiment. Despite what you may have heard, rationing is not some sort of oppression of the people here. Even if you were independent, you would still rely on imports from Earth, which are now constantly attacked by the enemy. Many commercial ships are destroyed on their way here from Earth. Right now, as we sit here, there are actually ships in orbit from the European Union, just waiting for the opportunity to attack the cargo vessels. They would be laughing right now, if they knew what you were doing."

"But you've already admitted that I haven't done any harm. Those ration books couldn't be used, and you could just re-issue more."

She sighed softly and shook her head. "There is a considerable process to producing those ration books to ensure they cannot be counterfeited. It will take time as a result. If we don't get those ration books back, we can't issue them, and it'll be several weeks before we can. You act like you're worried about people going hungry, and yet, you're now the cause."

I'd never thought of it like that, and while I was determined not to care, I felt uncomfortable now. "No doubt, when you pick up the others, you'll be able to get them back, so no real biggie, right?" I shrugged.

"What if they destroy the evidence before we pick them up? Have you thought of that?" She sighed, uncrossed her legs, and recrossed them in the other direction. "Kyla...Do you mind me calling you Kyla?"

I shrugged. "That's my name."

"Well, Kyla, you seem like a young lady who cares about her community. The actions tonight can potentially bring a great deal of suffering. If you would help me return these ration cards, it would go a long way to alleviate that. Do you understand me?"

"Oh, I understand. But it's whether I believe you, that's the question," I laughed humorlessly.

She studied me for a while before looking down to check her watch before looking back at me. "Let me do a deal with you. I'm really concerned about the effect this will have on New Brooklyn. I just want to help. If you would please tell me who your co-conspirators are, we can pick them up and return the ration books, and you can go home tonight, and I'll forget you're part of this."

"And what happens to them?" I scowled.

"Well, my dear, I think you should be more concerned about what will happen to everybody if you don't help me with this," she looked at me with deep concern in her eyes. "It really is in the best interest of everybody that you cooperate with me. We are not the enemy. We are here to protect you from the enemy."

I bit my lip as I looked down at my shoes and weighed everything in my head. The woman sat patiently, and eventually, I looked up. "They're my best friends. I can't do it. I know you're gonna find 'em in time, but I can't be the one who helped. Do you understand that?"

She sighed softly but maintained that smile. "How about this as an incentive? You help me, and I will see your family's rations are doubled for the next two months.

Whether you use those rations or pass them on to friends and family, it will be entirely up to you. You'll achieve what you intended tonight, but it will be legal this time."

I was no fool to realize that she was playing me, but not going to bed hungry every night is quite the incentive.

I tried to retain my resolve, but it was quite an offer. I started to wonder what Ben would do in these circumstances. His family had been hit hard since his father's rations were reduced. Would he refuse the offer to feed his family better for two months? No, he wouldn't hesitate. Desperate times call for desperate measures. I, for one, would certainly like to go to bed one night without being hungry. "How about we do this? You let me go, and I'll get you the ration books back."

The woman started shaking her head but stopped and looked quizzically at me. "You know, Kyla. I will take you up on that. However, there is a caveat to it."

"What's a caveat?" I asked, bemused.

"A stipulation, a condition. You do not discuss my involvement, and have the understanding that, should you betray the trust that I am about to impart in you, there will be serious consequences."

I shrugged. "Understood."

She smiled and rose gracefully to her feet. "In that case, Kyla, I think we have a deal."

She got up and called the guard into the room to unlock my handcuffs, and with the only sound being the clip-clop of her heels, we headed out into the hallway. My phone and other possessions were returned to me, and she led me to the front door.

"How long do you believe this will take?" She asked me.

I shrugged. "An hour, maybe more. It all depends on how quickly I can get them to answer a phone call."

"OK, my dear, if I don't hear from you in two hours, I will assume you are not returning." She took my phone from me and tapped her phone number into the contacts. "Feel free to call me anytime," she said with a smile, as she handed it back to me. I then headed out to the front door with the sound of her heels heading away from me.

It took less than an hour. I called Curtis first and explained that I faced going down the Sewanee for a long time, if he didn't turn over the ration cards. He wasn't stupid and clearly knew they were caught, but I assured him nothing would happen if he just gave me the ration books. I didn't actually know if that was true, as the woman hadn't exactly said she wouldn't continue to pursue them, but hey, I have no doubt they would have done the same to me in similar circumstances. So, don't think too bad of me.

We met several blocks away from the Broadway Building in case it was being watched, and with great reluctance, he handed them over to me. I was quite surprised by the amount he had. There must have been thousands of dollars' worth there. Giving him time to get away from me, I headed back to the sector house.

It would be the last time I hung out with the gang. My feeling of guilt at getting the extended rations really didn't sit well in my conscience.

True to her word, I was released and went home, and the next day, a package was left outside our door. My father got it, opened it, and looked surprised at the newly issued rations. He didn't understand what was going on, but they were clearly allocated in all our names. I played innocent and said nothing because, well, I couldn't exactly explain that this resulted from a crime and me working with the Department of Outland Security. However, there was also a card inside the envelope. A small plain white card with just four words, written in immaculate cursive. "With regards, Charlotte Kensett."

CHAPTER THREE

A GIFT HORSE

My father made no further mention of our little windfall, but to my annoyance, my parents immediately shared this bounty with the neighbors most in need. While I didn't begrudge them this, I did kinda feel like charity began at home. It's not like there would be more coming.

Within a week, my father had distributed all of the additional rations. I felt incredibly cheated, but I couldn't do much about it. The gang had decided to lay low, and we didn't meet up for a while. In fact, that was pretty much the beginning of the end of our association.

However, the breakup wasn't actually related to them, or over the incident with the rations. Well, at least, not directly. No, it was more about an idea I had that would ultimately change my life's course. I devised a plan that, if it worked out, could make our family much more prosperous. It was a gamble. I didn't know if it would work, but one morning I got up and pretended I was going to school, but instead, headed up to the surface.

I walked casually over to the Department of Outland Security building, ignoring the morning noise of traffic in the busy street as people headed out to work. As I strolled along, I pulled out my phone, looked down at my contacts, and saw the name she had entered. It read simply 'Charlotte.' I hit the call button and waited nervously, only to find it went straight to voicemail.

"Kensett, please leave a message." Was all she said in that cold, clipped English accent of hers.

"Umm! This is Kyla Lieberman here. Give me a call when you get a chance," I said and hung up.

I stood outside the Department of Outland Security, looking up at it, and then, with a dejected sigh, I turned away and headed back towards Broadway. It could have been no more than three or four minutes later when my phone rang, and looking down at it, I saw it said Charlotte. "Hello," I said, pulling it up to my ear.

"Well, it's nice to hear from you again, Ky. I certainly wasn't expecting it." She responded pleasantly.

"Yeah, well, I wanted to talk to you about something," I said uneasily.

"I'm listening."

"Well, you know I helped you all out the other night."

"Yes indeed," she replied cheerfully. "It was exceedingly helpful of you, and I really appreciated it."

"Umm..." I hesitated. "I was wondering if I could do anything else for you? You know, in return for more ration cards."

There was a long pause at the other end. Long enough, I thought we got disconnected. "My goodness, Kyla, you do surprise me, my dear. This is possibly the last thing I expected."

"So, what do you think of the idea?" I asked, trying to sound enthusiastic.

"Frankly, to be quite honest, my dear, you have taken me completely by surprise, and trust me, that's quite a remarkable achievement."

"Well, maybe we should get together and talk about it?" I suggested.

But there was another pause. "Alright, my dear. When can you come over?"

"I'm right outside now." As we talked, I'd walked briskly back to the Department of Outland Security.

"My, you're most definitely eager, aren't you? Come inside, and I'll send someone down to bring you up."

Minutes later, I was once more seated across from Charlotte Kensett albeit now in a much more comfortable position, not handcuffed to a table. And, once more, she was dressed in an expensive looking business suit, but this time one of dark blue. I couldn't help but wonder if she ever wore the same outfit twice. She most definitely didn't have the typical Martian 'make do and mend' attitude.

She sat back in her chair, legs crossed, with her arms folded across her lap, and she looked at me with, what could be described as an incredibly pleasant smile. "So, Kyla, what exactly do you want to help us do?"

"Call me Ky. Everyone does." I replied quietly.

Charlotte smiled again. "As you wish, Ky. What exactly do you want to help us do?"

I shrugged. "I dunno."

"I see. Well, let's look at this from a different angle. Exactly what commitment are you willing to make?"

"Look, to be honest, Miss Kensett. I honestly have no idea, 'cause I don't really know what you do, for the most part."

She chuckled lightly. "My dear, the Department of Outland Security is responsible for maintaining the interests of the United States off-world," she explained.

"But we're not off-world," I said with a frown.

Charlotte chuckled again. "My apologies. Usually, when we refer to off-world, we mean 'not on Earth'. Let's just say outside the home world."

"Earth may be your home world, Miss Kensett," I said defensively. "But this is my home world. Mars."

For the first time since I'd come in, that smile seemed to falter, but it was only a slight narrowing of her eyes. "Oh, I do so hope you're not a separatist, Kyla," she said with an air of disappointment.

"Why? Is that such a bad idea?" I frowned.

"Oh, to be honest, I don't know if it is or it isn't. I don't indulge in politics." She dismissed the idea with a shake of her head and a wave of her hand, which I now saw were exquisitely manicured and polished bright red. "However, Ky, as long as this war continues, it is in both the interests of Mars and Earth that we don't get distracted from the ultimate goal of victory against the European Union. Should Mars try to vie for independence now, it would remove a considerable amount of resources from the war effort. The matter of Martian independence can be discussed later, but it's vital that people don't upset the situation now."

"Honestly, Ms. Kensett, I have little interest in politics either. I don't care whether Mars is independent or part of the Pacific Alliance, or even the European Union, for that matter," I said dismissively. "All I care about is getting our daily bread."

The smile once more returned, and she said, "I take it you don't have particular religious convictions, considering what you just said?"

"Huh?" I looked at her, confused.

"You just quoted a New Testament, yet according to my records, you follow the Jewish faith."

"I'm not really sure what my religion has to do with anything. But considering my father cries out 'Jesus' whenever he hits his thumb with a hammer, I really wouldn't read anything into that." I stopped as something occurred to me, and I narrowed my eyes at her. "What's your point? Jews not allowed in your club?"

Charlotte laughed lightly and shrugged it off. "Oh, it's simply that I have found that people with strong religious convictions tend to have a moral compass that always points south."

A curious statement, to say the least. "And what direction do you want it to point, Ms. Kensett?"

She narrowed her eyes, but her smile remained. "Whatever way I tell it too. But you haven't answered my question."

"Well, if it really matters, I attend the synagogue with my family on Friday nights. I observe the holy days, but no, I don't have any particularly strong religious beliefs. However, let's be completely honest, I don't exactly have a level of patriotism toward the United States either. But is that really any different from anyone who works for someone else? One doesn't have to believe the same thing as their employer to work for 'em. If you're worried about my loyalty, and since we're being so honest with each other, I'll give you the same amount of loyalty you give me."

"Are you suggesting your loyalty would be personally pledged to me?" The smile turned into a smirk.

"Look, if what you told me the last time we met is correct, and the Peons are the cause of the shortages here, that's something I can get behind. My first interest in working for you is for the money or, rather, the ration cards, but if I could do something to help Mars get out of this situation, then I'm willing to do it. Just don't ask me to do it for America. I am not American, no matter what it says on my ID card. My loyalty lies with Mars, and then with Brooklyn."

She studied me carefully from behind those large, thick-rimmed glasses before saying. "Well, I can certainly work with that, but how much commitment are you able to invest? How much time do you have available to devote to this work?"

"Well, I have nothing to do in the evenings or weekends."

"So, you wouldn't be willing to do this full-time?" She looked somewhat disappointed.

"Oh, I'd be more than happy too, but I have to go to school, don't I?" I said a little sarcastically.

Charlotte glanced at her screen and then back at me. "Oh, I don't see why you should have to."

Now that certainly threw me a curveball. "Are you suggesting I drop out?" My eyes widened.

"Well, according to your record, you hardly attend anyway. You are listed as a chronic truant," she shrugged.

This was the first time I'd ever heard an adult suggest I didn't complete my education, and I was almost lost for words. "Are you saying I don't need to graduate?"

She smiled softly and weirdly affectionately. "Oh, Ky, with your current grades, you're not going to graduate anyway, so is there really any point?" She scrunched up her nose questioningly. "No, you will have far better prospects working for us."

Telling you all these years later and now having children of my own, I can't help but feel how unbelievably inappropriate this was. But I was now seventeen, and I hated school, and this was quite a dream. "I couldn't agree more, Ms. Kensett," I said, smiling genuinely for the first time.

"How about this? You come and work for me full-time, and I'll see to it that you get your graduation certificate anyway."

I couldn't help but grin. "You have yourself a deal with that, Ms. Kensett," I said, not even realizing we hadn't discussed what I was actually going to be doing.

"Oh, not quite yet my dear. We need to go through some tests. Don't look so concerned, my dear. They are just psychological profiles to see what areas you would be best at." I would later find out this wasn't exactly true. It was more about testing how loyal and dedicated I would be. Obviously, I passed. Otherwise, there would be very little point in telling you this story.

I spent the rest of the afternoon in front of the screen, answering random questions that didn't seem to make a lick of sense, and having images flashed at me while wearing a rather unusual pair of glasses which, again later, I would find out were monitoring my pupil reaction.

Several hours later, I was sitting back in front of Charlotte Kensett. "You need to spend a week in orientation. Just some basic training."

"What do I tell my parents?"

"Nothing. Just get up, as usual, each day and act like you're going to school. The record will show that you are present, but instead, you will come here. In fact, you are not to tell anyone that you're working for the Department."

"What exactly do you plan for me to be doing?"

"There are many people who have European sympathies, and we call those people traitors. They're the ones providing information about transports coming in and things like that, and we need to get them out of the picture. I will ask you to help me find them, so they can no longer cause any more harm."

Of course, she was really downplaying what I would ultimately end up doing. Charlotte Kensett was indeed quite the master manipulator, but I don't tell you that negatively, for ultimately, she was my mentor and taught me everything I knew.

With the profiles complete, I had to sit down and sign various documents on a small tablet she handed to me.

I didn't want to read them, but Charlotte insisted that I fully understood the implications of what I was getting into. Pretty much, I was signing up for an indefinite period of employment with the Department of Outland Security Martian division.

Something suddenly occurred to me, and I looked up at Charlotte questioningly. "Ms. Kensett, how can signing this even be legal? I'm not eighteen yet."

She simply smiled at me. "Mars has almost a twenty-five-hour day, right?"

"Sure."

"Well, that's not figured in when age is based on an Earth-time year. You have three hundred odd hours a year unaccounted for. Were you on Earth, you would be almost nineteen now."

"But we are not on Earth," I said haughtily.

"No, but Outland Security is based on Earth and operates within United States mainland jurisdiction. As far as the US government is concerned, you are eighteen."

"Then why does this say that you become my legal guardian?" I asked.

"In case your parents decide to challenge this through the Martian court system. If they declare you a minor, parental consent will become necessary for you to work for the Department," she advised. "Since we can't discuss this matter with your parents, we get around it by getting you to emancipate yourself and appointing me your legal guardian."

"But surely you need my parent's permission to even do that?"

"No, a judge can sign off on it, and your parents can file an objection if they choose to do so, and they will most likely win. However, I don't intend on telling them, do you?"

"You told me I can't." I frowned, and Charlotte just smiled back at me.

"It's just a minor legality, my dear. Just sign the form."

I did so, and Charlotte proceeded to countersign everything I had signed as my legal guardian... just in case. "I should advise you that your phone will be tracked from now on." She informed me. "This is as much for your safety as for the department's. Knowing where you are at all times will help us to help you in an emergency, so please don't lose your phone."

"I'm a seventeen-year-old girl, Ms. Kensett," I replied with a grin. "Where do you think I'm possibly gonna go without my phone?"

Charlotte chuckled. She told me to return the following Monday, giving me four days with nothing to do, but ponder what to expect. I still didn't have a good idea of what would be expected of me. I spent a lot of time online, looking up information about the Department of Outland Security, but most of it was just public relations bullshit, and the general idea of their operations securing American citizens throughout the Solar System. They appeared very big on telling taxpayers it was all for their best interests.

The weekend then dragged on until Sunday night finally came, and I lay in bed wide awake, wondering what was to come as I listened to my sister's snoring. I got up early, arousing my parents' suspicions but apart from an odd look, they didn't really say anything. I even left before I usually would. I would become much more cautious in time, but I was excited and nervous about my first day with the Department.

You can't imagine how pissed off I was when I finally arrived, only to find myself sitting at a desk, taking classes on a computer. This was worse than high school. At least I had people to talk to there, but no, here I was, sitting in what was clearly a classroom with rows of computer stations, but all alone. Most recruits were taken on at the same time twice a year, but an exception had been made for me, and thus I had no classmates.

However, as I got into the lessons, I found them most intriguing. The policy issues of what we could and couldn't do were boring, but when it actually came to the procedure, I found that I was entering some fantasy world of secret agents. It went through how to keep up a cover story and how to contact your handler without being caught. It even ran over the use of certain covert surveillance equipment and how to hide it when not in use. It felt like I was in some old spy novel.

I found my enthusiasm growing with the excitement of stepping away from my boring humdrum life and entering this intriguing world of espionage. It went through all the varieties of careers within this line of business, from technicians to interrogation to field agents, and I had no clue which Charlotte had been lined up for mr. At the end of the week, I had to sit an exam on everything I had been listening to, and for the first time, I passed with the equivalent of an 'A', if this had been a high school class. Ironically, the reports that my parents started receiving from the school I no longer actually attended started showing an improvement in my grades. I was disappointed that I wasn't getting A's and mentioned this to Charlotte.

"Honestly, do you really think your parents will believe a sudden overnight jump from not attending school to being a straight 'A' student?"

Yeah, she had a point.

Chapter Four

Ky Lieberman - Secret Agent Girl

The second week was much the same, but on the third, I was sent up to another floor, and a young man met with me. He was tall and good-looking for a man in his thirties. His accent wasn't much different from mine, but his tan clearly indicated he was not from around here. I couldn't help wondering if he was Jewish. We may have had a mixed culture here, but marrying outside the faith was still rare. It wasn't like I was thinking of marriage. It had simply become automatic for a couple interested in getting involved to check out if they were both kosher. However, in these circumstances, he had absolutely no interest in me and retained an extremely professional approach. His name was Keith Abbington, and it turned out he was from the real New York but, alas, non-Jewish.

"Nice to meet you, Agent Lieberman." It was the first time anyone referred to me as that, and I admit, I found it quite exciting, and to be honest, I struggled to maintain a mature perspective. "It's time to start putting into practice what you have been studying for the last two weeks. You still have a lot to learn, but you know enough to prepare for going into the field. I just need to know if you can pull it off."

"Oh, I'm quite certain I can," I said confidently.

"Well, that's for me to decide," he said firmly but smiling. He then slid a sheet of paper over towards me, which was very unusual since only arty-farty people these days used paper. I looked down at it. It had a name, address, and multiple details about some woman I'd never heard of. I can't remember the name now, so I will go with Betty Smith. Betty was apparently a year older than me, and it went through a detailed list of her interests, where she went to school, what she did now that she graduated, etcetera, etcetera. After reading it, I looked up at him questioningly. "You've got ten minutes to memorize as many details on that paper."

"Oh, I won't need ten minutes," I replied, quickly scanning the document and returning it to him. "Done." I smiled sweetly at him.

He looked at me suspiciously and started firing questions at me quite aggressively. I hadn't expected that, and it threw me for a moment. However, I managed to compose myself and started answering his questions.

"I'm quite impressed you got everything right, and not many people can do that the first time they're thrown into the deep end with me." I grinned back at him proudly. "However, I have to ask... do you have an eidetic memory chip? They're highly illegal, you know."

"I don't even know what that is, but if you are referring to how quickly I learned that, it's my eyes."

"What about them?" He frowned.

"Genetically enhanced replacements."

The effect that had on him was most surprising. He turned white and took a step back. "You're a GenMod?" he said uneasily.

"Fuck you! No, I'm not!" I said, completely insulted. "I was about three, when there was that chemical leak at the atmosphere processing plant. Caused me to go blind. To avoid litigation, Grant Industries supplied me with top-of-the-range organic replacements."

"So, you process things faster and in more detail?"

I shrugged. "I see everything within my field of vision, if that's what you mean?"

"Replacing the eyes doesn't mean your brain will process that information differently. How do you explain that?"

I looked at him with utmost disbelief. "How the fuck do I know? Do I look like a geneticist?"

He laughed. "I guess not, but this could be incredibly useful."

I had never even thought of that. I had no recollection of the Grant Industries event, and my eyesight was my eyesight. I never knew anything else and, therefore, never thought about it.

He didn't mention it again, and we spent the next week going through very similar scenarios and an array of equipment such as cameras, listening devices, and drop points to pass things on. While I didn't maintain a hundred percent in everything, I did pretty well. Towards the end of the second week, he actually took me out into the city, taking me far away from my local community so that no one would recognize me, and we role-played scenarios of where I would try to communicate with him, or find a place where to leave him some information somewhere, without anyone seeing me do it.

Then came the more exciting stuff. I was trained in the use of various types of weaponry. Guns, knives, low-yield anti-personnel explosives, you name it. I did raise the issue of if I would be expected to kill someone, but the answer was that I simply had to be prepared for any eventuality.

Then there was unarmed combat, which was more like advanced self-defense, and while I hoped I'd never have to kill anyone, simply knowing how to increased my confidence.

My parents didn't cotton on to what I was doing, and the weeks flew by. The only time it got a little awkward was when, towards the end of the month, another package of ration cards turned up at my family's house. However, my father simply took them and made some comments about his mysterious benefactor, but he wasn't going to look a gift horse in the mouth. Once more, he began distributing them amongst the neighbors. To be honest, I didn't really care now. I was too hyped up with the idea that my training was almost ending and what Charlotte would want me to do. Had I known, I probably wouldn't have been quite as excited.

The last Friday came, and when I went into the classroom to meet with Abbington, he simply informed me that I had passed everything.

"By how much of a margin?" I asked.

He simply grinned back at me. "Well, above average, but don't let it go to your head. You're not the best."

"But I will be." I grinned.

"Oh, we'll see about that then, won't we?" And that was the last time I spoke to him. I never saw him again.

He sent me back up to Charlotte's office, and she congratulated me as I came in. "Come in, take a seat. We have something we need to discuss." I did, wondering what the issue was. "There's some other training I want you to undertake. It's an advanced course, but having learned about your enhanced eyesight, I think it will be helpful. With your observation skills, I want to make you what we call a 'Grade One Observer'."

"And what exactly is that?"

"It's a position only GenMods usually fill, and I only know of two in the entire military. Usually, an unaltered human can achieve only a Grade Two. It's the ability to read people. Their reactions. Their intentions. Whether they lie or try to hide. Whether we can trust them."

"Sure, I know I see more in people's reactions than the average Joe, but it's not like I can tell if people are lying," I said, thinking the idea was crazy.

"Well, we can teach you," Charlotte smiled. "If you allow us to implant an eidetic memory chip in your head, we can literally upload the sum of knowledge of psychology."

"But Abbington said they were illegal?" I queried.

"Oh, we have what is known as 'special dispensation'," Charlotte advised.

"You mean we can just break the law, and no-one gives a shit?"

Charlotte pondered my question but simply shrugged, saying, "Yes!" with a smile. I laughed.

"Well, OK then," I replied. "Let's do it."

And that's how I became what is known as a 'Grade One Observer', and how I learned what an eidetic memory chip was.

There are a lot of misconceptions about these memory chips. They're more of a data retrieval device. For example, you can program someone with all the data on how to fly a space ship but can they do it? No, it can't replace training and experience. What it can do is give you access to data. Think of it as a mini internet in your brain. Anyone can read how to pilot a ship on a computer, even you, but could you then just go out and do it?

While some countries allow these for military use, the USA completely outlawed them. That didn't stop the Department of Outland Security from sticking one in my head. This required surgery and an overnight stay. Charlotte provided me with a new 'best friend.' The story was I was going to a sleepover. My new bestie was the daughter of another D.O.S. employee, and they had my back if my parents wanted to contact them. It was unnecessary, as my parents didn't give a flying shit about what I did.

The implanted chip was then uploaded with every aspect of psychology known to humankind, and combining that with my eyesight, I could now observe people in a new way. I could tell when they were lying by their body language. I could gauge personality, values, morals, interests, loyalty, etcetera, by the subtleties of what they said or how they interacted. It was a game changer in both my personal and professional life.

A week later, I met with Charlotte again. "Are you ready for your first assignment, Field Agent Lieberman?" she asked quite cheerfully.

"Absolutely, Boss." I grinned back.

She turned her chair back towards her terminal on the corner of the desk. "You'll be moving to Sector Twenty-six. We arranged accommodation for you in the district."

"Wait, what?" I said, sitting up sharply. "I'm leaving my family?"

Charlotte turned back to me, and she wasn't smiling now. "Do you really think you could operate around here? We can hardly put you undercover in a community where half the population may recognize you, my dear."

"But how the hell am I supposed to explain this to my parents?"

"We have that covered. You're about to receive a scholarship at Portman College for a month's course in something or another. I'm not sure of the details. You can call your family when it's safe to do so." She saw that discomfort in my eyes, and I saw a flash of anger in hers for the first time. "You're not going to try to renege on this arrangement, are you? We've invested a lot into you, not only time, but hundreds of thousands of dollars, and I would be most disappointed if it turns out it was all for nothing."

"Chill out, Boss, keep your panties on. I got no intention of backing out. I was just shocked, that's all," I replied irritably, and instantly, her smile returned. Then, I saw it. My new senses kicking in. Cold. Emotionless. Fear of failure, but confident all the same. She was seriously betrayed and can't trust now. Possibly a case of Anti-social Personality Disorder. Charlotte... Charlotte was now an open book to me. Well, almost. She was trained to hide her reactions from the likes of me, but everyone slips up now and then. It's human nature.

"You'll be leaving on Monday and staying with a couple called the Martin family. You'll pose as their daughter, Jennifer Martin. I'll send you the details on your phone of your cover. Basically, you've just moved here from New Philadelphia and are settling in. The job I have for you is set up at the Mars H2O facility. It's a water recycling subsidiary of Grant Industries."

"I know where we get our water from, Boss," I replied snarkily. "You don't need to explain it to me."

She looked a little piqued at me interrupting her at first, but that disingenuous smile returned one more time. "Good. You're starting an apprenticeship, and we'll give you a couple of days to settle yourself at the plant before providing further instructions."

"Why can't you tell me now?"

"Because you've never been properly field tested, at least not in the real world. You will be observed, although you'll probably not be aware of it. We have other agents present who will assess how well you're keeping your cover. We don't want to blow this by making your target aware we're coming after them. If we don't get a positive report back, I'll simply pull you and try another avenue." She let out a little smile, and for the first and only time, I believe she was truly honest with me. "I saw something in you when we first met, Kyla. Your recruitment wasn't done through our usual procedures. Normally, you'd be put on a waiting list and be tested with other candidates looking to do what you're about to do. When I argued for your case, my superiors made it very clear that my head is on the block should you fail. It's not a position I like to be in, so I expect excellent results from you. I don't like people disappointing me, and I don't expect you to let me down, but just in case you get cold feet or screw up, let me make it very clear – no-one likes me when I'm disappointed."

In some ways, despite the implied threat, it was a back-handed compliment, and I just looked her in the eyes. "Oh, trust me, Boss, I won't."

Sector twenty-six was pretty much like any other sector, except for one major difference. It housed both the air and water recycling centers. As a result, you could hear a low-level hum of the vast machinery that ran twenty-five/seven. This simple fact made property prices here vastly lower, and, as a result, it became a region that attracted socio-economic issues. In other words, it was a big fucking dump. The lowest paid and dregs of society that everyone else pretended not to notice. Unlike Earth, there was no such concept of homelessness. No, we hadn't created some wonderful utopia. We simply couldn't sustain non-productive people, so by law, families were responsible for their relatives. If someone became a bum, their next of kin was legally obligated to take them in. There was no welfare system. No one was permitted to be idle, no matter their situation. And while this shocks people from other worlds, it was simply a matter of survival. The reality and the dreams of making a second Earth were far apart.

As I arrived in the sector, I noticed the smell. It was that faint odor of decay that I would find out was caused by chemicals from the plants leaking into the air. God alone knows what we were breathing in, but it hung in the area with nowhere to escape. There was no wind on Mars. Well, I mean within the domes, that is. Nothing that could blow it away. It made me feel nauseous, and it took me several days to get used to it.

An unmarked department driver had dropped me off on the sidewalk, several blocks from where I was supposed to stay. Due to the lower-class nature of the neighborhood, there were fewer vehicles on the road, so I drew some mild attention as I got out of it. The moment the car drove away, I was officially Jennifer Martin. I would be expected to stay in that persona until the day I left the sector. I didn't really know what was going through my mind as I headed towards the complex where these Martin people resided. I was excited and anxious, and various scenarios rolled around in my head of what Charlotte would ultimately expect of me.

As I reached the front door of what appeared to be a two-story building not very different from those surrounding it, I pulled out the ID card bearing my photo and this "Jennifer's" details. It only then occurred to me to wonder if Jennifer Martin was a real person or completely the imagination of the Department of Outland Security. My identity may have been fake, but the ID card certainly wasn't. It was a genuine bona fide government-issued ID, so why I was nervous when I swiped it on the door, I didn't know.

Like many residential blocks, it was identical to my home back in Broadway House, with one difference. Mine had different graffiti painted over the walls. A lot of it was just random shit, but I couldn't help but notice the anti-American slogans, and in one case, someone had very carefully painted the head of the Statue of Liberty with red eyes and fangs. Hilarious.

I stepped into the elevator to be greeted by the stench of piss. Charming. I hit the button for the sixteenth floor. I felt a little uncertain, as I heard the elevator shudder slightly and grind its way down. I was quite relieved when I was able to get out. From there, it was easy to find apartment 1624, where I'd been instructed to go, and rather timidly, I knocked at the door. It was opened by a man, probably in his mid-fifties, with a kindly face and a welcoming smile. He was a slightly chubby guy, which was quite a rare sight these days, and had that horseshoe shape of grey hair that comes with male pattern baldness.

"Come on in, Jennifer." He stepped back for me to enter.

The apartment was identical to my family's. Most apartments used the same design for almost every block. However, this looked more homely than mine, nicely decorated. My parents had once taken a lot of care in the appearance of our apartment, but that had long gone with their spirits.

"I'm Luke, and this is Marie," he said, indicating a woman who stepped out of the kitchen. She didn't look quite as friendly. In fact, she was clearly nervous about something or other.

"Hi." I said, but she didn't respond, and an uncomfortable lull hung there.

"Let me show you to your room," Luke said, interrupting the silence, as he showed me to my room. Again, this was identical to my own room, with a major difference being that I was the only one sleeping there. A single bed with no bunks in alcoves made the room appear larger than mine. "Make yourself comfortable, and then come join us for lunch."

I simply nodded at him, and he stepped out and shut the door. I don't know what he expected me to do, because I simply chucked my bag at the bottom of the bed and sat down. I don't know why, but I was expecting something a little more secret agent-y about the Martins, not this middle-aged couple who looked like they worked in an office, filing insurance claims.

After a few minutes, I returned to the living room, where the woman quietly laid plates on the table. I couldn't help but notice the portion sizes of food were much larger than I was used to. It appeared the Department of Homeland Security paid well.

I sat mostly in silence, and it became quite uncomfortable, as I noticed Marie had failed to make eye contact with me. Something sus was happening here that I didn't know about and didn't think I wanted to know. I was starting to believe she wasn't completely on board with what was happening. As we reached the end of the meal, Luke Martin told me about the job at the processing plant.

I was joining as a general laborer, so I clearly would be facing some hard graft. It sounded a lot more like I was just getting a new job, rather than going into an undercover position, because the Martins didn't bring up anything related to Outland Security. Well, Marie Martin never even spoke to me at all. Even Luke Martin looked uncomfortable with her attitude. As soon as the meal was finished, I thanked her, retired to my room, and shut the door, wondering what I had gotten myself into.

Chapter Five

Grant Industries H2O, Mars Division

The next day, after an uneasy sleep, I got up and left before they were awake. I was early, so I walked around the sector for a while, trying to kill time. Eventually, I headed to the plant, where workers were clocking in through a gate. I showed my ID once more to the security man, and he called up to someone in personnel to come down to meet me.

A large bearded man in blue overalls took me inside a large processing plant, that was so vast you couldn't see one end to the other. Huge machines, like turbines, pumped away and the stench from outside grew stronger.

"You'll be working the typical 9-hour shift from 7 AM till 5:30 PM." He told me, as he led me in and out between the machinery like I was in some sort of maze. "You get 30 minutes for lunch, but you're not to leave until you hear the bell. In fact, we do everything by the bell here, but Moulton will be able to give you all those details."

"Moulton?" I asked.

He indicated to a man that we were approaching, standing in front of some piping large enough to fit three people inside simultaneously. He was gripping a vast two-handed wrench and tightening a massive bolt. He was in similar blue overalls to the supervisor, and was about average height but very muscular, with thick black hair and a matching beard. Looking like some woodsman I'd seen in pictures from Earth. He had bright blue eyes, but they looked tired and weary. I think he gave me a smile, but it was hard to tell under the mass of hair on his face. "Hey, Moulton, this here is Martin. She's new, and I want you to show her the ropes."

"Don't you think I have enough to do, Ken? Those lazy assholes on the night shift didn't do half what they were supposed to, and I'm already playing catch up."

"What if you spent less time complaining and more time working? Then, maybe it wouldn't be so bad," Ken said irritably. He then turned to me. "Don't mind, Moulton. He's a chronic whiner, but he's a good guy. You have a good day, and I'll check in on you later." And with that, he left me alone with the man who was glaring after him.

"I'm sorry if I'm putting you out," I said, maintaining a confidence in my voice that I didn't really feel.

He looked at me and shrugged, and then I saw that he smiled. "It's all good. It's that asshole that I'm pissed at."

He looked me up and down, and, placing his large wrench against the pipe he'd just been working on, he beckoned me to follow him. "Let's get you some pretty overalls so we don't mess up those nice jeans of yours." I couldn't help but grin as I followed him across the plant, headed up some old iron stairs, and into a small communal area. There were a variety of lockers and some tables for seating, and a small food preparation area. Clearly, the staff rec room. He asked me my sizes, and I told him, and he went to a back room and came out with a blue one-piece. "We'll get you some more at the end of the day, but this'll do you for now." He handed it to me and indicated a door marked changing room; minutes later, I was dressed like him.

For most of the day, I was fetching and carrying and didn't get much chance to talk to Moulton, whose first name, it turned out, was Terry. As the morning wore on, I found myself getting more and more tired. The little middle-class Jewish girl from Broadway House was not exactly used to hard labor.

By the time the lunch bell went off, the novelty of being a secret agent had long worn off. Terry took me up to the rec room again and introduced me to a couple of other people, and when he found out that I hadn't brought any lunch with me, he gave me one of his sandwiches. "What were you expecting? Some sort of fine dining service?" he laughed at my expense.

"To be honest, I didn't know what to expect, and I really didn't give it any thought," I said, as we sat at one of the tables with two others.

"Grant Industries motto – minimum wage, minimum benefits, minimum respect." He chuckled. "But it's okay. You can share some of your rations with me tomorrow." Now, to some of you Earthers out there, that may sound petty, but if you haven't got the idea yet that food was scarce, you better go back to the beginning of this tale and start reading again.

"No worries, boss, I got you," I said, biting into the cheese sandwich.

"I heard a rumor they're gonna cut the rations again." This was said by the woman sitting to his left. Shannon was about ten years older than me, and as she spoke, she looked incredibly irritated.

"And you're surprised?" Moulton snorted. "Those bastards won't be happy until we're all dead."

"There's a war going on. You know we all have to make do," growled the man on the other side of Shannon. "It's not our government causing these shortages, you know."

Moulton snorted again. "We don't see them going hungry on Earth. There's zero rationing there."

"Because they don't have to ship food across space for three months. It's the Peons attacking the shipping lines that are causing the fucking problem, Terry."

"Really, Dwayne?" Moulton responded, getting quite riled up. "How is it that we were almost self-sufficient before this war? There are literally hundreds of farming domes across this planet. Yet, we now have to import most of our food for some reason?"

"Domes don't expand, Terry, but populations do," Dwayne replied equally aggressively. "Maybe if we cut down on the number of people we keep producing here, we could get back to those days."

"'Population control' right, Dwayne?" Moulton retorted sarcastically. "What then? Maybe we should eliminate all the handicapped people or the elderly?"

"Oh fuck off, Terry, you know what I'm talking about is restricting the number of children people are allowed to have. It's all those damn Catholics and Mormons. They breed like fucking rabbits and are a drain on our resources."

"Really?" Moulton snorted. "I suppose your solution would be to deport all the non-Jewish people out of New Brooklyn and declare a state of New Zion?"

"Cut that bullshit out, Terry. If you just stop and think about it, you know what I'm talking about. Don't try to make it out that I'm some sort of bigot," Dwayne waved a dismissive hand at him.

"Then stop talking like one." Moulton snapped. "The only state I want to see is a free Mars. Independent of Earth. We're little more than a resource for them, and I'm telling you the day'll come when there'll be a reckoning."

"I'd be careful what you say," Shannon said carefully, and although she was speaking to him, she was looking at me. Terry and Dwayne fell silent as they also looked towards me.

"Hey, don't worry about me," I said with a shrug. "Politics bore the shit out of me."

Shannon grinned at me. "That's an excellent position to take. These two would make your ears bleed. Did you get the rest of your uniforms?" I shook my head. "Okay, let's go get them and leave these two to their ranting." I wanted to stay and hear more, but I didn't really have an excuse not to agree, so getting up, I followed her out of the room.

The moment the door closed behind us, her expression changed, and as we walked along, she glanced at me and said in a low voice, "That's your mark."

"Huh?" I replied, totally confused as we trotted down the metal steps.

"Terry Moulton. Outland Security believes he's part of a Martian independence group potentially working with the Peons to generate insurrection amongst the Pacific Alliance civilian populace."

It took me a moment to recover from realizing she was actually one of 'us.' She looked more like someone who would be the chairwoman of a women's group at my synagogue. "Why does he think the Peons would be any better?"

"Oh, their agents do a good job convincing these idiots that they would get their independence if they get the Pacific Alliance out," Shannon snorted.

"Okay, what am I supposed to do?" I asked.

"Befriend him. Get to know him. Get him to introduce you to his organization."

"I was supposed to have several days to get acclimatized before being told what my mission was. Why the sudden change?" I frowned.

"You started telling him you weren't interested in the 'political bullshit.' If I let you carry on with that, it'll make it a lot harder for you to suddenly have a revelation that you want to do something about it. It's not like this is a deep-cover mission, and you have a year to ingratiate yourself. Kensett has given you two weeks."

"How long have you been here?"

"About three months. Why?" She frowned at me.

"I was just wondering why you haven't done anything?" I shrugged.

"I tried. Let's just say he prefers his women a lot younger than me."

I laughed and said, "What do you expect me to do? Fuck him?"

She looked at me with a bewildered frown. "Well, yeah. If you have to." That left me momentarily speechless, as it wasn't something that was ever discussed. Sure, part of my training was attracting the attention of a target, but no-one ever talked about having sex with them. That was a big problem for me. It wasn't like I was a prude or anything, but I wasn't exactly the one-night-stand-type of girl. It was just... well... I'd never been with a man. I'm not good at long-term relationships, and my love life never went that far. She saw my reaction. "What were you expecting, Jennifer? This kind of work being all kittens and candy?"

"No need to be sarcastic," I muttered.

"Sorry," she said, sounding like she meant it. "I'm a little tense because technically, for me, this is a mission failure, and it won't reflect well on my record."

I shrugged. "You can't hardly be blamed if he doesn't fancy you."

"Yeah, well, try telling that to Charlotte Kensett." I wasn't sure what she meant by that, but then, I didn't know Charlotte as well as she did at that time.

"I'll do what I can," I said, unable to hide the unease in my voice.

"Well, I certainly hope that you do, because then we can both get the fuck out of here and go home."

Although the mission was to last two weeks, I was only assigned to Moulton for one week of orientation. This meant I had four days to ingratiate myself before the weekend. The following day I decided to step it up a bit. So, rather than wear a T-shirt under my overalls, I put on a button-up shirt, leaving the top four buttons undone and the zipper on my overalls down low, to reveal just the right amount of cleavage that would attract, but not look deliberate. I struggled not to smile when I met Moulton that morning, and his eyes instantaneously dropped to my chest. It was just for a moment, but enough to let me know I had his attention. However, I still hoped to pull this off without going as far as Shannon had suggested. I have to admit I'm quite good at flirting. Getting a boy to share his rations or pick up the tab in a burger place was quite an art. One that I had managed many times before. The trick is to give the impression that you'll put out without making it obvious, so they can't blame you when you eventually don't. Doesn't always work. Some guys can get pissy, mostly teenage boys who follow the conscience of their dicks.

As I worked with him that day, I chatted about innocent shit, but eventually, I said to him, "What was all that bullshit Dwayne was coming out with yesterday?"

I thought I blew it for a moment when he looked annoyed. Then I realized that it was his recollection of the conversation that was upsetting.

"I really don't get people like Dwayne. Do you have any idea of how we struggled to make Mars what it is today? Yet others still think the Alliance can come here and tell us what to do."

"And they always will as long as we don't do anything about it," I said it like an offhand comment, but he looked at me curiously.

"I thought you said you didn't care about this stuff," he said, with narrowed eyes studying me.

Again casually, I just shrugged that off. "Oh, I've learned long ago not to get into debates with the likes of Dwayne. It's a waste of energy. You can't argue with stupid."

His face relaxed, and he smiled as he turned back to the conduit he was working on. "You got that right, Jen. But people like that make it harder for us to gain our freedom."

"I guess so, but honestly, I don't think we'll ever achieve anything peacefully." I continued to sound casual and knew I was taking quite a risk being so forthright this fast, but I thought I had no alternative. I noticed him round on me, but he said nothing. This was the moment to drop the subject for a while, and we worked in silence before eventually talking about other innocuous matters.

At lunch, I returned the favor and gave him back the sandwich. Marie Martin had made it for me, and apparently, she'd had lunch ready for me the previous day, but I'd left before she got up and gave it to me. Dwayne wasn't present this time. The afternoon passed quietly with no further discussion on political matters, but as we left for the day, Moulton turned and said, "Look, a group of friends of mine are meeting up tonight for a few drinks. You should come along. Although we do talk about political bullshit." He grinned at that last line.

"Sounds like fun," I laughed. He told me where to meet up. We said goodbye, and I headed home. My official Martian ID still said I was seventeen, but fortunately, Jennifer was eighteen, which meant I could go into a bar without being kicked out for being underage. Regardless of what Charlotte said, I was still a minor on Mars.

I returned to my apartment and looked for something appropriate to wear. Seducing men had not been on my agenda, and I really didn't feel I had anything appropriate. I told Luke Martin this, and he simply replied, "Don't worry, I'll get something sorted." He went off and made a call, and two hours later, there was a delivery at the door. As I took the package into my room and opened it, I grinned at the obscenely short skirt, ankle boots, and t-shirt that was one size too small for me and would accentuate my attributes. I slipped a small pin-sized recording device behind the shirt's collar. It would automatically record everything said and upload it to the chip in my head.

Changed, I headed for the door and glanced at Marie, who was staring at me. I hadn't heard her speak once since I'd come here. It irritated me, so I smiled at her and said, "Don't wait up, Ma. I might be late."

"I'm glad you find this so amusing, young lady." It was the first time she had spoken to me. "When this is done, we are done. Understand me?

I shook my head and genuinely replied, "No, not really."

She stood up, her eyes filled with contempt for me. "Whatever my daughter did, we've made up for it. When will she be coming home?"

"MARIE!" Luke Martin hurried over to her as he came out of the bedroom. "Be quiet. She's a field agent. She has no clue about our agreement with the Department."

Tears came to Marie's eyes, and Luke quickly calmed down as he pulled his wife toward him and held her close.

"I just want Jennifer to come home."

Damn! This was awkward. "Look, I gotta go. Is she gonna be okay?"

Luke smiled softly at me and nodded.

I headed out, wondering what the fuck that was all about.

CHAPTER SIX

THE MARTIAN LIBERATION FRONT

Following Moulton's directions, I found myself down a dingy back alley on the surface. The bar was seriously shady, which was a surprise since surface-based establishments were usually premium places. Above ground was pretty exclusive. But apparently, the wealthy didn't want to do business in this shithole of a sector. The bar, like everything on Mars (well, at least in Brooklyn) was small and cramped, catering mostly for standing room only. However, there were a couple of booths where you would receive a surcharge on your drinks for the privilege of sitting down.

I was surprised to see no-one else in the bar besides the small group around Moulton, seated in one of those aforementioned booths. He saw me come in and got up to greet me. Some woman also got up with him, stepped past me, and threw a bolt across the door. A pang of unease ran through me as she did this. I looked questionably at Moulton. "Private party, don't worry." He grinned.

The woman turned to me, gave me a nervous smile, and offered me her hand. "Lucinda Braithwaite. You can call me Lucy."

Although she smiled, it was clearly with unease nervousness and a lack of trust. I took her hand and smiled warmly. "Jen Martin," I replied, and she indicated the table where three others sat. I walked over with her and Moulton and sat down. One of the men pushed an empty glass towards me, and the other lifted a pitcher of beer and poured me a glass. I glanced over to the bar, but I saw no one serving. "Not even a barman?"

"That would be me," Braithwaite said. "This is my place."

Everyone was staring at me, and I tried not to look uncomfortable until I realized being uncomfortable would be expected, with five pairs of eyes boring into me.

"Tell us about yourself," one of the men said, and it sounded more like an order than a conversational request, but I complied. I delivered my back story about living in New Philadelphia until recently, having moved here with my parents. I hoped to the Almighty that none of these people were familiar with New Philadelphia because I certainly wasn't. The city was the unofficial capital of the Pacific Alliance Martian colonies and was where all trade came in and out of. In fact, it was the only place you could get off the planet, unless you hitched a ride with a Peon. The Department of Outland Security had chosen it as part of my background because everybody knew something about New Philadelphia. I'd never left Brooklyn, but had

I just said I'd moved from a different part of town, that could be easily checked upon.

Although I wasn't aware of it at the time, I apparently have an engaging personality. I make people feel at ease. Charlotte would eventually tell me this is what helped her decide to accept me into their ranks. I'm also told I'm fairly attractive, and it's a matter of human nature to be drawn to attractive people. That's why the hot kids are also the cool kids.

As I chatted about my life in Philadelphia, the group around me relaxed a little, but there was still that edge. And tension grew once more when Moulton said, "Jen recently expressed a similar interest of ours." It was clear from their reactions that he'd already discussed this with them, but it was his way of raising the subject.

"You've known her two days, Moulton," Braithwaite said coldly.

"Which is why I brought her here to meet you," Moulton said dismissively. "She's already told me enough that can get her arrested. She can hardly report us without reporting herself."

"For fuck's sake, Moulton, she could be an agent of Outland Security and lying to get you on her side." Braithwaite snapped. My heart skipped a beat at those words, and I struggled to maintain composure.

Moulton scoffed. "Look at her. She's just a kid. Do you really think this little girl is a trained operative of Charlotte Kensett?"

Thinking quickly, I interceded. I acted like I was confused about what they were talking about and said, "Okay, what the fuck is going on here?" I said aggressively, looking as if I was getting ready to stand up. "I come in here. You lock the door and start talking like you're some sort of terrorist group, and who the fuck is Charlotte Kinsit?" I deliberately mispronounced her last name.

"Relax, Jen," Moulton said. "You're amongst like-minded friends here. You just have to understand my friends here have to be cautious."

Of course, they were being far from cautious, but what Mouton said was technically right. I had implicated myself in expressing an opinion that an armed insurrection was the only way for Mars to gain independence. If I really was Jennifer Martin, the would-be revolutionary, and I was to turn them in, it wouldn't take the authorities long to find out that I, too, had expressed treasonous thoughts.

"All I said to you was that Mars would never be free. We tried to do it by peaceful means. I didn't say that I would be a part of some...revolt," I said. Going in gung-ho shouting 'power to the people' was not the way to handle this situation. Force them to convince me.

"When did we say we were part of some revolt? "Braithwaite said coldly.

"Honestly, if you really thought I was a dumbass, I wouldn't be sitting here. Yet here we are, meeting in secret, in a locked bar, talking about Outland Security, and me having similar views to Moulton here. The only views I've expressed to him, beyond conversations about movies and fashion, are my political opinions. Terry, himself, said his friends would be discussing politics. So don't fuck with me!" I started getting out of my seat again, clearly intending to leave. I was praying to God the Almighty that they would stop me.

"Jen!" Moulton said. "Don't you want to change the way things are?"

"Of course I do!" I shouted back at him as I spun around and fixed my eyes on his. "But all I see here is a bunch of egos sitting around the table. Personally, I don't think you have the balls to do anything but just sit here and blather to appease your conscience. Convince me otherwise, Moulton, or I'm just walking out of here, because I'm not going to prison for talking about this stuff. If I go to jail, it's gonna be for something worthwhile."

"Do you remember the attack on that Department of Environment building a few months back?" asked Braithwaite, sitting back in her chair and folding her arms.

"The Roosevelt Center?" I said softly, and she nodded. A Silence hung there for a moment. "That was you?" I asked, looking impressed.

There was another silence before Moulton said, "That was us."

I smiled and sat back down. My smile was genuine for that moment. I truly believed I had just succeeded in my mission. That admission meant everyone sitting here could be rounded up and questioned, and the truth would come out. I had it all recorded, after all.

"So now you know we mean business," Braithwaite said firmly. "Now, what we need to know is, do you?"

"I sure do," I said enthusiastically.

"And we're supposed to just take your word on this?" She said, looking at me in a most patronizing way.

She was severely pissing me off, but I couldn't show it. "What do you want me to do to prove I'm more than willing to help you with your work?" To be honest, I was willing to agree to absolutely anything, because I now genuinely believed that when I left here tonight, I wouldn't be coming back.

"Do you believe you're able to kill someone?" One of the, as yet unnamed, men asked quite calmly. Of course, I made sure I knew everyone's name before I left the room that night.

"Well, it all depends on who you would expect me to kill," I replied with the right amount of unease. After all, I didn't want to come off as some psycho like Emma Dodgson, who I would encounter many years later. "It would have to be extraordinarily exceptional circumstances to kill a fellow Martian, but honestly, I don't think I have a problem killing one of those American fuckers."

"Well, we can't promise you that we would never put you in a situation where you can avoid killing a Martian," Braithwaite said. "In the bombing of the government building, we killed a lot of Martians. Sometimes sacrifices had to be made."

"If it comes to that, maybe it's possible, but right now, I can't even fathom doing it," I replied.

Her next words hit me right in the gut, and I thought I'd lost all the headway I'd made. "Then perhaps you're not the right person to join us."

"Hold your horses right there, Lucinda," said Moulton raising a hand to her. "You know full well we don't intend to have her kill a Martian to prove herself. She wouldn't be human if she didn't have doubts about harming a Martian."

"You want me to kill someone?" I questioned disbelievingly, and it was quite genuine this time.

"Call it an induction," said Braithwaite. "We've all had to do it, so don't take it personally. We need you to compromise yourself to cement the trust within the group. We have something on everyone around this table, and they can't betray us without betraying themselves."

"Do you think you can do it?" Moulton asked me.

I sat there mulling this over. At least, this is what I appeared to do because I had no intention of killing anybody. I just wanted to get out of here and put in a call to Charlotte Kensett to say, 'Job done, give me a medal.'

"Yeah," I said, eventually looking at each of them.

Moulton looked towards Braithwaite questioningly, and she returned the look before glancing back at me. "Let me be honest with you, Jennifer. There's something about you I don't trust. I can't put my finger on it, but my gut is telling me not to trust you, but I'm gonna give you a chance." She slipped her hand into her pocket, pulled out a slip of paper, and slid it across the table. It had a photo of a man in a suit named Jordan Wilson.

"Who's this?" I asked.

"Department of Outland Security Sector Chief, a particularly vicious piece of shit we want you to take out," Braithwaite sneered.

I looked up at her. "You want me to kill a Sector Chief? They're gonna come down on us like a ton of bricks. It was bad enough when you blew up the government building, but Outland Security will likely get a little pissed about taking out one of their own."

"We are well aware of the consequences, Jennifer," Moulton said. "It won't be pretty, but it'll get a message out there that Outland Security is not as untouchable as they think they are."

"And just how do you expect me to do this?" I asked. "Sector Chiefs don't generally wander around the city waiting to get shot."

"But they don't live in the sector house, do they?" said one of the men snippily.

"Think of it as an initiative test, as well as a loyalty test," Braithwaite said as Moulton slipped his hand into his jacket and pulled something out, which he slid across the table to me. I looked down at a snap pistol, the kind only used on starships with low-velocity jet-propelled ammunition designed to kill a person, but not puncture the hull. I stared at it for a while, then picked it up.

"Where do you expect me to put this?" I said, looking down at my clothing.

This brought a grin from Moulton, and he took back the weapon. "I'll walk you home and give it to you there."

I got up out of my seat. "How long do I have on this?"

Braithwaite shrugged. "There's no time limit, but you're not to come back here until it's done. Don't talk to any of us other than Moulton at work, until your task is completed."

I nodded and headed out, with Moulton following behind me. "That Lucinda is quite a bitch, you know that, don't you?" I said as we reached the street.

Moulton laughed at this. "When she gets to trust you, she's the woman you're gonna wanna have at your back. She would take a bullet for you."

"I'll take your word on that."

As we reached my apartment complex, I turned back and looked at him, and he looked down at me. I reached up and ran my hand along his collar. "I was hoping that tonight I'd get to know you better. I must admit I'm disappointed."

I don't know why I did it, but since my instruction had been to seduce him, it felt like I was completing the task. Maybe it was my own insecurity about whether I could have succeeded.

"Perhaps we can do that once this task is done. I'd like that very much." He smiled down at me.

I smiled sweetly, and reaching up, kissed him on the cheek. "Goodnight, Terry."

I turned to go back into the building, but he suddenly called me back. "Don't forget this." Turning to face him again, I saw the gun in his hand. Smiling, I simply took it and placed it in the band of my skirt at the back and covered it with my shirt. Stepping into the building, I remained in the reception, not intending to go to the Martin's apartment. I had someone to call, and it couldn't wait. However, despite my beliefs, this would turn out to be far from over.

The moment I was sure that Moulton had left the area, I headed back outside and, walking up the street, I pulled out my phone.

"I'm sure you're aware that it is not protocol to call me whilst you're undercover." Charlotte Kensett's first words were quite curt. "This better be serious, especially as you woke me up."

"Mission objectives complete," I said quite smugly.

There was a pause. "I will send a car for you, and we'll meet tonight at the sector house."

Still on a high with incredibly smug pride twenty minutes later, I was sitting in front of Charlotte Kensett, who made it incredibly hard to believe that she had only been woken up less than half an hour ago. Once again, she looked immaculate. I couldn't help but amuse myself, thinking she went to bed and got up that way.

"Okay, Ky, let's hear it." She said as she poured coffee for herself and handed me one.

As I told her the night's events, I sat back, feeling quite proud of myself. "I have the conspirators' names, and they have even admitted to blowing up the government building a couple of months back. It's all recorded. I got them banged to rights."

"My my, I didn't know this group was involved with that incident," Charlotte smiled quite genuinely for once. "We've been trying to find the conspirators for a long time, and you've done it in just two days. I'm impressed. Did you get the name of their network contact in New Philadelphia?"

"Huh?" I said, bemused.

Charlotte looked a little disappointed at my reaction and said, "No matter, you have done excellently well, and

I'm not taking that away from you, but your job isn't done yet. I need that name."

"Well, there is a snag with that, Boss," I said, feeling the euphoria I had diminish immediately. "They won't meet me again unless I prove myself to 'em. They've given me an assignment to do, and it's something that can't be done."

"Oh, don't be coy, Ky," she smiled. "Tell me. What is it that they want you to do?"

"They wanted me to kill a sector chief of Outland Security." I sighed.

She raised an eyebrow. "My my, that is certainly a difficult task they've given you there. Do you know the name of this sector chief, although I probably can already guess? Joshua Wilson, of their sector?" I simply nodded in response. "And do you have a particular problem in completing this task?"

"Well, yeah," I said, confused. "He's a member of our department."

Charlotte smiled softly and sat back. "You know, Ky, we don't live in a perfect world, and security matters are complicated. I need that name, and that name is more important than a Sector Chief that I can easily replace."

"You seriously want me to carry out this assassination?" I said, and I think my jaw was hanging down to my knees as I said it.

"Sacrifices need to be made for the greater good. Wilson is an adequate sector chief, but he's not one of my best people, and it's not like it will set us back in any way. Of course, we'll have to come down hard on the sector just for showmanship, but we'll even help you carry this out. I will see that Wilson is in a position for you to take him out quite easily." I hesitated to reply, and she frowned softly. "Do you have a problem with doing this?"

"Apart from the suggestion that I kill a member of my own team," I said sarcastically. "I've never actually killed someone before."

"Well, first of all, it's not a suggestion." She actually chuckled. "It's an order, and secondly," she paused and gave me the sweetest smile. "Killing people gets easier the more you do it. Trust me on that." Sadly, that would prove to be true but let me not get ahead of myself here.

"I'll give it my best shot," I said weakly.

"Oh, you'll have to, my dear, because you'll only get one." She grinned.

"That's not what I meant."

"I know, my dear, it was supposed to be a joke."

Wow. The cold bitch.

CHAPTER SEVEN

AN IGNOBLE SACRIFICE

I was dropped off, back in that foul sector which I'd hoped I would never have to visit again. Once more, it was several blocks from where I was staying, and it was almost dawn before I got into bed. I had about two hours of sleep before I had to return to work. Moulton didn't mention anything about anything, and there was an awkward silence between us for the next couple of days. I had nothing to do that weekend, other than wait for the call from Charlotte or one of her cronies.

On Friday night, I felt compelled to visit the synagogue. I always went with my family, but it was never by a particular choice, but more by routine. It's simply what we did on Friday nights. But now I was being asked to kill a man. While I'd never considered that something I couldn't do, finding myself in this situation played heavily on my conscience. I can honestly say I didn't really know what the religious ramifications of what I was doing would be, and it wasn't like I could ask the rabbi to discuss it.

I was greeted warmly as a newcomer to the congregation, listened to all the planned events, and was invited to various people's houses for dinner, as was the way. I politely declined, saying that I wasn't staying in the area for long, and avoided the many questions about myself. Several women tried to introduce me to their sons, and I went along with it.

Saturday morning came, and I didn't really want to hang around in that apartment with Marie staring at me. So once more, I went up to the surface and spent most of my day walking around the sector, deep in thought. Around lunchtime, my phone rang. I didn't recognize the number, but I answered it all the same.

"Agent Lieberman, you will listen to these instructions, and you will not speak, other than to confirm your understanding of them when I have finished." The voice was that of a man, an old one, and I complied with his instructions. "Your target will be leaving his apartment complex for a trip to the movie theater. He will be coming out around 2pm. You are to position yourself outside. You will only have as long as it takes for him to walk from the door to the car waiting for him. His guards will attempt to apprehend you, but will only do it for show. You will remain perfectly safe. Upon completing your task, you are to go down Miller Street, where a car will pick you up. It will then return you to the residence where you are currently staying. We have arranged for any cameras in the area to be offline at the time and will ensure that no police drones are in the vicinity. Do you understand these instructions?"

"Yes," I replied, even though I found it hard to get the word out as I was visibly shaking now.

"Good luck, Agent Lieberman."

Those were his last words, and then the line simply went dead.

I slowly walked back to the Martin apartment. I changed into baggier clothes to hide the gun in my waistband. It was one o'clock, and I headed to Joshua Wilson's apartment block. I waited patiently, trying to be as inconspicuous as possible, looking in shop windows. I couldn't move too far away as I would literally have seconds.

When he finally came out at about ten minutes past two, I saw the two plainclothes guards following him, but what filled me with horror was that a woman and child were with him. The child was barely six years old. A knot tightened my stomach, but I didn't have time to think this out. It was simply now and never. It was enough of a delay that I almost missed the opportunity.

Wilson opened the door to let his wife and child get in. I certainly didn't want to shoot with them nearby. I'd never fired at anything other than a target before. Once he closed the door, he started to move around the other side, and that's when I started walking briskly towards him. A moment of concern crossed his face as he looked up and saw me coming, and he glanced at his guards, who were standing further from him than they should have.

A sudden realization crossed his face, and he started rushing to the other side of the car, but too late. Stepping up behind him, I raised the gun and fired straight into the back of his head.

I was already turning and running before he even hit the ground. I didn't look back, but I could hear the footsteps of his guards following me and calling out for me to stop.

As soon as I turned down Miller Street, they carried on past as if they'd lost me. I continued along Miller Steet until I almost passed a car that flashed its lights at me, and jumping into the passenger seat, I saw Shannon in the driver seat. "Is he dead?" she asked me.

"Well, I didn't exactly stop to check his pulse," I replied sarcastically through heavy breaths from my exertion. We drove the rest of the way in silence, and I was back in the apartment room less than ten minutes after the incident.

He was dead, alright. There was no mistake in that. It was on the news less than an hour later, and, despite the stress I felt myself going through at having taken a life, I almost laughed as I listened to an incredibly bad description of me being read out. No doubt Charlotte's work.

There was a lot of commotion resulting from this. The police were going from door to door throughout the sector, and a lockdown was in force, where no one was allowed to leave their apartments for over a day. However, it quickly lifted since Charlotte ensured this was a crime no-one would solve.

There was literally no evidence to trace it back to me, and I'd even left the gun with Shannon to dispose of. I had trouble coping with what I had done, and got even less sleep over the next few days. The image of his wife and kid is permanently burned into my brain to this day.

Monday came, and I had to go back to work. Moulton said nothing about it, but he was looking exceedingly cheerful. I admit I was sullen and unable to focus. He clearly understood the situation and didn't give me a hard time. I was working alone now, so we didn't have much time to engage, but as I left that evening, he stopped me. "If I recall, you promised me a date?" he said cheerfully.

I felt this was so cold after what had happened that I wondered if he was related to Charlotte Kensett. But I still had a job to do. We met up that night in a different bar to the one run by Braithwaite, and to be honest, it might've been a pleasant evening, if I hadn't just murdered someone the previous day.

Maintaining the facade of someone enjoying a date was impossible, but Moulton clearly understood it. To make things worse for me, he talked about his family life. He was divorced but had a kid living on the other side of town and was a clearly devoted father. I tried to push all thoughts about that out of my head, knowing that he'd probably never see that kid again if I was successful.

As it got late and we stood to leave, I decided to play on the recent events, and as we stepped outside and started heading back towards my apartment complex, I turned and looked up at him pitifully. "Terry, I know this is probably inappropriate of me, but I really don't wanna be alone tonight. My parents are very suspicious of my sudden mood change, and I really can't get out of it. Please don't let me go home."

"It's fine. Everything's gonna be okay," he said, running a hand gently through my hair. "Come on, let's go back to my place."

His apartment was like every other. Except, for being single, he only had one bedroom.

I was hoping he would take advantage of the situation and seduce me, but I guess he was more of a gentleman than I realized. He got out blankets and pillows, telling me he would sleep on the couch in the living room.

I felt incredibly uncomfortable knowing what I was expected to do. It's really stupid when you think about it. Being more uncomfortable about fucking someone than killing a guy is positively ludicrous, but it was the case. He was about to say goodnight to me, and before I realized it, I had my arms up around his neck and was pulling him down to kiss me. He had that moment of indecision where his brain conflicted with his dick on the appropriate thing to do. So, I gave the dick some encouragement by grinding my body against his and running my hands over his back.

I felt his tense body suddenly relax. I knew this was gonna happen. I didn't exactly have any experience with this, and so I had to draw inspiration from a mixture of the romantic movies my mother watched, mixed with the scenes in some of Ben's porn collection. I felt him stiffen against my belly. He suddenly crouched down, lifted me into his arms, and carried me into the bedroom like some corny love story. Laying me down on the bed, he started to remove my clothes, and I struggled to find in my memory what I was supposed to do now, but he clearly took the lead. It hurt like hell when he finally entered me. I freely admit that I had no idea that I was supposed to be turned on during this process for it to be more enjoyable.

And that was how I lost my virginity. No love, no passion, nothing but an incredibly uncomfortable experience. Real romantic, huh? I even had to pretend that it was the best thing that'd ever happened to me. When he finished, I wanted to cry as he rolled back onto the bed beside me.

I couldn't help but reflect on what I'd got myself into. The idea that this was going to be some sort of wonderful adventure was a dream that was long gone, and at that moment, I hated myself. I hated Charlotte Kensett, I hated Outland Security, and I hated the world. This had been something that I'd dreamed about, dreamed what it would be like. My first time should have been with the guy I loved, but, instead of being an amazing experience, it was dirty and ruined forever.

And I had just killed a man.

A family man, a man I didn't know. He could have been the most heinous bastard you've ever met, or he could have been the kindest. It didn't matter. Somewhere that night, a wife and child were mourning the loss of that man, and I felt like shit.

"Are you okay?" Moulton drew me from my deep thoughts, and I turned to smile at him as he lay next to me.

"A lot has happened. You have to understand that."

"I do, but trust me, the more times you do it, the easier it gets." I wasn't sure if he was talking about killing the man or having sex. But it clicked in my head that he'd said exactly the same thing that Charlotte Kensett had told me. Were they so different?

"Tell me it's worth it, Terry. Tell me it's not just a group of five people who meet in some bitch's pub that make occasional futile attacks on government buildings. Is there a real resistance out there?"

"I promise you there's a network all over the planet," he replied reassuringly. "And it's not just us. There are even

Europeans out there in their communities that think just like we do. We're a growing network."

"But someone out there must be leading all this, coordinating everything," I said hesitantly, acting like I was still unsure of what I already knew to be fact.

"Of course there is," he said, trying to sound reassuring.

"Who is it?" I said, sounding desperate.

"Why do you want to know?" he said suspiciously. I glared at him and then jumped out of the bed, grabbing for my clothes. "Where are you going? I thought you were gonna stay here?"

I picked up a shoe and threw it at him, deliberately missing, shouting, "I just fucking killed a man for you! If you don't trust me now, then I don't know what'll make you."

"It's not that easy, Jen." He said, looking quite conflicted. "That sort of information is on a need-to-know basis. It could bring down the entire organization."

"I killed a man so that you would trust me now. I need to know that I can trust you and that you won't drop me in it. If you're not willing to tell me, all it tells me is exactly what you think of me, and it's certainly not good."

He sighed and looked down with a heavy sigh. "His name is Emilio Sanchez. He's a civil administrator in the government based in Philadelphia." He then glared at me as if I had just beaten a confession out of him.

I feigned relief, calming myself down. "See. Was that so hard?"

He already looked as though he regretted doing it. "I shouldn't have told you that. It was a mistake." I slid back into the bed beside him. "If anyone finds out..."

"Shh!" I said softly, putting a finger on his lips, and ran my hand down to his member, caressing it softly.

He moaned softly and closed his eyes. Turns out that a hand job is a good distraction when a man has betrayed everything he stood for. By the time he woke up, I was already gone.

Heading out into the street, I once more put in a call to Charlotte Kensett.

"You are a constant source of surprise to me," she said, and while she tried to sound cheerful, you couldn't mistake the irritability in her voice. "I suppose you're about to tell me that you now have everything I need." The sarcasm was equally noticeable.

"Emilio Sanchez." That was all I said.

There was a pause. "Are you seriously telling me that's the name of the man we're looking for?"

"Yes. Can I go home now?"

In quite a euphoric tone, Charlotte replied. "A car is already on its way to you."

It turned out that Emilio Sanchez was a member of the Martian administration. Quite a high-ranking one. This was certainly a feather in the cap for Charlotte Kensett, whose name quickly became well-known throughout the Department. Moulton, Braithwaite, and the rest of them were arrested in a raid on Braithwaite's bar a few days later. I stayed in some quarters in the section house until the rest of the week was finished, as I couldn't return home without explaining why I was coming back early.

For myself, there was no glory other than the praise of Charlotte Kensett. But the nature of my work was that it goes unsung. I didn't begrudge Charlotte getting all the credit for everything. I didn't really want it. I continued working for Charlotte Kensett for the next two years, breaking up various rings, and was quite successful at it.

I moved out of my parent's apartment, and as a reward for my services, I received accommodation on the surface that, in comparison, was quite luxurious. Although you Earthers out there would still consider it cramped, it was twice the size of anything else anyone I knew had. However, I was rarely at home and traveled to various cities on Mars to carry out my duties.

I never had to kill anyone again during that time, but I'll never forget Joshua Wilson and his family.

Two years later, my career as a spy on Mars ended abruptly. The Peons blockaded the planet, and all contact with Earth and the Alliance was lost. They cut off all supplies to everyone except their own European communities, and although some of those communities tried to supply us, it wasn't long before the civil administration had to capitulate, and any Alliance forces that could get off the planet did so, including Charlotte Kensett, who simply disappeared. I didn't know if the Peons had got her, or if she'd fled until many years later.

Chapter Eight

Operation Tangent

The Department of Outland Security had prepared for this situation. They must've known the war wasn't going their way, or they were significantly over-prepared. Operation Tangent was a pipeline designed to get everyone out should Mars fall to the enemy. When I say everyone, I'm only referring to members of the Department of Outland Security and other Alliance officials that weren't native to the planet or people like me, who the Peons wanted to arrest for our services to the state. I'd received an encrypted communication from the Department telling me to make my way back to New Philadelphia, which incidentally was the only place on the planet with facilities for launching crafts into space. I was stopped several times at checkpoints, but my fake I.D.s held up, indicating they hadn't entered our computer system yet. It was equally possible that the higher-ups destroyed the records before leaving.

The address I was given was kind of weird, as it turned out to be a small warehouse operating as a tire manufacturing storage place. It turned out it was a front for

Outland Security, and once I'd identified myself, I was led through a hidden door. There was no hanging around. They clearly wanted me in and out of there. A man was sitting behind a computer terminal at a desk in the middle of a room. It was clearly not designed to be an office, and was more of a storage area. Once again, it seemed like something out of a movie, for he was surrounded by stacked-up tires. They were moving so fast that there wasn't even a chair for me to sit on as I stood before him.

"Full name." He barked at me, like it was an order. Grim, angry at something. Didn't wish to be here.

"Kyla Eliana Lieberman," I replied, and he typed it in.

"Please place all I.D.s into this box." I removed all the fake I.D.s from my purse, but took my genuine one out of the collection and placed it back in it. The man looked up at me. "I said all I.Ds."

"This is my real one." I frowned.

"Oh, exactly what do you think is gonna happen if you're caught with that on you?" He said most patronizingly with an air of impatience.

Good point! I retrieved it once more and dropped it into the box, and he hit a button on the side of it. There was a flash of light, and everything in the box was instantly destroyed.

"You are a bit late to the party, Agent Lieberman. No Alliance registered ships are being allowed out. Just neutral and Peon."

"Well, I don't care if it's a neutral ship. Can't you pay someone off?" I said with a little irritation.

He looked at me like I was stupid. "I suppose you think the Peons will let you past their checkpoints with that accent of yours?" He looked back at his computer. "I suppose we could try and get you in a cargo crate. It's risky, and the chances you'll make it are slim."

Obviously, I didn't like the sound of that, but then something occurred to me. I tapped the side of my head and said, "I have this." When he looked at me questioningly, I elaborated. "Eidetic memory chip. If you can get your hands on some language files, I can be fluent in any language you like in thirty seconds."

He looked surprised at my reference to the chip, but made no comment about it, as he pondered a moment and then told me to wait in another room while he made some calls, and after about twenty minutes, he called me back. "We've got you on a Chechnyan ship. However, we don't have any Chechen language programs. You're gonna have to make do with Russian."

"Do Chechens speak Russian?" I asked. Truth be told, I'd never even heard of Chechens before. At least, I didn't remember having heard of them.

"Of course, otherwise there wouldn't be any point to this, would there now, Agent Lieberman?" he said quite tersely.

It took a couple of hours for him to find a tech with eidetic memory chip experience, but eventually, I was sitting in a small room with a nerdy little guy who raved on about the wonders of this technology. It took a little bit longer than thirty seconds. The language files had to be uploaded to a portable eidetic memory hub. Then the technician had to tap in the unlock codes that I provided, for my chip to access the Wi-Fi connection. There was a slight tingling sensation on the side of my head where the chip was. Upon completion, I looked at him and asked, "Eto srabotalo?"

He smiled back at me and shrugged. "I have no idea what you said, but it appears to have worked."

I grinned back at him. "That's exactly what I asked."

He led me back to the front desk, where I was once more greeted by Mr. Sunshine and his cheerful disposition.

"Stand over there in front of the screen." He grunted at me.

I saw where he was referring to and walked over, and stood in front of it, as another man snapped a picture of me. He then beckoned me to come back to the table. An I.D. card was printed out by the small machine at his side. He pulled it out and handed it to me. "Your name is now Ksenia Bortnick. You are a Chechen serving on board the Kamchatka, a civilian vessel that hauls waste. When you leave, you'll go to Starport Seventeen in the Northern District. A man named Peter Delaney will be expecting you." He then waved a dismissive hand at me and carried on typing.

I just looked at the I.D., confused. "If they're neutral, why are they helping us?"

He sighed wearily, as if he was being incredibly inconvenienced by my very existence. "Because we're paying them a lot of money. The Peons won't stop them from leaving because they don't want to bring them into the war against them, and it's really your only way out of here. Now if you don't mind, I must ask you to leave. The less you know about this place, the better."

I tried to say something else, but the guard that had led me in took me by the arm, an indicator that I had to leave. I complied. And when we got to the door, he simply said good luck and closed it behind me. I looked down at the Ksenia Bortnick I.D. again. Senia spelled with a K at the beginning. I wouldn't have known how to pronounce it if he hadn't said it himself. I couldn't help thinking what a cluster fuck this was as I jumped onto the tram that would take me to the docking port.

The New Philadelphia Interstellar Airport was hectic at the best of times. However, many people were trying to leave. The Peons had blocked any Martians or Alliance individuals from departing the planet, and as I lined up, I could see everyone ahead of me being turned away, and I grew nervous as I reached the front. You may think after two years that I wouldn't be scared of this sort of thing, but it was one thing going up against your own people with the authority of the government, and another to be going up against the authority of an enemy government.

The closer I got to the front, the more my nerves got frayed about when they spoke to me.

However, when I handed the I.D. over to the Peon soldier at the checkpoint, he looked at it for a long time, then looked at me and said something in French. I just stared blankly at him. He repeated himself in heavily accented English. "Do you intend to return to Mars?"

Again, I stared at him, even though I obviously understood now. "I'm sorry, I do not speak French or English,"

I said in fluent Russian that even a native would be unable to tell that I was a Brooklyn girl.

He sighed and pointed with his thumb for me to go through the barrier.

This was only the first of one checkpoint. The next one checked the contents of my bag, and I was relieved that the agent back at the warehouse had insisted I turn over all my I.D.s and equipment.

As I entered the main concourse, a board overhead told me where every ship was currently docked. Finding the Kamchatka, I started heading over to the bay. My heart sank as I stepped through. I looked up at the ship that was supposed to take me out of here. It was not a cargo ship. Even I knew that with my very little familiarity with such things. It was a trash hauler. Specifically designed for dumping waste into space.

I looked around for someone, but no one was there. All the airlocks were closed, and it looked for the world like the ship had just been abandoned there, waiting for a scrap dealer to come and take it apart. Suddenly, a voice came over the loudspeaker emanating from the ship. "Are you Miss Bortnick?" The voice asked in very broken English.

"Apparently so," I replied.

"Step up to the airlock nearest you, and I will come down and open it for you." I did as I was told, and a few minutes later, the door opened, and the cheery-faced, portly man greeted me at the door. "Come on in, Miss Bortnick. Welcome aboard the Kamchatka." He stood aside for me to enter. He then wiped his greasy palms on his pants and offered me a grubby hand, which I took without showing any sign of my disgust. It wasn't like I wasn't used to getting dirty by this time.

"You don't have to speak English. I understand your language," I said in perfect Russian.

He looked delighted by this, replying in Russian. "If you forgive me for the rush, but I think that now that you are aboard, we should get out of here as fast as possible."

I didn't feel reassured as he led me through the ship, because it was a complete wreck. It must have been well over a hundred years old. I've since heard Michael Phelkar talk about the state of the U.S.S. Lewis Puller, but it couldn't have been worse than the Kamchatka. The vessel was literally broken pipes, worn-out wiring, and rust. I was starting to think that going out as cargo may actually have been the safer option.

I noticed a faint unpleasant odor as I followed him, and it took me a while to realize it emanated from Peter. Gross! However, it would turn out that the water recycling unit was what he called 'a little shaky,' and showers were not an option.

He took me into a filthy cockpit with two seats at the controls. The room was covered with old coffee cups and the various stains where they had put them on the counter. It also looked like the floor of a movie theater at the end of the movie. Honestly, it was disgusting. He leaned over to the co-pilot seats and brushed it down a little bit before saying, "Please take a seat, Miss Bortnick." I did so. I was surprised to see some makeshift seat belts attached by someone who clearly didn't know what they were doing. "Please put those on."

"Don't you have inertial dampeners?" I asked nervously.

"We do, but they are a little shaky." He waggled his hand from side to side. Great! I had no idea how literal that statement was until we launched. He then reviewed some pre-flight checks before hitting on his communications to the docking authorities. "This is the Kamchatka," he said in his broken English. "We are looking for permission for immediate liftoff."

"You have clearance Kamchatka." A British voice came back. "You have a ten-minute window to clear Martian airspace."

"Oh, we will do our best, Control," Peter replied uneasily. "But please remember, we are an old ship, and you can't push an old lady too far."

"Do your best, Kamchatka. I will note the possibility that you may have difficulties completing this, but I can't guarantee what the Peons will do." It was then clear that Alliance personnel were still running things, but under observation by the Peons.

Then the engines powered up, and everything around me started to shake. As Peter slowly lifted the craft into the air, I was terrified we were about to break up, but there was a grinding of metal and a whining strain coming from the engines. I even closed my eyes and said one of my prayers.

Everything fell silent instantaneously. My eyes shot open, and I found myself staring out into an inky blackness, bespeckled with the small silver lights of the universe. I felt queasy as my body became weightless, but that didn't detract from the wondrous sight before me. I was in space. Mars was behind me, and an unknown future was ahead. "We have cleared Martian Air Space Control," Peter reported. "Setting a course for Earth. Arrival time six months, two weeks and four days."

"Copy that, Kamchatka. I hope one day I will see it again too." The voice came back dejectedly.

When communications were cut, I looked at him and said incredulously, "Six months? Even at its longest distance from us, the journey is about three months."

He chuckled at this. "Not in this ship, sweetheart, not in this ship."

There were only two crew members on board. Delaney and Petrov, who was the ship's engineer, but he doubled as the cook. He was a pretty good one. Although he made incredibly unhealthy meals, they were absolutely delicious. They were an older couple who had been together most of their lives and married soon after becoming partners.

I found myself mostly getting in the way until one morning, Peter said to me, "If you are really bored, Miss Bortnick, I can find you some work?"

"Actually, I think I can find my own work. Where did you keep the cleaning supplies?" I responded. He told me, and I set about cleaning that bucket of shit from top to bottom, and it may surprise you, but it took me nearly a month. Although it was a small ship, it was incredibly filthy, and with nothing else to do, I went at it with the idea that it would sparkle. I even stole Delaney's toothbrush to use to clean those hard-to-reach places. I just spent several days working on every room, cleaning every nook and cranny. I removed every stain and mark, and even went into engineering and polished the engines, which was quite dangerous while it was running. In the evenings, we would sit down and watch Chechen and Russian movies, mostly comedies, and they would laugh while I got quite bored. I didn't get Russian humor.

The life support system made me very nervous because it would often cut out. Peter and Petrov seemed quite used to this. Alright it didn't really bother them. They just went and jerry-rigged it back into working again.

I got Peter to invest in some maintenance programs, and logging into an Alliance comms buoy, I purchased and downloaded the schematics of the design of the Kamchatka's model, along with some manuals on electrics. Fully loaded, I set about making repairs. Of course, I could only patch things as a lot of things required replacing. Sadly that included the water recycling, so my dreams of a shower were to remain just that, dreams. Another thing I was unable to fix was the coolant system. The ship was incredibly hot. So hot that I ended up cutting off the legs of my jeans and turning my shirts into crop tops, choosing comfort over modesty.

As we approached Earth in the last four weeks, Peter started to turn up the gravity. He had maintained the Martian levels because it saved on power, but as he explained, continual low gravity that didn't match that of humanity's home world weakened the muscles, and by slowly bringing it up to 1G, I gradually started to notice the difference as the musculature of my legs began to become more fully formed and less skinny. Even my arms began to become more defined as things became heavier. The change was so gradual, that I didn't even notice the change in weight by the time we arrived on Earth.

Chapter Nine

The End of the War

I was prepared for all the changes, except one. New Brooklyn was, as was every Martian community, hidden behind a protective dome that filtered out the dangerous aspects of the sun, such as radiation and U.V. rays. This meant everything was a lot darker than it was on Earth. As a result, when I stepped out on Earth for the first time, it hurt my eyes. I had to wear sunglasses, regardless of the weather outside.

Of course, we landed in Chechnya. Grozny, to be precise, and my I.D. now couldn't pass muster, since they had no records of a Ksenia Bortnik. So I was immediately arrested. However, the Chechens had been growing more sympathetic to the Pacific Alliance cause over the last few years, and indeed, eventually, they would join the war on the Alliance's side. But that wasn't now, and I remained in custody for several days. Eventually, to my surprise, they offered to release me and transport me to the United States.

"I have no reason to go to the USA. I'm not an American. I'd rather stay here." I told the official as he was sorting out my release papers.

"Are you refusing to leave Chechnya?" He asked me curtly.

"No, but I have no interest in going to America." I insisted.

He looked confused. "But you are an American."

I took immediate offense at this. "I'm damn well not. I'm Martian." I snapped.

He looked even more confused. "Devushka, there is no such nationality as a Martian."

"Tell that to a Martian!" I growled.

He smiled and shrugged. "I think I just did."

"Oh funny, ha ha," I replied sarcastically, but then took a deep breath and calmed myself. "Is there any reason I can't stay here?"

"Well, the law, for one thing. You will need a job and a sponsor. A Chechen citizen willing to take responsibility for any expenses you may incur from the government." And with that, ten minutes later, they allowed me to call Peter.

"But my dear Ksenia," he said. "We are not staying on Earth. We are going back out into space. That's my job."

"Then let me come with you! I have nothing here." I implored.

"You really want a career as a garbage hauler?" He asked incredulously.

"Peter, it's no worse than the garbage I was doing for the Alliance, and to be honest, I think I'm done with that life now. And hey, it's not gonna be forever. Mars is gonna be open to me again one day," I paused and sighed before adding, "I hope." Then imploring once more. "Come on,

Peter, you must admit I'm a hard worker, and we get on well. I don't even want paying. Just feed me and buy me some new clothes."

"Tell you what, I'll talk to Petrov and get back to you."

"Thank you, Peter. You won't regret this."

And it turned out to be a done deal, as a couple of hours later, I was released, and in the reception, I was greeted with hugs from Delaney and Petrov. I returned to the officer who was signing me out. He then slipped a card over the counter, and I looked at it. It was the I.D. of Ksenia Bortnick. I looked up at him questioningly. "Don't ask any questions. Let's just say there are people here that sympathize with your plight. It is now official, and legally you are Ksenia Bortnick, a citizen of Chechnya."

We stayed in Grozny for several weeks, and I got to see that beautiful city and the wonders of a blue sky, but that was nothing compared to what I would see over the next eight years. I traveled the Solar System with two of the best friends I've ever had. No, that's wrong. They became family to me, like two favorite uncles. I saw the wonders of the Solar System. The rings of Saturn to the Eye of Jupiter. The sulfur lakes of Titan to the ice geysers of Enceladus. All this time, collecting vast amounts of garbage and dumping them into space.

Things got a little more hairy when Chechnya joined the Alliance and entered the war. It affected our profits by reducing the number of systems we could visit, as we were banned from doing business with Peon colonies. It got even harder as the ship continued to age, and replacing spare parts became too expensive. I think towards the end, we held that thing together with glue and tape.

Then it all came to an abrupt end.

We were in transit back to Earth for the first time in a couple of years, and we received the news that America had surrendered to the European Union, followed the next day by the U.K. Then, like dominoes, everyone else followed suit. We waited for the inevitable, and finally heard it four days later. Chechnya had surrendered too.

"What the hell are we gonna do now," I said as the president finished his announcement.

"We go home, and we see what we will see." Peter shrugged.

"I'm still wanted by the damn Peons," I hesitated. "Well, at least I assume I am. So what's gonna happen if they're in control of Chechnya?"

"Maybe it won't be so bad if the war is over?" He shrugged. "Why would they even want you?"

"They're charging me with war crimes, Peter. People don't forget that." But he had no answer, and we continued on course, as there was nowhere else to go. And that is when we picked up the broadcast from Jenna Plural.

"This is Major Jenna Plural of the U.S.S. Lewis Puller, calling out to all free allied forces throughout the Solar System. We have chosen not to recognize the treasonous Pacific Alliance leaders who signed their surrender to the European Union and their functionaries. We call on our allies to rally to our cause and fight European imperialist oppression. We will rendezvous at coordinates that will be encrypted and transmitted after this message. The time has come to decide: Live under European Union oppression or be free once again. Please acknowledge this communication. Plural out."

"I think we have the answer. We head for those coordinates." Peter told me.

"That message was for military personnel, not civilians," I said testily.

"Well, what is she going to do if we turn up? She's hardly going to shoot us down." He laughed.

Oh, what irony those words would become.

It took us several weeks after we changed course to reach the rendezvous point, and we were pleased to discover that we weren't alone amongst the civilians who'd responded. I stared out in awe at a vast ship called the Twilight Wanderer, which was apparently a luxury cruise liner that traversed the Solar System with self liberties and rich assholes from around the Solar System. But that was nothing to the humongous military vessel, the U.S.S. Constitution, which hung in space like an avenging angel.

Ships of all sizes, makes, and models, both military and civilian, from all Alliance nations, came. A civilian administration was quickly set up under a man called Michael Phelkar, and we received a visit from a couple of the people from his office who were assessing what we had to offer the fleet. As we could have told them ... absolutely nothing.

That was soon to change.

Not only had we civilians picked up the message, but so had the Peons, and it was soon announced that a vast fleet had been gathered together and was on its way to take us out. There was quite a panic among the civilian ships that were mostly kept out of the loop, especially when we saw all the best ships heading away. Were we being abandoned? We couldn't listen to any communications, as the military now communicated on highly secure networks. Then, about a day before the Peons were due to engage us, there was suddenly some bizarre burst of communications as if every ship was talking at once, but amidst that, there was a short-range call directly to us. It would turn out this was all for our little garbage hauler's benefit. They wanted to hide the message that we would receive amid the chaos.

"Kamchatka. Please be prepared for an umbilical connection. This is a priority order." A woman's voice came over the radio. Peter and I looked at each other, unsure of what was happening. He reached over to the communication switch, and to my surprise, he answered in Russian. "Um, hi there, can you hear us? This is the Kamchatka. What do you want?"

"This is shuttle one four nine seven. Please be prepared to receive us," This time, the response was that of a man who spoke Russian like a native.

Again, Delaney looked towards me, but I merely shrugged, as bemused as he was. He turned back to the small microphone that extended from the console. "Oh, okay, um, we weren't really expecting company." He said in his broken English, and I had to stifle a laugh.

There was a pause until the uneasy response came. "Yes, well, this is a priority situation. I assure you we do have the authority to be here. However, I'm not going to discuss anything else over an unsecured channel. Please prepare for us to dock with you."

"Oh, okay then," Delaney said, looking extremely anxious at this turn of events. "We will be prepared to have you aboard. Would you be staying for dinner? Petrov gets really pissed if we don't inform him beforehand, or if there are any changes."

"Petrov?" The man responded, sounding somewhat perplexed.

"The ship's cook."

"Well, Kamchatka, you let Petrov know we'll be there for some time, and to prepare for three guests."

"Will do. We are looking forward to meeting you. We haven't seen anyone in months. It would be nice to have some company. Kamchatka out." He switched off the comms and swiveled in his chair to face me. "What do you think this is all about?"

"No clue, and I don't like it." I looked over at the video screen, at the various maneuvers of the fleet and once more listened to the comms chatter that was lighting up. "It might even be possible they're gonna commandeer our ship for something."

Peter snorted. "Well, we are certainly not going to let that happen. I am happy to work with these Alliance people, but the Kamchatka is our ship."

"Our ship?" I said with a warm smile.

"Oh, Ksenia, you have become like a daughter to me over the years. We are a family, and what's mine is yours, and what's yours is mine." He reached out, and patted my knee. I reached over to him, kissed him on his forehead, and hugged him tightly.

"Come on, we have to go prepare for our visitors." And by prepare, I meant I would go into the cargo hold and get out our snap pistols. This was our home, and we would not give it up without a fight. I checked they were loaded, and I handed one to Delaney, who stuck it in the back of his pants. Considering what I was wearing was barely clothing, I placed mine into a small recess behind the airlock door that they would be coming in from. I then delivered another to Petrov, who we agreed would remain out of sight as a backup, if needed.

It took them about an hour to dock with the Kamchatka and ensure our airlocks were sealed tight.

I found it quite insulting when they spent almost thirty minutes checking the airlock seals between them and us. But that was nothing compared to my surprise when the door opened to reveal the commander of the fleet standing there, flanked by a woman in full United States Marine uniform, packing a firearm at her side. A man stood on her other side dressed as a civilian, in dress pants, a collared shirt, and a tie. He and the major smiled warmly at us, while the other woman appeared to check us out in the typical security surveillance style.

What stood out more than that, was that the major was an undeniably perfect-looking person with immaculate chiseled features and looked barely older than a woman in her early to mid-twenties. And given there were no Majors in their twenties (ever!), I could only come to one conclusion.

She was a fucking GenMod.

I'd never known much about them before I went to Grozny. Earthers may have studied the Grozny Uprising in their high school history classes, but it certainly wasn't on the Martian curriculum. However, there wasn't a Chechen alive that didn't either remember the revolt of the GenMods or had a relative who experienced it. By the time it was crushed, a quarter of the population of Grozny lay dead, and it took three weeks to get the fires under control. Chechens hated GenMods with a fiery passion and had passed that prejudice on to me.

"Welcome aboard the Kamchatka. I'm Captain Peter Delaney, and this is my co-pilot, Ksenia Bortnick," he said in broken English.

"Captain, let me introduce the fleet commander, Jenna Plural." The civilian said, and Peter's jaw dropped, while I grew more suspicious about what was happening. Despite being gay, Peter was still a sucker for a pretty girl.

"Seriously?"

She smiled at him. "Relax, Captain, your name will go down in the history books in the next few days. Who knows? They may even start naming high schools after you in years to come. Let's go to the bridge, and I'll tell you what's happening." He led the way, as Plural asked, "How many crew do you have aboard?"

"There are just three of us."

"Forgive me, Major, but I must question why you come here?" I asked quite curtly while maintaining the accent of my adopted country. "When the surrender order came from the Chechen government, we did not know what to do. I did not want to end up in a European labor camp.

109

We considered this a safe harbor when we intercepted your message for military vessels to rendezvous at this point. However, a battle is now imminent, and the leader of the free forces is on our ship? So, forgive me again. I just want to know we are safe."

"I understand your concern, ma'am," Plural said in soft tones, but her voice then grew hard. "None of us are safe. Not while the predatory European Union enslaves our homelands. We are at war, and we must all play our part. I won't insult your intelligence by saying you're not at risk. I will do whatever I can to ensure you are safe, but I can't promise it."

I felt somewhat relieved knowing they wouldn't commandeer our ship, just our services. It didn't even occur to me to identify myself as a former officer of the Alliance. Eight years meant that I barely thought about my days as Kyla Lieberman. "Well, I must say your honesty is more reassuring than any attempt to reassure me."

"What is the nature of your operation on this ship?" The man who I would come to know as Michael Phelkar asked.

"We just spent the last six months dumping radioactive waste from the mines of Saturn's moons," Peter replied.

Michael gave the marine a concerned look. "I will check for radioactivity." She turned to the captain. "Would you direct me to the cargo bay, please?"

"Sure. Ksenia, would you take the young lady down to the cargo hold?" I nodded, and we headed in the opposite direction.

Anna Grayson was a marine who didn't appear to have a personality. She was grim-faced, and barely spoke. I took her into engineering, and she began to examine the gauges. "Do you really think we are stupid enough to allow radiation leaks within our ship?"

"Forgive me, ma'am, but when the safety of the Major is my concern, then I'm not taking any risks," she said, not looking back at me.

"But she is a GenMod, is she not? You could stick her into a reactor, and she'd come out unharmed."

"Actually, that's not true. A lot of things about Gen-Mods are a myth. And you must admit Chechnya has probably the most bias against GenMods."

"What exactly is that supposed to mean?" I responded defensively.

She did look up at me this time. "Correct me if I'm wrong, but Chechnya is the only country where genetically modified people are executed for just being there."

I couldn't deny this. Given the slanted history of Gen-Mods I'd learned from Chechnya, I even approved of it. However, I wouldn't reveal this to Jenna Plural's bodyguard. "So it is your opinion that I would kill us all due to some prejudice against the genetically modified?"

She stared at me momentarily before turning back to the gauges. "Just let me do my job, ma'am, and then it won't be a problem."

Oh, I wanted to punch the patronizing bitch! But I just stood in the corner, crossed my arms, and watched her every move. If I intended to be intimidating, it certainly didn't work. Eventually satisfied, she turned and indicated

111

to the door, and I led her back to the others. I met Delaney coming the other way, and indicating where Grayson was to go, I said, "It's not like you can get lost around here." Without a word, she headed off, and I followed Delaney down to where we would find Petrov.

"She is using this ship to avoid becoming a target in the coming attack by the Peons," Peter told me. "We have just become the command ship for the entire fleet!" He laughed at this idea. "Maybe an American high school will be named after me, like she says."

"Don't get your hopes up, my friend. You do realize she's a GenMod?"

He looked up at me questioningly. "I thought that too at first, but GenMods can't become Majors because the Prague Convention restricts them from holding a rank higher than a Lieutenant."

"Oh, and do you think they make twenty-year-old cheerleaders into Majors?"

He pondered this and shrugged. "She is quite the beauty, isn't she? Maybe there is some truth to what you say, but what do we do about it?"

That was an exceedingly good question, and one that I didn't have the vaguest answer for. "We go along for now, but we don't lower our guard, and we certainly don't trust her." I stepped into the kitchen with him and asked him. "Why have we come down here?"

"Her ladyship wants some dinner."

"Those military types assume we have endless food supplies," Petrov said as we entered. "I heard what you said out there. Do you honestly think I'm willing to cook for a fucking GenMod?" He spat aggressively.

"Well, you could always go up there and try to kill her but be prepared to get past a very determined Marine," I said sarcastically, and Petrov just snorted in return. I looked back to Peter. "You know, I might work on that civilian a little bit. To see if I can get him to open up."

CHAPTER TEN

THE BATTLE OF DEEP SPACE

We were seated with our visitors less than an hour later, and rather than join in, I sat back and studied the GenMod's reactions as she chatted casually, like she was just one of the crew. It totally creeped me out, as I soon realized she was unreadable beyond her obvious reactions, which of course, anyone could fake.

"We were heading back to Earth after being out here for two years," Delaney told her. "We were mighty pissed--excuse my language--when the report came in that we had surrendered, and we were tremendously pleased when we heard your transmission. We had no idea what we were going to do. We had no orders to return to Earth or turn the ship over to anyone."

"I hope you don't have any problems that we rig the ship for military use now?" Plural asked.

Peter shook his head. "Not at all. We can't do much, but we will do anything we can."

Plural smiled at him. "That's the attitude we need to win this war, Captain. You and your crew are true heroes.

I wish everyone had your sort of dedication in the United States."

I rolled my eyes as Peter seemed to enjoy this idea. "I never really thought about myself being a hero before, but if it means I can get back to Grozny, I'm ready to fight."

Plural dropped her fork onto the plate as she finished her last mouthful. "Well, that was certainly a delicious meal. Thank you. However, we're rather tired. I'm assuming you don't have spare rooms for us?" She sighed heavily.

"You can have my quarters. Sorry, but it's not much," Delaney said. "I'll bunk down with Petrov, and your crewman can have the first officer's room."

"Oh, we don't mind sharing. We are marines after all, Captain." Plural smiled.

"As you wish, Major."

Peter took Michael to show him the rooms as Petrov cleared away the dinner things. Left alone with Jenna and Grayson, I was surprised when Jenna casually looked at the marine and said, "Go check out the quarters with Mr. Phelkar, would you? I want to have a word with this Miss Bortnick here alone."

The young marine made no reaction to this order and simply got up and left. Jenna stared at me momentarily before saying, "Who exactly are you, Miss Bortnick?"

"I have no idea what you mean, Major," I said, trying to hide the discomfort in my voice, and attempting to sound more like I was confused.

"You said nothing during that entire meal, but your eyes barely left me. You're clearly studying both the reactions of myself and Mr. Phelkar, and I want to know why."

"I have no idea what you're implying, but that's positively ludicrous," I said innocently.

"Don't play games with me, Miss Bortnick. You are no doubt aware that I'm genetically modified. As a result, my eyesight and hearing exceed that of regular people. Not only did I see that you're looking at each of us, but you were also looking specifically at our eyes. A method only the genetically modified can call upon when trying to detect deception. You're clearly genetically modified to some degree. And you wouldn't have passed a childhood medical, let alone grow to adulthood as a modified Chechen. On top of that, your accent is virtually perfect, but I did pick up inconsistencies in it. American?"

"I am not a GenMod," I said, fixing my eyes on her intently, and resorting to my training to ensure that she couldn't see any deception in my eyes, I controlled their reactions. It's easy to do, really. You simply tell the truth. "I had a childhood illness that caused me to go blind, and my eyes were replaced with perfectly legal genetically grown ones. They're perfectly legal, even in Grozny. I spent many years on Mars in an American community, speaking in English. I developed the accent in my youth and can't really shake it, even though I now speak the language of my country. So, Major, I can clearly state to you, without a single doubt that I am Chechen, and I am not a GenMod." All of it was true. After all, the Chechnyan government had given me citizenship, and I never said I wasn't born there.

"So why the examination?" She asked, but I could tell she was relaxing.

I laughed at that. "Because I'm a Chechen, and you are a GenMod. No doubt you can understand my concern. You'd come into my home, putting us at considerable risk. We are simple people, and we live simple lives, and everything that is going on here... It's frankly hard for us to take in."

A smile crossed her face. "Forgive my concern, Miss Bortnick. It's been a long and uncomfortable journey to where we are today, and I hope you understand that I have to be cautious."

"And I hope you understand, but I must be cautious too," I smiled, trusting this woman even less now.

"Tomorrow, we're going into a battle that will establish whether we'll prevail, or if this is a lost cause. I appreciate your cooperation and understand those concerns, but would it help you to know that I was at Grozny when the uprising happened?"

"Well, my dear Major, that all depends on whose side you are on." I chuckled.

She smiled at this. "The United States, and therefore, in support of the government of Chechnya. My partner, Rocky, and I were tasked with infiltrating the insurrectionists. Officially, I signed up with the GenMod resistance group. My task was to provide information on their activities while they thought I was part of their revolution. I wasn't. And the result of my information meant that when the fighting started, the forces of the government and its allies were able to bring it down," she paused to smile and shrug. "I'm not bragging about my part in this. I just wanted to let you know, because not all of us think like they do. However, you've got to understand, when you grow up different from other people, you turn out one of two ways. You either yearn for that normal life or resent those not like you. Some, like the reactionaries in Grozny, believe that means superiority over others. As you probably realize, I fell into the category of genetically modified people who just wanted a normal life. I've lived for almost two hundred years. More of the people I have known in my life have died, than those who are living. Watching your friends grow old, become infirm, and die isn't pleasant. You never get used to it, Miss Bortnick. It means you do become somewhat jaded in your outlook on life. However, when the uprising ended, I became a second-class citizen when the Prague Convention outlawed genetic modification and restricted what we could do. Am I bitter? Yes. Am I now someone who wants to rise up and take over the Solar System? No. However, all I want is a fair and equitable society where I can live, just like anyone else. There aren't many genetically modified people left. So many were murdered in the post-Grozny panic. I don't want to see that sort of chaos again, and I certainly don't want to see the rise of the oppression of my people, and by my people, I mean Americans. Despite everything, I'm a patriot, but I am loyal to you as an ally, and I hope in the coming days I'm able to earn your trust."

Unless she had training like me, she clearly didn't lie. She meant what she said, but she was still a GenMod. "An interesting story and very nice words, Major, but I'm someone who trusts actions. But... you will have my sup-

119

port, until the time comes that you prove unworthy of the faith I've put in you."

She actually grinned. "I can live with that, Miss Bortnick."

Once she retired to her room, I headed up to the bridge, and I sat in the Captain's seat, watching the twinkles of the little ships moving around, getting in position and ready for the coming battle. I was tired but couldn't sleep, and I sat there all night pondering what the future held for me.

Towards dawn, I made myself a pot of coffee and placed it on the bridge console before returning to my seat. However, I never got to drink any, as I finally succumbed to my weariness and fell asleep in the Captain's chair.

I don't know if Phelkar imagined it when he described me as having 'strong Slavic features' in his book *Jenna Plural Wants You*, but I certainly don't. I guess he was unconsciously prejudiced by my assumed ethnicity.

He woke me up when he entered the cockpit, but I pretended I didn't notice him. I opened my eyes and watched the back of his head as he helped himself to my coffee.

"Good morning, Michael," I said in Russian, knowing full well that he understood me.

"I'm sorry. I didn't mean to disturb you," he responded with a smile. "Unfortunately, a caffeine addiction made that coffee just too inviting."

"Don't worry about it. We are not on one of your United States military ships now." I chuckled, realizing I now had my chance to get him alone. "And I appreciate the company. I don't get many visitors in my line of work."

He sat in the copilot seat and turned the chair toward me. He took a sip and was startled as he realized that the coffee was actually delicious. "It is good, isn't it?"

"Indeed." He replied

I shrugged. "This is not glamorous work, but I like the occasional luxury."

He made to put the cup down. "I'm sorry, perhaps I shouldn't have...."

I laughed. "You are fine, Michael. You need to relax. As I said, this is not a military ship. I'm all too willing to share my coffee."

"Well, thank you. How long have you been out here?"

"Do you mean out here in the Solar System, or since we were last back home?"

"Either."

"Well, it's been about three months since we last made landfall. But just over two years since we were on Earth."

"That's a long time to be away from home."

"It's a living of sorts." I yawned slightly and stretched my arms out behind my back. He stared at my breasts as they pushed against the tight crop top.

"Sorry to interrupt this cozy little meeting," said Plural as she stepped into the cockpit. She gave me a cold look, and I quickly realized her relationship with this man was more than professional. "Perhaps you can see about getting us some breakfast, if you would?" she asked. I gave her a sarcastic salute and smirk, and left the cockpit.

I headed down to the kitchens where Petrov had laid breakfast on the table. Delaney looked surprised, as I entered alone. "Are they not coming down to eat?"

"No, it would appear her ladyship wants room service." Rather than be annoyed by this, he started to gather up a couple of plates. "Oh my God, Peter, you have it bad for her, don't you?"

He flushed quite pink and said sheepishly, "I don't know what you're talking about, Ksenia." Even Petrov laughed at that response, and Petrov hardly ever laughed.

He barely got to the door, when Anna Grayson suddenly appeared in front of him. "You're needed in the cockpit."

Plural jumped out of the pilot seat as we ran into the Control Center, allowing Peter to sit.

"Take us in with the fleet carefully, Mr. Delaney," Plural ordered softly, looking out grimly at the ships moving into formation. "We're just one of the crowd."

"But keep her near the rear, captain," Michael said. "Don't let anyone get suspicious of our activity."

"I'm just going to mosey along like it's a walk in Gorky Park," said the Captain, as he pulled the ship in line with the others heading towards the Peon fleet. As soon as the Peons realized that we were coming up from the rear, they began to turn around, but stopped when they realized that Addison's alpha fleet was heading back towards them. Our forces took advantage of their confused situation. We swept between them from all sides, and our ships were first into the battle, launching troop pods at battleships. Plural whooped as reports came in that nearly all the pods had hit their marks, and our forces were burning into the hulls to board.

Smaller ships engaged other smaller vessels, and the sky was filled with thousands of tiny glowing dots, as flying troopers from both sides jetted across the abyss. The first ship to fall victim was one of ours. A cutter lit up the night as its ion drive detonated.

"Open all radio frequencies, Captain!" Plural ordered.

He turned to look at her like he didn't understand her. "But Major, there are hundreds of communications! It will all be a blather."

Plural didn't take her eyes off the window ahead as she studied the situation. "Captain, things will go much smoother if you don't question me."

Peter shrugged and turned back to his console, and seconds later, an unintelligible cacophony of voices came out of the speakers. "Bring up incoming reports on every screen you can give me, please, Ksenia."

"Done," I said, turning over all our monitors to fleet control.

Streams of reports started coming in, and I have to admit I was amazed at how Plural absorbed the data over the radio and on our screens as she leaned over my shoulder. I looked up to see her eyes darting here and there with an unnatural speed, without once asking for us to have anything repeated or even slow it down. She barked orders and frequent instructions for Peter to change the radio frequency. She appeared to have memorized every civilian and military ship and their radio call signs.

Suddenly she stopped and stiffened. "Repeat that, Stacey." She said, somehow having isolated one voice out of the melee. "Isolate that call." She ordered Peter.

I heard an Australian woman urgently shouting out. "Major, the Chesty is under heavy attack! Much more than other ships."

"They must think you're aboard," Michael said to Plural.

"At the very least, they're working off that possibility," Plural replied tersely. "Get me the Lewis Puller on the line."

"Yes, ma'am," I said and auto-hailed for the named ship.

As the connection was made, you could hear the sounds of explosions and gunfire, but the calm, professional voice of a Japanese woman came online. "Are you holding your own, Tomi?" Plural asked.

"That's a negative. We are compromised with Dutch commandos on board. Engines destroyed. We have lost key personnel. I'm losing troopers faster than we can download them. Implementing self-destruct."

"That is a negative, Sakamoto! I repeat, that is a negative!" Plural shouted, "You are to abandon ship. Do you read me?"

"That is not protocol, Major. My duty is to ensure this ship does not fall into enemy hands."

"Fuck protocol, Sakamoto! You are of more value to me than that piece of shit ship. They can grow goddamn tulips on it for all I care. I want you alive!"

There was a long pause before Sakamoto returned, "The ship's captain is the last to leave."

"Damn it to hell, Tomi, I won't continue repeating myself! Get off that ship, and that's a fucking order!"

"What about the rest of the crew?"

"Evacuate as many as you can in the life pods and eject the M.E.T. Anyone who doesn't make it then tough luck, but I need you, Batty, and Harlow off that ship. No more talking, do it!"

"Harlow is already dead, Major."

Plural tensed and closed her eyes. It was the only emotional reaction she'd had all through the battle. Harlow must've been really special to her. Then she softly stated, "Get yourself off that ship."

"Yes, ma'am." The line went dead.

"Keep an eye on them and update me on the situation," she ordered, returning her attention to the battle.

The formations began to break up as both fleets' ships entered what was known as "the dance of death". Ships on both sides twisted and turned to either make a purchase on their enemy or avoid them.

The Lewis Puller went up in an explosion minutes later. Then another ship went up, then another. "They're not trying to board our ships! They're simply planting mines on them and blowing them up!" Plural snarled. "Give me an open line Captain. Plural to all ships, break protocol, NOW! Bring your ships in close to the enemy. They are not trying to board, they're trying to blow you out of the sky. Ensure you stay close so they have to destroy their ships to get to you."

She watched as her ships drew closer to the Peon vessels, which immediately began trying to back away to carry out their plan. The fleet seemed to be in chaos, but then two more of our ships disintegrated in front of our eyes. It really wasn't looking good.

CHAPTER ELEVEN

THE DEATH OF KSENIA

There was good news – we had taken control of three Peon heavy cruisers from their crews.

"Get those ships out of the fight." Plural commanded. "As soon as you have control of an enemy vessel, take them out of here." Several inquiries came in about prisoners. "I made it clear. We don't have the resources to take damned prisoners! Don't accept any surrender, and don't leave survivors."

As Plural continued dishing out orders, the tide slowly began to turn. Ships started flashing their transponders, and Plural grinned and cried out, "The damn shit-eating motherfuckers are running away!" She laughed as the Peons began to disengage.

However, Plural's joy turned to fear after a radio message came in. "The last two Peon cruisers are heading directly for the U.S.S. Constitution. Collision speed."

"Turn us around. Turn us around now!" Plural snapped, and Peter obliged.

. "Full speed ahead!" Plural shouted.

"I'm giving you full speed! Kamchatka is an old lady who's doing her best."

"Sorry, Captain." Plural rested a hand on his shoulder. "Would you get me the Constitution, please?"

"You are through, milady." He responded.

"Tracker, you have Peon cruisers coming in on you. Can you get anything online?" There was no reply, so she had Peter switch the frequency. "Addison, disengage the Los Angeles now and protect the Constitution."

"Major, all ships are in the process of picking up troopers." Came the response. "We've got thousands of shuttles out there in space. If we stop now, we'll lose a lot of our men and women."

"Damn it to hell! I won't lose that ship." She turned to Peter. "How good a pilot are you?"

"I can do at a pinch." He shrugged.

"Get us in there. Get us into the docking bay. Don't spare the thrusters. Carry on, Addison, disregard my last order."

Suddenly a large Peon heavy cruiser overshot us. "Holy crap!" Delaney stared wide-eyed. "They're going to ram her!"

Plural looked about for a ship that could intercept it. Just as all hope appeared to be lost for the behemoth of a warship, a sleek silver frigate passed over us, coming into view and filling the viewport. Peter struggled to keep control as we were caught in the wake of its afterburners.

"I.D. that idiot." Plural snapped. "What the hell do they think they're doing?"

"Ma'am, it's the U.S.S. Lady Liberty," I reported.

"Stacey!" Phelkar stepped up behind me. We all stared in silence, waiting to see where the Liberty was going.

"Stacey!" Plural muttered as her eyes began to widen. Then she shouted, "Stacey, you dumb Australian fuck! Don't do it!"

The Liberty plowed into the side of the frigate. "For Harper and Wagga, you fuckers!" Her voice came over the comms, the sound of grinding and twisting metal almost drowning her out. As both ships started to break up, she barked orders at her crew. "Okay, you pack of rabid dingos. Time to disembark this joy ride. Abandon ship, I repeat, abandon ship. Move it, you shits, that's a fucking order."

"Stacey Grant, I love you!" Plural laughed, and to my amazement, I saw a tear running down her cheek. "Don't die, or I'll bring you up on charges."

"Ahh, you only get all kissy-kissy when I save your genetically designed arse from hot water. Love to chat, but I gotta get these arseholes moving to the escape pods."

The line went dead.

"Addison, make picking up Stacey's escape pod a priority."

"But Major..."

"Just do it!" Plural snapped irritably. "And send out as many troopers as possible to board the Constitution."

"On it, Major."

The Kamchatka bucked and weaved as Delaney tried to keep away from the jetsam of the exploding ships.

"Captain, what personal arms do you have?" Plural asked.

"Just our sidearms, milady."

"Are you prepared to board the Constitution and fight with us?"

"I can't speak for Petrov, milady, but I can assure you, Ksenia, and I will be there with you."

"Thank you," she turned to Grayson. "Go find out if Petrov is willing to fight and see about fetching their sidearms."

The captain swung the ship toward the Constitution's main cargo hold. "Bay doors are closed, milady. We are not getting in there." Tiny dots of people came out of the last Peon cruiser and headed toward the Constitution.

"Call the Constitution. Tracker, come in, please. Plural to Tracker."

"Reading you, Major. Sorry for not responding earlier," Tracker responded. "We had trouble with the communications."

"You have inbound bogies. Is there anything you can do to stop them?"

"We are working on it, Major. I can't say anymore because we've detected the Peons are intercepting our calls." Suddenly, the U.S.S. Los Angeles passed overhead, causing us to shudder in its wake, and it began releasing its troop pods at the Constitution.

"Can you open the cargo bay doors?" Plural asked urgently.

"Yes, ma'am, opening the doors now," Tracker replied.

"We'll see you soon."

Peter swung the ship towards the cargo bay doors as they slowly opened. It was quite a maneuver, considering we were still going at full speed. Flying a ship, it's not exactly difficult. Flying a ship while in combat is.

The Kamchatka groaned, as Peter slammed on the retro thrusters trying to slow the vehicle, which was suddenly helped by slamming into the docking bay floor, sending the ground crew running for their lives. A painful screeching hit our ears as the craft's underbelly was ripped against the mercuranium lining of the Constitution's flooring. He then spun her to one side to reduce momentum even further, until the vessel lay motionless and silent as he killed the engines, which seemed to whimper as they died. I swiftly got out of my seat and headed to my quarters, where I quickly changed into an unmodified pair of jeans and a shirt before coming out again. I met up with Peter and Petrov to find them in the middle of an argument.

"Are you a crazy fool, Peter?" Petrov was saying urgently. "You're not a bloody Marine! You're going to get yourself killed."

"I will be fine, my love. Do not worry about me."

"He's right, Peter," I said urgently. "We are not soldiers, and this is not our responsibility."

"My sweet darlings." He looked at us with a warm, yet sad expression. "All my life, I've collected garbage. Sure, I've got to see the Solar System, meet interesting people, and visit interesting places, but I have done nothing that I can say I'm truly proud of. This is my chance to make a difference. Do you understand that? The two of you stay here, and I'll be back."

I sighed and picked up my snap pistol, and checked its load. He looked at me curiously, and I just rolled my eyes at him. "Someone has to keep you alive, Peter. Come on, let's go." He reached up and kissed Petrov softly, and I couldn't help but see a tear in Petrov's eye as Peter turned away and headed out the door. I put my hand out and squeezed Petrov's hand. "I'll do what I can to ensure he stays alive. I promise."

Plural's people were already putting up a good fight when we stepped aboard, and Plural went ahead despite Michael's protests. "I took the ship away from Americans. I'll be damned if I let the Peons take it away from me." She said to him.

"Wow," Peter said as he looked around at the brilliant cream-colored walls lined with chrome. "You sure have a fighting ship here, Major."

"Why, thank you," replied Plural. "If we make it through this, I'll find a place for all of you on its crew if you want."

Before he could reply, a sudden burst of electricity danced along the chrome.

"What was that?" I asked uneasily.

Plural looked ecstatic. "Oh, that beautiful girl has ionized the hull," she said, referring to Tracker. "There'll be no more Peons landing or leaving."

"Tracker to Major Plural, I have done what I can. We only have a few Marines on this ship, but we gotta move fast. I'm picking up distress signals from escape pods. They're homing in on this ship, but they'll get fried if I have the full field on."

"Patch me through ship-wide." Plural barked.

"Ship-wide communications open."

"This is Major Jenna Plural. All the enemy troops landed on the starboard side. Concentrate your defenses there."

And with that, we headed down into the corridors, opening fire on any Peon uniform we saw. Realizing that they had lost any opportunity to return to their ship unless they took this one, they fought almost frenziedly.

Tracker came online again. "Major, are all your troops wearing tracer pins?"

"No, I have the crew of the Kamchatka with me. Why do you ask?"

"I think I've got internal defense systems back online, but you gotta hurry. We have Peons pounding on the door down here."

"How long can you hold out?"

We heard an explosion, and Tracker cried, "They're through!"

"Set it off, Tracker. Set it off now!" Plural screamed.

A large double-barreled machine gun dropped from the ceiling ahead of us. Jenna pulled Grayson and Michael in front of the Kamchatka crew. I guess she hoped it would block us from the incoming assault.

The machine guns began to work as they powered for firing, and Michael suddenly threw himself against me and took me down to the ground covering me, but it was no good. I saw Peter go down, riddled with bullets, but I was too busy getting hit to care. The pain shot through my body as the armor-piercing rounds struck me. Then strangely, the pain stopped, and I knew it was all over. I would die on the floor of the Constitution, alongside a man who was more father to me than my own father. Michael leaned over me, and concern filled in his eyes. Over his shoulder, my eyes met with that bitch.

"Watch out for that Jenna Plural," I whispered in Russian that only he could understand. "That genetic freak has no soul. We remember Grozny." Then everything went dark.

When I awoke, everything was blurry, and I couldn't move. Various tubes ran up my nose and down my throat. I was lying on something soft, possibly a bed. Light danced in front of my eyes, and it took me a while to realize it was the movement of people in my room. I struggled to focus, and as I became more aware of my surroundings, I felt my body wrapped in intense pain. I wanted to cry out and scream, but nothing came. I tried to move but was too weak, and then the blurry image of a face came before me.

"Hey there, don't try to move." The voice was male, soft, and I thought it was Australian. Well-spoken, educated. My trained instinct to collect information was alert, even if the rest of me wasn't. "Don't try to speak. You have a ventilator down your throat, and it's the only thing keeping you breathing right now. I've gotta be honest, it's unbelievable that you're alive, but you are, and we're gonna get you back on your feet, but it's gonna take some time. But don't be afraid. You're in good hands. You're on board with the Twilight Wanderer in the emergency medical center. You were brought over here from the Constitution after you got shot. I'm really good at what I do, so don't worry."

Another face came into view. Well, sort of. It was still blurry, but I could make out a woman with blonde hair. "I've got an I.D. on this patient, Dr. Cooper," she said, looking down at a small tablet in her hand.

"Awesome, thanks, Hannah. We can finally give Jane Doe a name," he smiled at her and then turned that smile back to me.

"It's quite interesting, actually," Hannah said. Accent, affluent, an upper-class wealthy Australian. Confident. Not subordinate to the doctor. "Her D.N.A. links her to the fact that she's a Martian of American descent. She was employed by the former Department of Outland Security. Her job is classified, but no doubt my security will be able to get the locked files, if you want them."

"Well, I don't think that'll be necessary," The doctor responded. "But what's her name?"

"Kyla Eliana Lieberman. However, the interesting thing is that her record ends eight years ago when the Department of Outland Security listed her as 'Missing in Action, Presumed Dead.'"

"Well, well, she must have a story to tell." The doctor smiled as he looked at me with curiosity.

"It gets even more interesting than that, doctor. Her D.N.A. is linked to a second person. Ksenia Bortnick, a Chechen free trader working aboard a garbage hauler."

"A garbage hauler?" The doctor's eyes widened.

"Yeah. The record says she was born in Grozny, but there's no other record of her between her birth date and prior to eight years ago."

"Well, it looks like our mysterious friend here changed her identity," the doctor mused. "I wonder why?"

"I think that's easy to work out, Doc," Hannah stated. "Eight years ago was when the Peons took control of Mars. Our little Martian friend worked for Outland Security and probably changed her identity to escape arrest. However, that doesn't answer why she didn't check in with her superiors upon leaving the planet."

"Does it list the next of kin we can contact?"

"It does." And Hannah smirked at that. "However, I find it highly unlikely they are actually related."

"Color me intrigued, Hannah. Out with it." The doctor raised an eyebrow.

"It states her mother is a woman called Charlotte Kensett. But considering Charlotte is barely ten years older than her...well, that's fucking impossible."

"Adopted?"

"I highly doubt it. I know Charlotte Kensett. She's a former employee of the Department of Outland Security. As I understand it, she now works directly for Major Plural."

The doctor once more looked back at me. "Well, aren't you an interstellar woman of mystery, Miss Lieberman?"

"Do you think I should have my staff contact Kensett and tell her about this?" Hannah asked.

The doctor shrugged. "She's listed as the next of kin, and it's not my place to question how, why, or what is going on."

"I'll have someone call her office. Anything else I can do to help, Doc?"

"Sit with her for a few minutes." The doctor replied. "Reassure her. I've gotta move on and see other patients."

He disappeared from my view, and the face of the newcomer turned towards me, as she sat down on the side of my bed and took my hand in hers.

"How you doing, mate? You sure surprised the Doc. He was convinced you were a goner, but it looks like you're gonna pull through. He's asked me to talk to you, but I don't really know what to say. I don't normally do this, but today I'm helping out the Doc. I've never been a nurse before. I hope I never will be again. The battle is over. We won, but they keep bringing in more dead and wounded. You can't imagine the horrors I've seen today," she paused, flushed slightly, and then said softly. "Huh, would you listen to me, mate!? I just get to see the results of this war, and here I am whining at you about it, who's clearly been through it. I'm sorry."

An alarm from nearby suddenly went off, and I heard the voice of the Australian doctor again. "Hannah, can you give me a hand over here?" His voice was full of urgency, desperate. The woman released my hand and stood up. "I'm coming, Doctor Cooper."

She disappeared from my view, and I lay there alone, trapped in my useless body, unable to move and talk. However, I was only concerned about one thing. Was Peter okay? My lack of energy overcame me, and slowly, the noise of the alerts died down as, once more, I fell into unconsciousness.

The next time I opened my eyes, I could see clearly. The tubes had been removed from my nose and mouth, although several still went into my arms. However, I was completely distracted by a face I hadn't seen in eight years. But the immaculately groomed hair, that perfectly applied makeup and those large librarian-like glasses looked down at me with a smile. "Hello, Ky." Charlotte Kensett said with her perfectly clipped upper-class English accent.

"Did I die and go to hell?" My voice was a little more than a rasp as my throat was dry.

"Well, I must say, Ky, that wasn't the welcome I was expecting," Charlotte said with a grin. "It's not like we parted on bad terms or anything. In fact, I can honestly say that I've missed you for these past, what is it, almost nine years."

"You missed me?" I said disbelievingly

"Of course. You were one of my best operatives. You would have been very useful over there last few years of the war."

"Oh, that makes more sense." I wanted to laugh, but it hurt too much.

"You appear to have had some of your own adventures since we last met. I tried to check on you, but there was no trace of Kyla Lieberman on Mars or anywhere else. You were expected to report in after you departed Mars."

"Sorry, never got that memo," I replied with a hint of sarcasm.

She ignored it. "Now, Ksenia Bortnick, I have been able to find a record of her. An interplanetary garbage hauler? I must admit I had higher expectations for you."

"Isn't cleaning up shit what I've always done?" I replied.

Charlotte smiled. "Oh, most amusing, Ky. Come see me when you get out of here. We have a lot to discuss." With that, she turned on her heel and, with the clip-clop of her heels, left my room.

I cursed as I forgot to ask her about Delaney and Petrov. But clearly, Charlotte had told the staff outside that I was awake because the nurse rushed in, followed by a doctor. He wasn't the one I'd seen last time. They checked me over and asked me a bunch of questions before giving me the news about Peter's death. Unfortunately, they had no news on Petrov, who had remained behind on the Kamchatka. Eventually, I discovered that Jenna Plural had assigned techs to the ship and made repairs. Believing Peter and I were dead, he took the ship out of the Constitution and right out of the fleet. His last known course was heading to the outer Solar System, but something about the communication jamming or some other bullshit meant he wasn't contactable.

As for myself, I'd been in and out of consciousness for about eight months, and I had multiple surgeries. I had my heart, a lung, and a kidney replaced. When I asked who was picking up the bill, I was told it was payment for services rendered. This might make you believe that Jenna Plural knew that I was alive, but it turned out that she didn't. I missed too much of that year of my life, being mostly unconscious, but I was in no hurry to leave as I had nowhere to go. However, the day came for them to discharge me, and they asked me who I should call to come and get me. I pondered this for a long time before I – and with a reluctant sigh – said, "Charlotte Kensett."

CHAPTER TWELVE

THE INNER CIRCLE

It turned out that Charlotte was still aboard the Twilight Wanderer in offices given to her by the ship's owner, Hannah Grant. The very Hannah that sat with me by my bedside. Charlotte offered to send someone up to come and get me, but I was fit enough to walk on my own, and the nanobots in my system had been severely upgraded from my time on Mars. They made sure my muscles hadn't atrophied while I lay there. She gave me directions, and thanking the medical staff, I headed out.

I'd never seen such luxury as the Twilight Wanderer. Even the corridors were wider than your average apartment back on Mars. I wanted to go exploring, but realized I would quickly get lost, and so I stuck to the directions Charlotte had given me. Unlike her office back in New Brooklyn, there was no name on the door, just the room number, and I thought for a moment that she'd given me the wrong information, but when I knocked, her distinct voice called out for me to come in. Although the dimensions of the office were different, everything she had was laid out identically to what it was when I had first met her.

Clearly a sign of a compulsive mentality. She immediately stood up as I entered and came around to shake my hand. "Good to see you up and about, Ky."

"Thanks," I said, taking one of the seats in front of her desk. "Let me be upfront with you. I'm only here because I have nowhere else to go. I'm not looking to rejoin the service."

"Well, technically, you never left, my dear," Charlotte said warmly as she returned to her seat and crossed her legs. "You were listed as missing, although actually A.W.O.L."

"In that case, let's go back to Earth, and you can court-martial me," I said coldly.

"Most amusing, Ky," she responded, clearly unamused. "You can't be court-martialed as we're not military. However, you are right about one thing. America is no longer recognized as a legal entity, and as such, Outland Security is a defunct organization. No, we have a new role in the new Solar Confederation as the Ministry of Internal Affairs."

"And the difference is?" I asked.

"We now answer to Jenna Plural, instead of a bunch of elected wet losers on Capitol Hill." She shrugged. "I really would like you to rejoin me. We're going to save the galaxy or something like that."

"Not interested." I shook my head.

"Oh, I think I can persuade you if you give me the opportunity," she smiled.

"I'm not a dumb little Martian girl you met back on Mars, Boss. I've grown up, and I've changed." I said firmly. "But you're more than welcome to try."

"The whole Solar System has changed, Ky, most of it while you were out of it in the medical center. The Battle of Deep Space was a resounding victory for us, and we certainly packed a punch into the enemy's fleet. We've taken a base on Enceladus, and Jenna Plural has turned a ragtag bunch of basically lost-cause doughboys and turned us into a powerful fighting force."

"I don't see what this has to do with me, Boss," I interrupted. I had no interest in any of this bullshit.

"Let me finish. Over the past year, things have begun to change on Mars. The Peons decimated fleet has been unable to maintain its blockade of Mars, and the independence movement has grown quite strong."

"Oh, that must piss you off," I smirked.

"Oh, Ky, I thought you knew me much better than that. I frankly don't give a shit about the politics of the situation. I simply work to ensure the agenda of my superiors is fulfilled. As I said, much has changed. An independent Mars allied to us will be the death blow to the European Union. And that is something my superiors want. We've been negotiating with the acting governor for some time now, and we're taking the U.S.S. Constitution to Mars for high-level talks with Jenna Plural."

I tried not to hide my excitement at the idea of going back to Mars, but I really didn't know what Charlotte wanted, so I maintained my calm exterior. "Well, it would be nice for you to go back to the old place. Make sure you let me know how it goes."

Charlotte sighed. "We can play these games all day, but you know full well that I want you to be on that mission.

I don't trust this new Martian government, and although Jenna will be taking her own military security, I want my own people on the ground. And you know Mars better than any of my people. Jenna Plural has to succeed in this mission if we are to bring peace to the Solar System. You and I will be there to ensure nobody takes her out. The problem with an enigmatic leader is that we don't have a replacement on hand. Should she be killed, the Solar Confederation would fall to pieces in a few days."

I was about to say no. Why did I give a fuck about Jenna Plural, if she lived or died? She gave the order that killed Delaney and almost killed me. However, something occurred to me. "I'll agree on one condition."

She sighed. "Oh, you know I'm not fond of conditions, Ky, but let's hear it."

"I get to go to New Brooklyn and check up on my family sometime during this assignment."

"Oh, I don't think that will be a possibility, and the chances are your family is already dead." I'd done some cold things, but I couldn't believe the callousness with which she just said that. "I really can't have you wandering all over Mars with everything happening."

I nodded. "I understand, Ms. Kensett," I replied.

Charlotte smiled back at me. "Good, I will arrange for your transfer over to the..."

"Oh no, Ms. Kensett, I don't think you understand. I said I understood you, but I didn't say I agreed with you. If it's impossible for me to visit my family, then I'll accept that, but there is really no reason for me to go, so I won't."

The smile quickly faded. "I think I've made it very clear to you the reasons you need to go. But consider this. You are on a Peon wanted list, and if we lose this war because Jenna dies, then you're not going to find a safe place in this Solar System."

"Last time I checked, you are much higher on that list than I am." I snorted. "However, Jenna Plural gave an order that killed my best friend and almost killed me. I bear her no love, and I bear her no loyalty. Now the question is simple. I've always been loyal to you, and I'll remain so, and you know that I've never been one to join a cause, but that's never stopped me from doing what I need to do to complete my job. So despite my opinions on Jenna Plural, you know full well I'll carry out my task efficiently, professionally, and with dedication. However, my price is that I get to visit my family. It's not up for debate, discussion, or argument. In fact, because of your procrastination on this matter, I'm gonna add another condition. Once this mission is concluded, if I choose to, I'll get to stay on Mars and not come back." I rose to my feet but continued talking to her as I did. "You have a simple choice, and nothing'll sway me from that. I don't know where I'll be, but I'm sure you'll be able to find me when you've made up your mind." And with that, I turned towards the door.

"I will give you twenty-four hours, no more," she said softly. I admit I had a smirk before I turned back to her, and she knew, as I looked at her, that she had just revealed a weakness. She needed me more than I needed her.

"Seventy-two," I said, turning back to her.

Charlotte scowled at me. "That, my dear, is frankly ludicrous. There would be no point in you coming. We don't intend to be there more than a week."

I shrugged and gave an embarrassed smile. "Well, honestly, I expected you to meet me in the middle at forty-eight."

And as I said those words quite sheepishly, she actually chuckled. "Fine, forty-eight, I'll arrange for a shuttle to take you to the S.C.S Spirit of Freedom." Not having heard of that ship, I looked at her curiously. "It's the new name they've given to the former U.S.S. Constitution."

I nodded. "I can't say it's gonna be fun working with you again, Boss, but it's always interesting when you're around."

"Well, I'm glad I entertain you."

Quarters were arranged for me in the S.C.S. Spirit of Freedom, and I got a transport over there that same day. I was surprised when Charlotte joined me for the flight. "I want you to observe everybody at the mission briefing tomorrow," she said as we sat together in the first-class lounge, which I assumed was being paid for by the state. It wasn't a military shuttle and was owned by the company, Grant Industries, but it was clear by the lack of other passengers, that it was some sort of private charter. I had no idea that Charlotte had some sort of arrangement with the C.E.O. of that company, and at the time, I had no idea that Hannah Grant was the same Hannah I had seen in the hospital.

"Might I be looking for anything in particular?"

"No, I just want a second opinion. Perhaps we can discuss it after the meeting."

Transferring from ship to ship is not a simple task, and it took several hours before we docked aboard the Spirit of Freedom. I felt a little sick and had a tight knot in my stomach, as I entered the familiar corridors of the ship where Peter had died. Someone from the office of Commodore Addison, who was apparently Jenna Plural Number Two, came and took me down to quarters. Apparently, Charlotte had offices and quarters on this ship too. It was a simple affair this time because I was only expected to stay there a couple of nights. I had a decent meal provided for me, and I got up early to prepare for this mission briefing. Charlotte had suggested smart casual and provided me with casual black slacks and a white blouse. I couldn't help but think, "I only needed three-inch heels and a pair of glasses to be a clone of Charlotte."

I met up with Charlotte the following morning, and we headed up to the command deck and the captain's briefing room, where we were to meet. We arrived a little early, but we weren't the first. Michael Phelkar was seated at the briefing room table, reviewing some documents on his tablet with what appeared to be a young aide. They both looked up as we came in, and he smiled. "Good morning, Charlotte."

Interestingly, I'd never heard anyone address Charlotte Kensett by her first name. I looked from him to Charlotte. Although she smiled, her reaction was generally as passive as it was with anyone. I wondered if there was any true emotion behind those large thick-rimmed glasses. On the other hand, Michael was clearly attracted to her, but I couldn't help but notice a hint of trepidation. He was scared of her, and that possibly turned him on. He stood up as he noticed me and waited for Charlotte to introduce me. "Mr. Phelkar, let me introduce you to agent Kyla Lieberman."

"Good morning, Miss Lieberman," he said with a beaming smile as he stepped around the table to shake my hand. The smile disappeared, replaced by a slight frown. "Excuse me for saying so, but have we met before?"

"Yes, Michael." I smiled warmly at him. "The last time you saw me, you left me for dead in one of the corridors out there." I caught a glare from Charlotte, who clearly didn't share my amusement at the situation or my comment.

His eyes widened. "Ksenia?"

"Yes, that was indeed the name I went by."

Jenna Plural swept in before he could further comment, followed by her little entourage. "Good morning. I'm hoping we'll be productive in this meeting, because this is the last opportunity to get everything sorted out."

There was quite a celebrity turnout for the meeting, with most of her inner circle present. While I didn't know them then, they were very much household names by the time I wrote this.

In her role as executive officer Claire Addison chaired the meeting. Helen Tracker was in attendance as head of technology. Tiffany Mahoney, the scientist Dodgson found on Enceladus, joined as a senior science representative. Michael Phelkar in his role of Chief of Civil Affairs. Dodgson and Thompson as the security.

I couldn't help but think that this was a rather unusual choice of people. I'm neither a politician or diplomat, or even a military strategist, for that matter. However, even for me, the inclusion of the chief technician of the fleet, a scientist, and the head of internal security did seem a little odd for what was apparently to be a diplomatic mission.

My biggest surprise, though, was the attendance of Hannah Grant and Bronwyn Donovan representing Grant Industries. I couldn't help but wonder why they were included.

The only one missing from this group was Captain Stacey Grant, who, in recent months, had been effectively relieved of all duties until after the birth of her child.

Plural was the consummate professional officer. However, she was always concerned about the comfort of the people who worked with her, making sure everyone had the drink of their choice. She always engaged in idle chatter, asking how everyone was doing before getting to the point.

"Well, ladies and gentlemen, considering the recent communications I've been having with the government leaders on Mars, what I'm about to say to you will probably not come as a surprise. Mars is about to declare its independence officially. The Peons have tried to thwart this on many occasions. However, even though it's almost a year since we disrupted Peon communications and sent them into chaos, they still haven't recovered. Their attention has been squarely on us, and they've missed the unification of the Martian colonies, who have effectively taken control of the Peon defense systems of the planet. However, Mars does not intend to remain isolated, but I will turn the meeting over to Commodore Addison, who will give you more background on the situation."

Addison rose to her feet. "As I'm sure you already know, Mars has over forty countries represented among its colonies and is the second most populated planet, after Earth. About halfway through the war, the Peons gained their superiority, and we lost contact with Pacific Alliance colonies, and effectively came under European control. However, the successful destruction of the Phobos base left the planet somewhat isolated during the last days of the conflict, before the surrender of the United States and the Allies. The planet Mars has found itself in a unique position. They're declaring independence, but it's not a self-sustaining world. It's still relying on massive amounts of imports from Earth and the outer worlds. So, in an ironic twist, they want to be independent, but also form an alliance. At present, their only option is being ready to do a deal with the European Union. At least that's what they believe."

At this point, Plural came back. "Thanks to Mr. Phelkar's negotiations with the provisional government of Mars, we've offered them an alternative. We now have the potential to have Mars as an ally. This is a game changer, boys and girls. The resources of Mars will mean we're knocking at the door of Earth once more. Mr. Phelkar, your report, please."

Michael rose to his feet. "It took some work to convince them, but the provisional government has agreed to talk with us. It is not an opportunity we can just pass on. However remote the possibility is, we must seek that alliance with the Martians. There is a caveat to their agreement to talk to us. The Martians want to talk to Jenna Plural directly, in a face-to-face meeting. To do this, we must go to Mars."

Chapter Thirteen

Psychology 101

"Is that really worth the risk?" Charlotte interrupted. "You're basically taking our leader out of the fleet into potentially enemy territory for a whisper of hope."

"The danger is present, but the potential is something the Admiral is willing to risk." Addison put in.

"It really is an opportunity we can't ignore, Charlotte," Jenna stated. "Mr. Phelkar tried to negotiate alternatives to my attendance, but their attitude was quite simply, "if I can't be bothered to come to them, why should they listen?" They currently hold all the cards, and I know you like to have an ace up your sleeve and stack the deck in my favor, but I think on this occasion, that's not something we can do."

"This is all well and good," said Hannah with more than a hint of irritation in her voice. "But I'm neither a member of your military, nor your government, and I would appreciate it if we could get to the point of why I'm here?"

"Trade will clearly be an integral part of any negotiations," Jenna replied. "And to be quite honest, there's

no-one on my team with your level of business knowledge."

Hannah snorted at this. "To be quite fair, Admiral,
I simply direct policy. I have no particularly exceptional
knowledge in the area of business. However, Bronwyn has
been running the company for the last year."

"Which is why I asked you to bring her. However, you're
still the face of Grant Industries, since your predecessor,
the chairman, passed away in that accident recently. It
would be quite a snub to just send Miss Donovan."

"Nothing personal to you, Miss Donovan, but there
some proprieties that need to be upheld," said Michael.

"That is, of course, unless you want to stay here for your
sister, who I understand is due any day now," Addison
added.

I was surprised by Hannah's negative expression at the
mention of her sister, but if anyone else had noticed that,
it was quickly gone with her next statement.

"I would have thought holding the mother's hand
would be the father's job." She looked squarely and un-
equivocally at Michael.

I was sure he paled slightly before responding, "The
parentage of Captain Grant's child has not been established, Miss Grant."

Hannah raised an eyebrow, and there was a slight grin
on her face. "Are you implying that my sister is some sort
of slut?"

Michael's face flushed bright red at this statement. "Not
at all, Miss Grant. However, it is a matter of fact that I was

not the only person Stacey had been intimate with within a period sufficient to make the parentage unclear."

"Yes, well," Addison interjected as I noted that Jenna was staring very coldly at Michael. It wasn't a secret from the inner circle that Jenna and Michael had been in a relationship, and it was equally not a secret that they'd broken up, and now I thought I knew why. "This is a personal matter between those involved, and it doesn't have a place in this meeting. Are you saying, Miss Grant, you'd be unwilling to join the team going to Mars?"

"If the Admiral is going to promise me that any trading agreements will be the exclusive domain of Grant Industries, than I'm more than happy for myself and Bronwyn to join your little party. I'm sure such agreements would be quite lucrative for my company."

Jenna shrugged. "I'll leave that for you and Mr. Phelkar to sort out. Honestly, I have enough to worry about than get involved in commerce." She turned back to the group. "We'll be taking a small retinue. Addison will remain here in the fleet, taking command in my place. The team will consist of myself, Mr. Phelkar, Tracker, Thompson, Dodgson, and Kensett," she then looked over at me. "Ms. Lieberman will join us too. Both she and Thompson are Martians, and Lieberman will be an advisor on Martian issues under the auspices of the Ministry of Internal Affairs."

As all eyes turned to me, Hannah frowned and then smiled. "Hey, I remember you from the Twilight Wanderer medical wing. Good to see you up and about."

I smiled back at her. "In no small part to you, Ms. Grant."

"You should take more guards than just Thompson and Dodgson," said Sakamoto. When she said this, I looked over at Emma Dodgson. I was surprised that she looked very concerned, but as she noticed me looking at her, the concern turned into a relaxed smile. It was kinda odd, looking back now after all this is over, that I'm now confident that I was aware of what was concerning her at that moment.

"It'll be fine, Sakamoto," Plural replied, sounding a little frustrated. "Kensett and Lieberman will also be responsible for security." She turned back to the group. "This mission also means we'll be taking the Freedom out of the fleet to transport us to Mars."

"I still don't like that idea," said Addison. "It makes the ship a target and leaves the fleet vulnerable."

"It can't be helped, Claire. It's expected that I'll arrive aboard the flagship. However, you have my full confidence that you can keep my fleet safe."

"Oh no, Admiral, if you intend to take the Freedom to Mars, then I intend to command that vessel," Addison stated firmly.

Jenna raised an amused eyebrow at her. "And since when has it been your call to decide who does and doesn't lead my fleet?"

Addison shrugged and smiled back. "Article Seventeen of the operating procedures the Solar Confederation military, signed off by you when we started re-organizing everything. The executive officer has the exclusive judgment of making safety decisions for the Admiral of the fleet. I'm the executive officer, and I've decided I'm coming with you."

Jenna frowned at her. "I signed so many documents in those days. I didn't read everything and trusted everything was in order."

"Everything is in perfect order, Admiral." Addison grinned.

"I could fire you, you know?" Jenna chuckled.

"Look, as interesting as your witty banter about your personnel allocations is, if we're done with this meeting, may Bronwyn and I be excused? If you expect us to go to Mars with you, we've got shit to prepare for," Hannah said with clear annoyance.

Jenna gave her a cold stare. "You may go. This meeting is dismissed."

Rather than return to Charlotte's office, we went down to a small mess hall that was rarely used. It was an intimate bar for officers only, and while neither Charlotte nor I were military, Charlotte had the status of an officer. She'd clearly used this before because after ordering drinks, she asked the barman for some privacy, and he simply nodded, smiled, and left the room. We sat in two comfortable chairs, and, in her typical fashion, Charlotte sat back and crossed her legs.

"So, what's your assessment?" She asked.

"Well, quite an interesting group of people," I responded lazily. "Where would you like me to start?"

"Why don't we start with, say, Hannah Grant?"

"Usually, it's impossible to gauge the reactions of a GenMod, however, Hannah was very easy to read. Which means she's probably the age she appears to be and is entirely unaware of people like me. She could very easily control her reactions. In comparison, Jenna Plural was completely unreadable. However, Hannah is very confident and self-assured. Borderline narcissist. She's clearly very close to her companion Donovan. But doesn't trust anyone else in that room, including Jenna Plural. I would assess that she once held her in the highest regard, but that's started to wane. She positively loathes Michael Phelkar, to the degree that she'll actively try to undermine him at any opportunity. They, however, have a history, possibly an intimate one."

Charlotte looked surprised. "How do you know this?"

"Mr. Phelkar's reactions to her. He's uncomfortable in her presence, to the point that it's obvious that she clearly did something to embarrass him. This could really be anything, except that he's clearly attracted to her and doesn't want to be. She is very ambitious. Despite being in charge of the most powerful corporation in the Solar System, you'd think she'd settle for that, but she doesn't. She's fully aware that she's only in that position due to inheritance. This leaves a void in her that she wants to achieve something she truly calls her own. Were the Solar Confederation a democracy, she's likely to want to run for president or something like that. However, that's not a problem, since we're not."

Charlotte sighed. "There's a lot of pressure from the civilian community to form an elected government, and while Jenna is resistant for strategic purposes, the pressure will probably be too much for her to refuse."

"Well, in that case," I responded. "I'm fairly confident Hannah Grant will be at the top of the list of nominations for president, or whatever you plan to call it."

"And what would you assess Miss Grant's chances of winning an election, should she stand for it?"

I looked at her, bewildered at the question. "I'm no political analyst, but she'd probably lose. Anti-Gen sentiments would be difficult for her to overcome."

"You say that, yet Jenna Plural has virtually universal support and very few opponents. She's a GenMod too."

I couldn't help but smile at this. "Isn't it true that presently it's Jenna Plural's administration that controls the media?"

Charlotte smiled. "This is so."

"And I take it that you're very diligent in silencing any opposition to her authority?"

"Of course." She shrugged like it should go without saying.

"If we take a political road, then Hannah or anyone is a potential threat to the Admiral's leadership. If we follow the same conventions as Earth, Admiral Plural would be excluded from running for office because she's military."

Charlotte seemed to mull this over and then asked me, "Let's get back to this current mission. Do you envision Hannah being a problem?"

"Well, she clearly has her own agenda, and she's made that pretty clear, but the fact she's open about it implies that she'll be loyal where she claims she'll be loyal, and not where she won't." I stopped and narrowed my eyes slightly before asking, "Boss, you're more experienced at this than me, and no doubt have your own assessments of the situation. Why are you asking me about this?"

"You are correct. I have indeed made my own assessments, but I'm not perfect, and a second opinion is always helpful when assessing a situation." Before I could respond to that, she changed the subject. "Mars is going to be a test of our abilities, Ky. Despite the assurances of Michael Phelkar, who is quite idealistic, I don't have the same confidence as him that this will go as planned."

"Have you expressed this to the Admiral?"

"I have," she said with quite a frustrated sigh.

"I take it you didn't quite get the response you hoped for," I said with genuine curiosity.

"Oh, she agrees that that is possible, but she states we have no choice. Control of Mars will give us superiority around the inner planets as the base of operations for the ultimate assault upon Earth."

"Control of Mars?" I said with a frown.

"A turn of phrase, Ky, don't concern yourself. This is to be resolved with a diplomatic solution, hopefully. What is your assessment of Michael Phelkar?"

I didn't pursue it, but I could tell there was more going on than Charlotte was willing to share with me.

"Well, I'd already met him on the Kamchatka during the Battle of Deep Space. He's intelligent and well-educated, but he's quite the sycophant. Correct me if I'm wrong, but he's been involved, at least sexually, if not emotionally, with the leader herself?"

Charlotte looked impassive as she replied. "That would be correct."

"I thought as much. However, he cheated on her with this Stacey Grant, and also with Emma Dodgson."

At that, Charlotte raised her carefully sculpted eyebrow. "Well, frankly, Ky, you're blowing my mind here. How could you possibly know that? I can confirm that he did cheat on Jenna Plural with Stacey Grant, but Emma Dodgson...This is the first I'm hearing of that."

"Simple reactions, Boss. When Hannah Grant talked about the impending birth of her sister's child, everyone in that room reacted differently. Mr. Phelkar was embarrassed. Jenna Plural was angry, and Emma Dodgson couldn't take her eyes off him, and although it could just be a fantasy on her part, I have a feeling it's not. Michael Phelkar is a womanizer, even though he doesn't believe himself to be. He's easily led astray by a nice piece of ass. However, despite this, he remains fanatically loyal to Jenna. But he's not exactly going to take a bullet for her, even though he'd make you think he would."

"So all in all, considering everyone in that room, is there anyone that Jenna should be concerned about?"

I couldn't help but smile at this, and pondered for a moment whether I would answer honestly or not, but I thought I had nothing to lose. "There's only one, Boss."

A line of concern crossed her face at this. "And that is?"

"You, Ms. Kensett."

A flash of anger swept across her face, but retaining her calm and level voice, she said, "That's quite an allegation, Ky. Would you care to elaborate on that?"

"Of course. Frankly, you have absolutely no interest in the cause. You couldn't give a shit about who's in charge, as long you maintain your role and the power over the lives of others. Putting it bluntly, you suffer from an Anti-Social Personality Disorder, or you're what the layman would incorrectly call a psychopath. The only loyalty you bear is to the status quo. While you're not a threat to Jenna Plural, you're equally not loyal to her, beyond the fact she's the one who's currently in charge. If Jenna Plural was replaced, you would carry on business as usual, answering to them, if given that opportunity."

The coldness in her eyes instantly evaporated as I finished, only to be replaced with a smile. "Well, aren't you a useful wealth of information? However, you're sort of correct. I'm a civil servant who must adjust to regime changes. Within the United States, that would happen with an election every four years where policy could swap between the left and the right. But you're wrong in one aspect. I believe Jenna Plural is an exceptional leader, and I would do everything within my power to ensure that she retains her position."

"Understood, but even so, should you fail in ensuring she retains her position, you would quickly adapt to the new circumstances under a new leader. Your first loyalty is not to yourself, as I first thought, but to the power and authority of your organization. I take it that Jenna Plural gives you unfettered authority to independently make decisions in the best interests of her and the fleet?"

"That is so." Then her eyes narrowed. "Ky, let me be very clear. My psychological profile is on record, and the Admiral is aware of it. You cannot use this against me."

I shrugged that off, but promptly added paranoia to the list of her attributes. "Oh, trust me. I have absolutely zero loyalty to Jenna Plural. She was responsible for the death of someone very dear to me. Someone who was trying to help her in his own limited way, and she did so without concern."

"So this opens the question for me. If you have such contempt for Jenna Plural, why should I trust you on this mission?"

"Do you remember the reason why I joined your organization? Was it out of my love for the Pacific Alliance or even the United States of America?"

"No, if I remember correctly, it was for payment in ration cards."

"Exactly. And did I prove my loyalty to the department and yourself? Did I ever give you any reason to doubt me?"

"No." She replied simply.

"And that hasn't changed. My opinions on Jenna Plural are neither here nor there. I'm still not a part of any cause. I'll continue to do my duty and fulfill the mission's requirements, in return for the conditions I've already laid down and agreed with you. However, if you no longer trust me, I will gladly withdraw."

And with that, Charlotte smiled. "Oh, I'm quite sure the time has come for you to go home, and it should be an interesting time at that."

Chapter Fourteen

Mars

As soon as I heard that I could see Mars with the naked eye, I went up to the observation dome at the top of the Spirit of Freedom before anyone else was awake. Well, apart from the night crew. Each day it grew larger and larger, and the warm feeling filled me as I could start to make out the lights of the cities. I couldn't make out new Brooklyn yet, as it was too small, but I knew exactly where to look for it. Each day I continued to try until, with great excitement, I saw the faint dim light of where I grew up. It wasn't the greatest town on Mars. It was just an average little community, but I called it home.

However, as the day approached when we would go into orbit, I grew uneasy as to what I would find down there. In case you're wondering what else I did during this voyage, I carried on working for Charlotte, mostly running psych profiles for all the suspects, nothing really exciting.

Then the call came for everyone going down to the planet to meet at the shuttle. As I approached the docking area where we were all to meet to take the shuttle down to Mars, I heard voices in the room ahead of me. I'm not particularly nosy, well, apart from when I need to be professionally, but I couldn't help but stop and listen on this occasion.

"Look, Phelks, we've been through this." The strong Australian accent clearly belonged to Captain Stacey Grant. She'd temporarily been relieved of her duties as a frigate captain because she was now eight and a half months pregnant. Admiral Plural had had her transferred to the Spirit of Freedom, where we had the best medical facilities. "I don't know who the dad is, and honestly, I fucking don't care. This is my kid, and I don't want anyone else to be part of it! You understand me?"

"You know it doesn't work like that, Stacey," came back the stilted British voice of Michael. "Not only do I have a right to be part of my child's life, but it also has a right to have a father."

"You just called my child 'it.'" Stacey snapped back. "For fuck's sake, Phelks, that really fills me with confidence."

"You know full well I only said that because I don't know the gender of the child."

"I have repeatedly heard you admit what a bad father you are. You're not even in contact with your daughter. She wants nothing to do with you."

"I will openly admit my relationship with Kayleigh is somewhat strained. However, you simplify it way too much." He responded sheepishly.

"Well, let me simplify it even more for you, Phelks – you can fuck off. I really don't want a lying, cheating cunt to be an influence on my child, and whether it's yours or Cartwright's doesn't matter. I don't give a dingo's piss."

"We will see about that, Stacey," Michael said curtly.

"Yeah, yeah, whatever, go fuck yourself!" This last line from Stacey was coming closer to the door, and she walked out. I continued to enter, trying to look natural. As our eyes met, her face was red with anger, and she could barely walk, with her swollen belly looking like she was about to give birth to a football team. "G'day, umm...?"

"Kyla," I responded, shaking her hand.

"Cute name," she muttered and walked away. As she left, I stood alone in front of the shuttle with Michael Phelkar.

His broad smile appeared as he saw me, and it was as if he hadn't just had an altercation with anybody immediately before my arrival. "Good morning, Ksenia." he beamed at me.

"Good morning, Mr. Phelkar," I replied. "And it's Miss Lieberman." I wanted it clear that I would treat him professionally and not use first names.

"How are you doing?"

Before I could respond, Plural came in, flanked on either side by her personal security in the form of Dodgson and Thompson. Close behind was Addison, the first officer. They were going through a bunch of routine last-minute decisions about things but stopped as they reached Phelkar and me. She turned towards us. "Good morning, Mr. Phelkar. Ky," Michael smiled, and I gave her a nod.

You couldn't help but notice the coldness between the Admiral and Michael. It was pretty much an open secret that the two had been involved in a relationship that had turned sour. While I didn't officially know the cause of their falling out, I felt fairly certain Stacey Grant's swollen belly probably had a lot to do with it. However, they maintained a very professional relationship when working together. The sudden echo of the clip-clop of heels drew all our attention. It had become the signature noise of the arrival of Miss. Charlotte Kensett.

I almost wanted to laugh as I saw her in her long black slacks, blue pullover, and business-style jacket. Even in the current state of events, the impeccably dressed head of internal security still managed to get the latest high-end fashions somehow.

"Good morning, Charlotte." Plural smiled at her. "I think this is the first time you and I will be working together directly since you served aboard the Lewis Puller."

"Indeed, it is Admiral. It should certainly be entertaining, to say the least."

Michael and Plural went up the ramp, and he glanced back at me before entering. They were closely followed by Charlotte and Dodgson. Charlotte wanted me on last, having observed the demeanor of everyone around. When Hannah Grant and Bronwyn Donavon arrived, I got a slight nod acknowledging my existence before she headed up the ramp.

We still had to wait for someone, and I was getting quite antsy standing there as the minutes passed. Plural was pretty reasonable in her authority, but even she could be pushed at times, and you didn't want to be on the wrong side of her when that happened. Finally, Helen Tracker came running in. "I'm sorry! I got held up by some issues in the computer room," she said.

"Not a problem. Would you please go aboard?" It wasn't like she had to explain herself to me. I was just a dumb schmuck civilian. For Tracker, it was just old habit s.There were a lot of rearrangements of positions once the Solar Confederation was officially formed, and basically, Plural had raised the people she had worked with the most and trusted. She clearly had quite an intense and loyal following amongst what was informally called her "inner circle".

As I followed Tracker up the ramp, I saw Plural and the others seated in the shuttle's first-class accommodation. Dodgson gave Thompson a nod, confirming to each other that all was secure, without disturbing anyone else. And with that, Thompson went up to the cockpit and informed the pilot that we were ready to leave. I was going home to Mars, and I don't know why, but I felt some trepidation.

A lot of emotion was going through me. I'd lost contact with family and friends. I didn't even know if any of them were alive. I had shut thoughts of it out of my mind for a long time, but now, I was on a shuttle going home to a world that no longer considered itself affiliated with either side of the conflict.

"Penny for them?" With those words, I came out of my deep thoughts and looked up. Michael had been heading for the bathroom when he saw me.

"Huh?"

He smiled at me. "Your thoughts. It's an English saying when you see someone who appears to be deeply concentrating on something."

"I know what it means, Mr. Phelkar. We have the saying too." I smiled at him, but it was more out of politeness, as I certainly didn't want to share with him what I was thinking. "You just startled me, that's all."

Unfortunately, the seat next to me was empty, and he sank into it uninvited. "Something clearly seems to be bothering you, and I'd like to help if I can."

"It's nothing, don't worry."

"Sometimes it helps to share concerns."

He was starting to irritate me. However, I found myself blurting out my anxieties. "It's my first time going home in eight years, and honestly, I don't know what to expect. I haven't heard from any of my family in all that time. Eight years under Peon rule is a long time, Mr. Phelkar. Anything could have happened. Will it even be the same as I remember it?"

Michael sighed. "Well, things are very complicated politically, aren't they?"

"They always have been. I see myself as a Martian. You see me as an American."

"Well, the definition of an American is very grey now. With the United States now being run by quislings in league with the European Union, they claim to be the patriotic Americans, and we claim to be the patriots. Jenna realizes that we need to have an identity separate from the nation that is now effectively our enemy."

"I see her point. But I'm not sure if I agree."

A moment of silence fell, and I hoped it meant discussion was over, but he said, "That's not the only thing that's bothering you, is it?"

"I can assure you that it is."

"Ksenia, you are going home to Mars, where you were raised. But there's now a clear path, and you're going to be forced to choose whether to stay with us or join the Martians. If you're telling me that it's not on your mind, I'm afraid I would have to call you a liar."

"Or it could be, Mr. Phelkar, that I just don't wanna discuss my feelings on the matter." I certainly wasn't going to talk about where my loyalties lay when the supreme leader of this new organization was near at hand.

"I can understand that, but to be honest with you, Jenna asked me to check in with you and find out your thoughts."

I frowned at this with concern. "Is she concerned about my loyalty? Does she think I'll run off and join the independence group?"

Michael raised a hand defensively but smiled again, and I felt like slapping him. "No, no, don't get yourself worked up. It's nothing like that."

"Then why does she want you questioning me?"

"Calm down. I can assure you that if Jenna had the vaguest doubt about your loyalty, you wouldn't be on this mission. It's too important." I couldn't disagree with that now that I thought about it. She wasn't stupid. "It's simply that she's concerned about you. She knows you will probably want to contact your family and possibly others you knew here."

"Is that a problem?"

"Not at all." It wasn't Mr. Phelkar that now spoke, and I looked up, startled to see Plural standing there smiling at me. She looked at Michael and inclined her head to indicate that he give her the seat. He did so without a word, and Jenna Plural slipped into it, sitting next to me.

"Did you honestly think I hadn't looked into your background when Charlotte named you as her associate on this mission? Obviously, I know that you're a Martian."

"To be honest, I thought you might have other things on your mind," I said softly.

"Kyla, you made an extreme sacrifice in the Battle of Deep Space, and I won't ever forget that."

That riled me slightly. "I can assure you it wasn't by choice, Admiral. If I could go back in time and save Peter, who was like a father to me, I would."

"I understand that, and I appreciate your honesty. However, willingly or not, you made a sacrifice that day, or rather...I made it for you, but I want you to understand that it wasn't an easy decision. The alternative would have been to have lost the ship and the battle. I had to decide between your lives, and the lives of hundreds of thousands of people, possibly millions, if our cause ended that day. I'm truly sorry that I had to do it, and if I could change it, I would. I don't know what we will encounter going into this negotiation. There may not be an opportunity for you to contact your family. However, I'll do my best to honor Charlotte's agreement with you." At my look of surprise, she smiled. "Yes, Charlotte's told me everything. I don't have a family. My parents died over a hundred and fifty years ago. And...I must admit, there are times I miss them...even now."

"Well, I certainly appreciate that, Admiral." I was doing everything I could to read her, but nothing. Part of me wanted to trust her, and part of me knew that was probably never going to happen.

"Admiral, could you please come up to the cockpit? Mars Command is making communication with us."

"Never a moment's peace." Plural muttered, sighing. Then, smiling at me, she said, "Don't worry, Kyla, we'll work something out." And with that, she got up, and she and Michael entered the cockpit. I wondered about what she said as I turned and looked out the window. Below us, the brown-red rust of my home world and the cities spread across it, lit up like beacons. I smiled softly. However, it didn't last long as I suddenly saw a sleek white fighter coming into view, and it clearly started following us. I couldn't identify the type, as it really wasn't my area of expertise, but I distinctly recognized it as a Peon design. I started to rise out of my seat when the craft's captain came over the line. "Don't be concerned about the Interceptors following us. They're merely Martian defense command escorts."

It still unnerved me to see a craft of European design, even if the Martians used it. Slowly, we began to descend upon Olympus Mons. The vast city had been named after the mountain on which it was built. I had only been there once as a child and remembered it as quite an exciting place to be, a bit like visiting New York, if you grew up in the country. Slowly, the yachts descended on their Dark

Energy repulsors, and both Dodgson and I started to get out of our seats. By this time, Plural and Michael had returned to their own and were deep in a quiet conversation. Dodgson took the front of the ship, and Thompson went back. Routine secondary checks on a ship they had already checked a dozen times. When we finally settled, I headed to the door as Thompson unfastened the locks. Plural and Michael came up behind me and waited patiently, as the soldier went through the routine. Dodgson was just behind them, and the others remained in their seats.

There was a bunch of political bullshit to go through, as our head of state set foot on the planet. I looked at Plural, and she sighed deeply.

"I'm a fucking Marine," she muttered. "I hate all this bull crap pomp and ceremony."

I waited until the shuttle's captain confirmed that the Martian authorities were ready to receive her. Thompson took one last look at Plural, and opened the door.

There was a cacophony of clicking noises, as Martian media started taking photos immediately. Although I stood to one side, my eyes constantly scanned the crowds for signs of danger, as Plural stepped down with Michael at her shoulder. Dodgson followed behind, looking quite good as a representative of the Solar Confederation Marines in the black uniform. As Plural reached the bottom of the steps, a man stepped forward and introduced himself. They shook hands and talked for a few minutes at the bottom of the steps before he started leading them away. At this point, she was Dodgson and Thompson's responsibility. My attention returned to the remaining passengers. Hannah Grant and Bronwyn Donovan went next, and thanks to their celebrity status, the camera started clicking away again as Hannah was all smiles and waves. That just left me, Charlotte, and Tracker. We left together, but the cameras didn't bother clicking as the media was already following the VIPs. We were, however, greeted by a small group of officials. "Welcome to Mars." The one in charge said, shaking each of our hands in turn.

"Delighted to be here, Sir," Charlotte said surprisingly pleasantly. I didn't relax until we got out to the ground cars, and I could see Plural again. Only when I got into the limousine behind hers, did it truly begin to sink in.

I was home.

CHAPTER FIFTEEN

UNWELCOME REUNION

Before the war, New Philadelphia was known simply as Olympus Mons, named after the vast extinct volcano it was built upon. It had been a joint venture between the Americans and the Europeans long before the current troubles. Once the war started, it came under Pacific Alliance control, but it was still a multicultural city. It was divided into German, French, Dutch, and American sectors. It wasn't intended as segregation, simply a reflection of each country's architecture. The streets we now drove down reminded me of pictures I'd seen of old Germany. The limo was spacious, and there was quite a bit of room between me and Charlotte. Also, joining us in the car was the leader of the small group.

He had a typical Martian accent. It was a blend of American and French. However, because I'd grown up in a predominantly American community, I didn't pick up the Martian accent. I can't emulate it for this recording, so you'll excuse me if I speak it in my generic American dialect. Of course, you could simply be reading this, but really, who does that these days?

It was about a fifteen-minute drive, during which time the Martian official was waxing lyrical about Mars's new independence and the golden future ahead of it, but I wasn't listening. Apart from looking out for signs of potential danger I was taking in the sights of the city and how much it had not changed in my absence. We pulled up outside the New Philadelphia Hilton, and our driver exited the vehicle. It was probably the most exclusive hotel on the planet. It was certainly well beyond my pay packet. Dodgson and Thompson got out of Plural's car first and checked the immediate area discreetly before nodding to each other. With the all clear, a Martian official opened the rear door. Plural exited, closely followed by Mr. Phelkar. Behind them was Hannah Grant's vehicle. Stepanchikov and Lucan[TB1] got out and performed similar checks. Then Grant and Donavon stepped out to join Plural.

"So far, so good," Charlotte said softly next to me. "Ahh, there he is."

My eyes followed to where she indicated the First Governor coming out of the hotel with a small retinue of staff to greet his honored guest. "Oh fuck!" My heart skipped a beat, and I slid down in the car. I stared in disbelief. I recognized that face. He was older and no longer had a beard, and a scar over his eye made it look uneven against the other, but there was no way I'd ever forget that face.

"Give me your glasses." I said hastily to Charlotte as I put out my hand. She didn't hesitate. One of the aspects of our work was that situations change, and you couldn't always sit and debate them.

"I take it you know someone over there," she said quietly.

"Yeah," I replied as I put the glasses on. Everything became such a blur that I could only make out undefined colors. "What the fuck, Boss? Are you actually blind?" I said, pulling off the glasses and quickly popping out the lenses.

"This had better be good," she replied snippily. "It's not like you can buy frames off the shelf. I had to have those custom made."

"Get your eyes fixed or replaced. I'm pretty sure you can afford it," I said, returning the frames to my face.

"Hell will freeze over before anyone touches my eyes." I'm sure she actually shuddered at the thought of it. "Anyway, which one do you recognize?"

"The First Governor. It's Terry Moulton."

Charlotte started at him momentarily. "Am I supposed to recognize him?"

I looked up at her incredulously. "He's the first person you had me set up back when I first started with you."

"You say that like I'm supposed to remember everyone I had arrested back in the day," she sighed. "Do you think it's likely he'll recognize you?"

I glanced at her disbelievingly. "I fucked him, then turned him in to Outland Security. What do you think?"

"Well, that could be quite embarrassing," Charlotte sounded almost amused.

"I assumed you had them all killed."

She raised an expensively sculpted eyebrow at me. "Really, Ky, you suddenly have such a low opinion of me."

With my eyes still on Moulton, who was now shaking hands with Hannah Grant, I snorted. "Are you telling me that you don't have people killed?"

"When necessary, of course, I do. However, I'm not some avenging angel of death sweeping over the Solar System. Moulton was a low-level functionary. Once incarcerated, he wasn't considered a problem. Who you have eliminated or don't is a careful consideration. You certainly don't want to make martyrs of anyone."

"Yeah, well, it appears that the Peons must have released the anti-Alliance terrorists."

"Actually, this could work to our advantage," she mused.

"How so? Seeing me again will probably cause considerable tension." I frowned.

"You have an insight into the man that we don't."

"I knew him for less than a week, Charlotte. What insights do you think I have? I'll tell you this, he passionately hates the Alliance. However, since the Alliance no longer exists, I guess it's not an issue."

"On the contrary, Ky. People who don't recognize our Solar Confederation refer to us as the Alliance remnant. This sadly only arouses my suspicions about the governor's intentions."

However, we couldn't speak anymore as the first governor led Plural up to the main door, and it was time for Charlotte and me to get out of the car. Charlotte went ahead of me to ensure she was in hearing range of their conversation. However, due to the possibility of being identified, I hung back. Abigail Thompson looked at me curiously, and then at Charlotte, clearly confused about why I was wearing her glasses, but she said nothing, fortunately.

I quickly checked the body language of the governor's staff. While I noticed some tension or discomfort in a few, there was nothing to indicate any sort of danger. Of course, Plural and Hannah drew the most attention due to their flawless features, but then so did Bronwyn Donovan, with her artificial eye and the metal plate covering half her face. I'd heard that forty percent of her body was now cybernetic, but only the facial adornments gave that away. Dodgson was talking to one of, what I assumed, was the provisional government security. She then disappeared ahead with them and got into the elevator. It was her job to check out the residents before we arrived. Her counterpart, Thompson remained behind me so she could keep everyone in her field of vision.

As we stopped in the reception, the First Governor chatted with her for a while, and they posed for more pictures.

"Admiral Plural," called out a reporter. "What are your first impressions of Mars?"

Plural smiled back at him. "Your question assumes that this is my first time here," she replied. "I've been to this beautiful planet many times, but it's certainly wonderful to be back."

"There will be plenty of time for your questions after our meetings," said Governor Moulton pleasantly. "Our guests have traveled a long way to be here. Let's give them time to rest and freshen up to prepare for, what I hope, will be very productive talks tomorrow."

And with that, Plural was led to the elevator. At this point, I moved ahead to ensure I got in with her. There were more pleasantries with the First Governor outside, before the hotel manager and some government flunky joined me, Plural and Michael, inside. At the last moment, Charlotte slipped in too.

I tensed as the elevator started going down. "I thought I made it clear in my communications with your security that we wanted above ground accommodation," Charlotte said to the hotel manager.

"But, Madame," the manager stated, looking quite surprised. "Our best suite is on the lowest level."

"All the same, we would prefer it if we were above ground." She insisted. Both Plural and Michael were watching her, but didn't interfere. The manager shrugged as the elevator stopped at the 73rd sub-level, the lowest you could go before reaching the environment and life control levels. "I'll see what I can do to change the accommodations. In the meantime, can I show you to your quarters while I get this sorted out?"

Charlotte wanted to say no. We would be effectively trapped down here should anything untoward happen above us, but Plural placed her hand on her shoulder. "It will be alright for a couple of hours. Don't worry."

And with that, we stepped into the most luxurious suite I've ever seen. It even exceeded the accommodation Hannah Grant called home on the Twilight Wanderer. A large spacious living area with various bedrooms leading off and even offices. The manager gave a few more pleasantries before he departed. Then all the smiles disappeared.

"They've totally fucked us over!" Plural said angrily, as she threw herself into a chair as Grant and Donovan entered.

"Calm down. I'm sure we can fix this," said Michael.

She glared at him. "And just how do you propose to do that?"

"What is it?" Charlotte asked, taking a seat by Plural in a more dignified manner. Plural looked up at Michael as if to say, 'Go on, tell her.'

Michael sighed. "The governor told Jenna that the Martians aren't just negotiating with us. They're going to auction their support. He who offers the best deal will get Mars's backing."

Kensett didn't look at all fazed by this. "I guess we should have seen that coming." she said quite casually. "However, we have planned for an alternative."

"Yes, we have." Plural snapped back. "That is to be a last resort, not our first."

Whatever the Admiral had discussed with Charlotte, I certainly wasn't privy to it and couldn't help but wonder what the mysterious British agent had in mind.

"I suggest we go along with it and see how this plays out," Michael said in his 'I-am-the-voice-of-reason' tone that I was going to become very familiar with.

"Personally, Mr. Phelkar, I'm of a mind to pack up and go straight back to the Freedom," Plural was in one of her moods where she couldn't be easily placated.

"All that would achieve is handing Mars over to the Peons. Even if we are to lose a negotiation, we could significantly up the price to cost them dearly for their prize."

"The prize, as you put it, Mr. Phelkar, could mean the difference between a victory and a loss in this war. To have this planet as the staging ground for the assault on Earth would give us a massive advantage. If the Peons do a deal with them, then it's game over for us."

"The Martians are aware of this, which is why they are playing hardball," said Mr. Phelkar. "I'm quite sure that if we were in their position, we'd probably do the same."

Plural stared up at him. "I find it highly unlikely that I would auction the Solar Confederation without any ethical consideration of who I was getting in bed with, Mr. Phelkar."

"And it's not necessarily that the Martians are doing anything other than that." Bronwyn Donovan said. "The chances are they've already decided on whose side they'll come in on, and they're just using this as an opportunity to up the price at the bargaining table."

"You mean even the auction is a sham?" Plural frowned.

"Possibly," added Hannah. "In fact, I think it's more than likely that it's been decided whose side they'll take. However, a bidding war will get that side to up its offer in return for their support."

Plural looked at Charlotte. "Are any of your sources able to confirm or deny this idea?"

Charlotte's eyes widened, and a slight defensive smile crossed her face. "If I'd even heard so much as a rumor of this, I would have told you."

"Sorry, Charlotte," Plural said, deflated. "Of course, you would." She looked around the suite. "I would ask, as Stacey would say at this point, that someone find me a bloody drink?" As Michael approached the small bar, she sighed. "I think we should get an early night and prepare for the morning."

"Actually, no can do," said Michael. "You have to attend the gala reception tonight. It's expected of you."

Plural scowled and threw her head back. "Exactly why is any of this necessary? It makes no sense."

"We have to observe the social niceties of the occasion," he responded while pouring some liquor into a set of glasses.

Suddenly a wry smile crossed Plural's lips, and she said, "Actually, I can't do it. I have nothing to wear for a formal occasion."

"Actually, Mr. Phelkar called me about this the other day," Hannah stated. "I took the liberty of putting together a selection for you from one of the more exclusive boutiques aboard the Twilight Wanderer."

Plural glared at her. "That's most appreciated, Hannah." However, her tone was quite venomous. "However, you don't even know what sizes I wear."

"Oh, Mr. Phelkar was able to provide those as well," Hannah said with a grin and feigned surprise, implying something inappropriate.

Plural looked quite surprised, and looked up questioningly at Michael as he handed her a drink. "I simply called your steward."

Plural snorted. "I guess that's what happens when you get Brits as both your counselor and your steward."

"Either way, your wardrobe is being unloaded from the yacht and transported here," said Donovan.

Michael handed drinks around, and when he reached me, I raised an eyebrow and looked at him questioningly, as if he should have been aware that I don't drink on duty. Plural noticed this. "Take a drink, Kyla. Only one of you needs to be on duty, and at the moment, that's Dodgson." She looked over at Dodgson standing in the corner of the room, still rigid with her hands behind her back. "You don't mind, do you, Dodgson?"

Dodgson smiled back at her and then at me. "N...N...Not at all."

Michael turned and offered me the drink again, and I shrugged and took it. "Thank you, Admiral," I said.

"Actually, we have another problem." Charlotte said carefully. "The first governor is already known to us, and more specifically, Kyla here was involved in an assignment where he was the suspect. She trapped him, and he was arrested."

Plural looked up at me. "Now, that's going to be awkward. If he bears any animosity towards you for that, then it could turn against us."

"I can't disagree," I replied. "He was locked up for at least two years before the Pacific Alliance evacuation. I'm fairly certain he'll be pretty pissed to see me."

"Now is probably a good time for you to go and visit your family. You'll be taking Mr. Phelkar with you."

"I will?" I replied, unable to hide both my surprise and abhorrence of the idea.

"It's already been arranged," Charlotte said, sounding almost conspiratorial. "We need to kill two birds with one stone. There will be a lot of media coverage at this event. We want it focused on the situation."

"If Mr. Phelkar and I are seen at this social event together, it'll only increase the rumors that we're involved. With him at my side, it would look like I'm taking a date. We already discussed it and we won't be attending any social functions together unless necessary. So, you can take him with you."

I think I was standing there open-mouthed, because Plural chuckled. I looked up at Michael and then back at her. "Well, I, um, I don't know what to say." I downed the liquor in one. This was all a little too much.

"It's a date, then," Michael smiled at me.

"It certainly is not." It came out before I had time to think about it, but it brought a chuckle from all around.

"Thompson is also from here," Michael continued unabashed. "Maybe we can all head out together?"

I looked at Thompson with surprise. "Well, at least part way. I come from Lindon City."

So it was that when my luggage arrived, I found myself in one of the bedrooms changing. I'd only thrown in jeans, a T-shirt, two sets of formal business suits, and a pair of sensible shoes. As I was doing up my laces, there was a knock at the bedroom door. I called for them to come in, and was surprised to see it was Charlotte Kensett.

"Do you have a moment to spare, Ky?" she said, as her heels clip-clopped along the wood panel floor towards me.

"Sure," was all I said in response.

"As you know, it's not legal for anyone other than the security forces to carry a firearm on Mars, but it would be quite neglectful of me to let you go out there undefended." At this point, she opened her purse and took out a small white snub pistol. "Especially as you're with Mr. Phelkar." She held the weapon out to me, and I took it and turned it over in my hand. The substance it was made of was unusual. "This is a three-round porcelain firearm. The inside is lined with an anti-reflective lining. All but the best scanning equipment can detect it."

"While I appreciate it, Boss, it would cause quite the diplomatic incident if I was caught with this."

To this, she smiled. "How on Earth do you think you could be caught with it? We all have diplomatic immunity. If there is a diplomatic incident, it will be because someone tried to search you. Anyway, it's not an option, and my supplying you with it has the Admiral's approval."

"Well, there's another problem."

"Which is?"

I indicated the clothing I wore. Jeans and a t-shirt. Charlotte smiled and reached into her purse again. She pulled out the smallest holster I had ever seen and handed it to me. "Just tie this around your leg between your ankle and the calf, and it will be clearly hidden."

I pulled up my trouser leg. I did exactly as she suggested. I then pulled it back down again and checked to see if you could see it under the material. I couldn't.

"I appreciate it, Boss." It would have been odd going out without a weapon. I haven't been in that situation for almost eight years.

"It has come in useful. One of those saved the life of Stacey Grant once, and had it not, none of us would be standing here today, not even Jenna."

Chapter Sixteen

Return to Satan's Anus

O f course, it wasn't like we could just simply walk out and stroll around Mars. Well, technically, I could since I was a citizen, but I hadn't revealed it, and that would have possibly negated my diplomatic immunity. However, when Michael discussed it with the appropriate civil servants dealing with our visit, he managed to get the approval. Barely two hours after Jenna had suggested it, we were on the intercity transit train, which held the record as the fastest land-based transport in the Solar System. We were seated in first class, which was odd for me, but I was willing to put up with a little bit of luxury, as Michael insisted we had to maintain appearances. We were about halfway there, when I realized another passenger was occasionally looking in our direction. Whoever he was, he was a poor excuse for a surveillance operative. "We're being followed." I quietly informed Thompson and Michael.

Phelkar sighed. "Yes, well, Charlotte did say that would be a possibility. Actually, no...She said it would be a certainty. The level of trust between us and the Martians is on a knife edge."

"That's assuming it's a Martian," I responded.

"What do you mean?"

"Well, for all we know, it could be a Peon."

I felt him tense and saw him glance uneasily over at the observer.

"Oh, for fuck's sake. Don't look, Mr. Phelkar!" I muttered as I picked up the menu. We'd hardly had time for a meal, and I only did it to cover his actions.

"Yes, well, I was having a relaxing journey until you told me that."

"Oh, quit with the damn whining, Michael," Thompson said with annoyance.

"Why are you always so irritable with me?" He responded.

I stuffed the menu back in the seat, as Thompson said irritably, "I'm not."

"Yes, you are. When we work together, you hardly even talk to me unless you absolutely have to. Or if it was about Bridgette." Michael sounded frustrated.

"Oh, you remember her name, do you?" Thompson snapped sarcastically. What the actual fuck! Was I watching Thompson and Michael have a domestic? I stared out the window, pretending I couldn't hear what was right in front of me.

"And what exactly is that supposed to mean?" Michael snapped.

"When was the last time you tried to see her?" Tempers were rising now.

"I wasn't aware that I was supposed to."

"You're still her legal guardian, Michael... Unfortunately."

"Am I?" he said, quite irked. "I don't recall signing any papers to that fact."

"It was part of the general orders signed off by General Plural, as part of the emergency after the fleet's formation. A lot of children were orphaned after the Battle of Deep Space, and guardianship was to remain with those who had accepted the responsibility, until more formal arrangements could be made, especially in the case of Bridgette. That was you, Michael."

There was a long silence as he thought this through. Finally, he said, "You have to realize I wasn't around for much of that. I was sitting in jail, so on Earth."

She turned to face him square on. "That's really not the point, Phelkar. The point is, you took responsibility for Bridgette when we booked her from Phobos. Did you not?"

"Well, technically, it was more of an order from Jenna than volunteering."

"Mr. Phelkar, we can debate its technicalities and legalities until Mars turns green. You were responsible for that child, and you let her down."

There was a long silence between us as she turned away, unable to look at him anymore. Eventually, he let out a sigh and said softly, "I'm sorry. If there was something I could do to change that, I would."

"You can't change the past, but you can change the future. Nearly everyone around her is a woman, and it wouldn't hurt for her to have a positive male role model in her life," Thompson calmed herself. "She's really struggling. She's got no friends because she's considered a Peon, and all she ever hears in the media is anti-Peon propaganda. It wouldn't hurt you to take some time out to spend with her." I could almost see his brain ticking over as he thought about what she said, before she added, "If you can't do that, at least do one decent thing." She paused as he looked at her questioningly. "If you want nothing to do with her, sign the paperwork for me. I've been her mother for nearly a year now, in all but name."

"And you've done a fine job in very difficult circumstances. I'll be honest with you, I'm probably not the best role model for her, male or otherwise. I didn't see much of my own daughter growing up, and it's been a number of years since we've even spoken. I am squarely to blame. I could have made more of an effort, but I didn't."

Before anything more could be said, we were interrupted by the announcement that we were pulling into New Brooklyn, and my mind immediately switched back to my own parents, who I was about to see. I started to think that I should have called ahead, rather than just turned up on the doorstep, but somehow it just felt...wrong calling them out of the blue, and honestly, I didn't know what to say if I did call. As we exited the train and walked through the foyer, I noticed a man standing there with a sign that read 'M. Phelkar.'

I glanced up at Michael. "Oh, I forgot to tell you I arranged for a car to pick us up."

Thompson turned to us and said pleasantly, "You two have fun now. I have to catch my connection to Lindon."

We waved her off, and I looked back at the expectant driver. "It's less than ten minutes away," I told Michael. "I prefer to walk." He simply nodded in reply, went up, and spoke to the man who walked off as Michael returned to me.

"Lead the way, Miss Lieberman."

I headed out into the familiar streets. The memories came back of shopping trips with my mother, outings with my father, and riding my bike up and down the streets with my sister. "I think it'll be kinda odd if you call me Miss Lieberman in front of my parents. I really don't want them thinking we have some sort of social difference and make them feel uncomfortable."

"That's absolutely fine, Kyla." He grinned at me.

I scrunched up my nose and grinned back at him. "The only time anyone has ever called me Kyla was when I was in trouble with my mother. It's Ky."

"Fair enough, Ky, but please don't call me Mike."

Now that made me chuckle. I checked around to see if the guy from the train was still following us. He wasn't. That didn't mean we were no longer being followed. It just meant they may have switched.

I saw the disgust on Michael's face as we entered the graffiti-filled lobby of Broadway, and the faint stench of urine permeated the area. Michael drew some attention with his expensive suit, and I thought I probably should have said something about that, but hey, I had other things on my mind.

A couple of kids followed us into the elevator. Typical little punks that hung around the neighborhood. However, these two kids were particularly quiet. Suspicious. They kept looking at each other, although the girl kept glancing at Michael, who was clearly oblivious. Once the elevator stopped moving, it happened quickly. A knife quickly appeared in the boy's hand, and the girl moved to stand behind Michael. Bam! My hand was quickly around the boy's neck, and I slammed him against the wall. His knife was now in my hand. Michael looked startled, and the girl backed away against the wall.

"Sorry, buddy, you picked the wrong target today," I said with a satisfied smile.

"I didn't do nothing," he said, feigning a picture of pure innocence.

The girl started moving slowly toward me, and I glanced at her. "I seriously suggest you stay where you are." I hit a button on the elevator controls so it would stop at the next floor, before we reached our destination. As it did, I instructed the girl to get out, and as she did, they were both expecting me to let him out too, but I didn't, and she looked terrified as the doors closed with her on the outside. I let us go up another few floors, and then I stopped it again, and roughly I spun him around, threw him through the doors, and tossed the knife after him. He glared death at me as the doors closed.

"Oh my God, was that an assassination attempt?" Michael said, looking quite terrified.

I actually chuckled at this. "No, Mr. Phelkar. That was just your run-of-the-mill shakedown. They were more interested in your ration card than your life."

"And this is where you grew up?" He asked, as if this was some great revelation.

"Welcome to Satan's Anus, Mr. Phelkar. That's what the locals call it."

"Oh my, you must have been very happy to get out of here."

I studied him carefully as he said this, but I said nothing. This was my home. These were my people. Of course, I never wanted to leave it.

Again, all thoughts of everything else left me as we stepped out of the elevator, and I faced my parents' apartment. I took a deep breath, steeled myself, and knocked.

We seemed to have to wait for an eternity before the screen on the front door flickered into life, and a very low-res image of a woman appeared. It was hard to make out her features, but it was far too young to be my mother. "Yes?" the voice said impatiently.

"Hi, uh, do Carla and Jacob Lieberman still live here?"

There was a long pause before she answered. "Who are you?" the voice asked uneasily.

"Kyla Lieberman." Almost immediately, the bolts started to be thrown back, and a short black-haired woman in her early twenties stared up at me wide-eyed.

"Is it really you? Mom and Dad said you were probably dead."

As I looked into those large brown eyes, it clicked who this could be. "Sam?"

She would have been eleven years old the last time I saw my sister. She suddenly grinned. "The one and only." I wasn't sure whether to move in and hug her, so I stood there awkwardly. There was a dumb silence until she stepped back and said, "Well, you better come in."

"Sam, this is a friend of mine, Michael. Michael, this is my sister Sam."

He offered her his hand, which she took. "An absolute delight to meet you, Miss Lieberman."

The grin widened across my sister's face. "Damn, if that isn't the sexiest accent I've ever heard," she said, and I'm sure he actually blushed. "Come through to the living room." She led us into the small living room. A small child, probably less than a year old, was sitting on the faded carpet wearing nothing but a diaper and banging some blocks together. He looked up at us disinterestedly before going back to banging his blocks. "I don't have much in, but I can get you some tea or coffee if you want."

I didn't answer her as I looked around and said, "Where's Mom and Dad?"

The smile disappeared from her face as she looked at me sadly. "I thought you would have been informed. Dad passed away about six years ago, and Mom last year. She hoped that with the war ending, you would be coming home if you were still alive." That hit me like a brick, and she saw it in my face, for the next thing she said was, "I'm sorry I shouldn't have told you that."

"No, no, it's fine," I replied, but it wasn't. I felt sick and wanted to throw up, as I sank into the old chair my father would sit in every evening to watch TV.

"I'll get some tea," she said softly.

She headed into the kitchen, and Michael slipped an arm around my shoulder. Normally I would have shaken that off. I'm not exactly a touchy-feely person, but I barely noticed as I thought about my parents.

"Are you okay?"

I sighed and tried to pull myself together and looked back at him. "I will be." I looked at the little kid again and called out to Sam. "Who's the kid?"

"Oh, that's my son, Duke," she called back.

I scratched my nose. I managed to smile up at Michael. "Duke Lieberman! Poor kid. I actually hope he has his father's last name." He smiled back at me and patted my shoulder. I headed into the kitchen, which was barely big enough for the two of us to stand in. "You live here alone?"

"No, my husband Winston lives with me." It pleased me when she said that. It wasn't so much that I had any ethical values on marriage or otherwise. "What about James? Ever hear from him?" I asked, referring to our brother. Sam put down the teapot that she was holding and turned back to me. "Right. Um..." She said uneasily. "James was actually never arrested for draft dodging. He was killed, evading arrest. Our parents never told us."

It bothered me that I didn't have a more immediate reaction to this news. They say that absence makes the heart grow fonder, but it doesn't. It just makes you more distant. Eight years is a long time for someone who is now only twenty-seven years old. "I'm sorry I was unable to get in touch."

She smiled and returned to making the tea. "I often wondered what you are up to. I was really sad when my big sister left. I always knew there was a possibility that you were dead, but I never used to think about that."

"Excuse me, but would you mind if I turned on the television?" Michael was standing in the doorway. "Jenna should be just about arriving at the gala."

Sam frowned for a second as those words sank in, but then nodded. "Sure, go ahead."

She looked at me questioningly as he disappeared into the living room. "Is that something to do with you?"

"What do you mean?" I asked. I was sure what she meant, but I wanted to clarify before saying anything.

"Are you with this state visit from the Solar Confederation?"

I tried to read her feelings in her expression, but I couldn't, so cautiously, I said, "Would that be a problem?"

She shrugged. "Honestly, I don't understand all these politics. I personally believe that, now Mars is independent, that's the way we should stay."

"Jenna has no intention of interfering with Martian independence. I can assure you of that."

Sam's eyebrows raised. "Jenna?" She then smiled. "You know her well enough to be on first name terms with her?"

"I wouldn't go that far. It's more habit, as my boss calls her Jenna. I've been serving with her for the last five years."

"You surprise me. The Ky I remember, wanted nothing to do with the military. I would've thought you would've taken the chance to come home at the first opportunity." I couldn't answer that because I've never really thought about why I'd stayed. I'd simply followed along with everybody else. Even now, I couldn't honestly say that I was really into the cause to liberate Earth. Earth wasn't my world, not really my concern. This was my world. Fortunately, I didn't have to answer, as lifting a tray with four teacups on it, she said, "Come on, let's go join your friend and see what Jenna is up to."

We headed back into the living room, and I sat on the couch next to Michael, taking my cup from her before she moved on to him. As I took a sip, I looked up at a small TV screen that showed outside the Grand Theatre. It was pretty much where every major political and social occasion took place, as nothing else on a similar scale had ever been built anywhere on the planet. It occupied a lot of otherwise potentially usable land. The media was once more out in force, and there was a red carpet, as if it was some actress arriving.

A commentator was talking about the history of Jenna Plural, with references to her long career in the military and the nature of genetic modifications. Martians didn't really have any animosity toward GenMods, but they did uphold the rules of the Prague convention.

The same limousine that picked us up from the port pulled up, and the traditional uniformed doorman went and opened the door. Jenna stepped out with a radiant smile, waving back to the people that waved to her from behind the barriers. I noticed Dodgson get out of the other side of the vehicle, trying to look inconspicuous despite her Marine uniform. Jenna was wearing a long thin golden dress that was quite plain, except for a bit of lace around the collar, which was high on her neck. Behind her, Hannah Grant stepped out in a ridiculously expensive two-piece jacket and skirt. I, however, was watching Charlotte get out the other side with Dodgson.

The first governor and his wife were there to meet her, and he stepped up to shake her hand, but that's when it went wrong. A shot rang out, and I jumped to my feet as I saw Hannah Grant go down. She'd just stepped up alongside of Jenna, and I was sure she had just taken a bullet for her, albeit unwittingly. Smoke was starting to go up, and I saw Dodgson leaping over the hood of the limo and diving on top of Jenna, but just at that moment, another shot rang out, and Jenna went down.

Michael was at my side, and Sam was staring open mouth at the screen and then looking at us. The screen suddenly went blank, and after a few moments, the commentator said, "I'm sorry, we appear to have lost transmission at this moment. As soon as we can find out what is happening, we'll let you know. However, it appears that the leader of the Solar Confederation has been shot. Currently, we don't know if she is dead or alive."

Chapter Seventeen

Buried Alive

"We have to get back." Michael was saying, but I was already pulling out my radio.

"Viper Four to Viper One, do you read me?" I asked, using the code phrases for myself and Dodgson. I repeated this several times, but no response came, and I clipped it back to my belt. "I'm sorry, Sam, but we gotta go."

"It's okay, I understand." She said, looking as shocked as us. She picked up the baby and followed us out to the elevator. As Michael hit the button, I turned around and gave her a big hug.

"If I can, I'll come back, I promise. I love you, Sam."

"I love you too, sis." I kissed her on the cheek and then on Duke's head.

It was only then that I realized the elevator wasn't coming. I looked up at the numbered lights, which were not moving from the ground floor.

"I've never known these elevators to break down. Is that something recent?" I asked Sam.

"No, never," she replied nervously, clearly confused about what concerned me.

"I don't believe in coincidences, Mr. Phelkar. I'm not happy about this."

"You think this is deliberate?" he asked me, the nervousness clear in his voice.

I looked at Sam. "Do you have something to carry him in? Something that would be easier for you to move with?" She nodded. "Go get it. Mr. Phelkar, go with her. I'm gonna check out the emergency stairs."

He nodded and followed her back into the apartment. The Martian authorities knew where we were, and not knowing how secure that information was, for all I knew, the Peons did too. They had once gone to a lot of trouble to get Michael, and I was certain if they took out Jenna, they would want to take him out too. As I headed for the door to the stairs, the concept that Jenna could be dead refused to sink in. She was the rallying force of the Solar Confederation, and I could see it splintering very quickly without her. Before opening the door, I reached down, pulled out the miniature three-shot gun, and checked it. Two bullets in the grip, one in the chamber. I slowly opened the door and could hear distant voices speaking very softly a couple of levels above us. It was a mixture of Martian and some European accents, which I couldn't identify. Shit on a stick. The elevator was the only way out of here. I backed out and closed the door softly, and headed quickly back to the apartment. Sam had just strapped a baby carrier onto her chest, and Phelkar was helping to strap it at the back. He looked up at me questioningly with concern in his eyes as I entered. "We've been trapped down here all right.

I'm not sure who's coming after us, but there's definitely Peons among them."

"Is that all you've got?" She indicated to my firearm.

"Unfortunately, yeah, it is, and it only has three shots."

"Wait here." She quickly disappeared into the bedroom, leaving us confused, but returned within seconds and, to my surprise, carried a large shotgun and a heavy-duty handgun. "Which one do you want?"

I stared at her, totally bewildered, but took the shotgun. "I thought firearms were illegal on Mars?"

"Not if you're a cop," she replied.

"Your husband is a cop police officer?" Michael said.

"No, my husband is a delicatessen manager. I'm the cop," she made to give him the handgun, but he just looked at it and then at her.

"Frankly, Miss Lieberman, you probably know how to use that better than I do."

"Michael is a bureaucrat, not a fighter," I muttered.

Sam seemed to ponder this, and then strapped the weapon belt around her waist. She then passed him the baby carrier.

"What are you doing?" Michael asked.

She looked at him almost contemptuously. "If you think I'm going to go into the line of fire with my baby in front of me, frankly, you're probably the stupidest man I've ever met."

"Mr. Phelkar knows a lot of stuff, but on many accounts, he's still pretty dumb," I said, unable to stop a grin from crossing my face. She handed him the baby, which he looked at like he was about to explode. We both helped strap him in.

"You want to stay behind us," said Sam. "At no time, put yourself in the line of fire. If my kid gets hurt, you better hope you go down with him because, trust me, I don't care who you work for. You'll be a dead man."

"I can assure you, that at no time, will I put myself in any danger."

I rolled my eyes. "That's one thing you can trust him on."

"Come on then." Sam told me, "We'll go ahead while he stays here. Once we're certain that we have an escape, we'll come back for you."

As we reached the door, Michael said, "What if you don't come back?"

I shrugged and said, "Let's hope you do a better job with Duke than you did with Bridgette."

He scowled at me, and I gave him a wink before my sister and I headed back into the corridor. As we got to the stairwell door, we could hear the soft voices behind it. Sam nodded towards one side of the door, and I nodded back and took my place at the side of it. She took the other side, and I checked my weapon once more. She was doing the same with her handgun. We waited. Slowly, the door began to open. A man stepped out, followed by another. The one in the front spun around towards me with his weapon ready, only to receive a whole hell of a lot shot straight into his chest. He went down immediately as another shot rang out, and the second guy joined him with a bullet wound to the side of the head. We weren't sure if anyone else was behind the door, and so, didn't move. Suddenly a small device was thrown into the corridor, and Sam cried out, "Flash-bang!" I spun away, closing my eyes and covering them with my arm, but even so, the glare came through, and I was momentarily distracted. I heard Sam's gun firing several times, and a single shot returned. As my vision cleared, I saw her bending down over the bodies and searching them.

"These are Martian Defense Force uniforms," she said, distressed. "I hope I haven't just killed one of our own."

I bent down to search the jacket pockets of one of the men, but there was nothing. I then reached under his collar and allowed myself a smile, as I pulled out Peon dog tags. "Not unless the Martian Defense Force is recruiting German Marines," I said, sharing my find with her.

"Seriously? Oh, thank Hashem."

We both stepped carefully into the stairwell and looked up. My heart sank, as we heard more running feet. "This is a no-go."

"This is the only way out, other than the elevator."

"There's the trash chute?" I said with a shrug.

Sam scrunched her nose. "The hatch is pretty small. Do you think we'll fit?"

"We can try. We're not exactly that big."

"What about your friend?"

"He just spent the last three or four months as a prisoner of war. Trust me, he's lost a lot of weight."

We headed back past the apartment and called Michael out. We made him go ahead, since any attack would now come from behind, as we raced down the corridors past many other apartments. It occurred to me that no-one had come out when they heard the gunshots. Yeah, that was the type of place I grew up in.

The garbage chute ran up to the surface. One would drop their trash in, and it would fall through to a container, and once every couple of hours, D.E. generators would come online, and the trash bags would float up to the surface, where they'd be taken for recycling. The problem was, we couldn't just jump in and fall down with the rest of the garbage, because it was at least another twenty stories down.

"Shit. We have about 7 minutes before the next lift," said Sam as she checked the time.

"We just have to hold them off," I said, turning away from the drop chute and looking down the corridor. Fortunately, it had a slight gradient and disappeared within about twenty meters. Pushing Michael behind me, I made him crouch down and turn away from us. Basically, that meant he was more likely to take a bullet and shield the baby. I listened carefully for the slightest sound of noise. With the deaths of their comrades discovered, they were certainly not going to be taking any more chances. I heard a shout go up. This time, it was definitely in French. "They've found the apartment empty. They're looking for us. They were supposed to take us out before they shot Jenna."

I checked the time. We had three minutes left to wait. Sam started unfastening the baby from Michael.

"You won't fit through with him attached to you," Sam said. "I'll pass him up once you're inside."

Before I could say anything, an armed Peon came around the corner, and I managed a blast from my shotgun. As the echo died, I could hear scampering footsteps of men backing up and staying outside. Next to me, I heard the faint hum start up from the way chute.

"Go! Get in!" I ordered Sam.

"Yeah, I'm not going in there while my kid is still here."

I was about to protest, but you don't bait a mother bear, and I knew it would just be a waste of time. I heaved myself into the hatch after handing Michael my shotgun. It was awkward trying to turn in the tight tube. I was about halfway through when I reached back and took the firearm back again. If you're wondering why I didn't send Michael first, well, simply because I didn't know what to expect when we got to the top. There was a weird sensation when half my body was in gravity and the other half was inside the waiting wave of dark energy. I was already starting to move up as I pulled in my legs. It was much slower than I thought, but it made sense. Dark energy generation uses a lot of power; the less you use, the cheaper it would be. Moving garbage wasn't exactly an urgent matter.

The one thing that hadn't occurred to me was that, obviously, trash would be moving up with me. However, I stayed ahead of it, but the same couldn't be said for the others. I heard gunfire from below. It was Sam's handgun, and I prayed, hoping they were okay. This was kind of odd, considering I was an atheist, but people fall back on familiar patterns when in weird situations.

I looked up and could see the dim light ahead of me. I tensed myself, because I didn't know how I was gonna exit this tube. Would I come to a stop, or would I fly out as if on the top of a geyser? It turned out it was the geyser method, and I was lifted above the ground as I came out into a large room filled with bags and bags of household waste. That gave me a soft landing, which was quite fortunate considering I had the indignity of landing flat on my ass. It was difficult standing up, as it was almost like I was trying to walk across one of those children's bouncy castles as I made my way back to the vent.

I was too far away now to hear anything from my companions. I had no idea what was happening until I heard an excited child's laughter. Duke came flying out of the top with the expression of a kid on a ride in Disneyland. He started coming down some distance away from me, and I made a dive that if anyone had seen it, would have established my place in the Football Hall of Fame. Oh, the innocence of childhood. He giggled and laughed up into my face as, with him held tightly against my chest, I turned back to the chute just as Michael came flying out. He landed in a similar fashion to me, but took a lot longer to get up and balance himself. Then I waited...and I waited. My heart began to race as there was no sign of Sam.

"What was the situation when you came up?" I asked Michael.

"She was engaging the enemy. She was unhurt when I left." He said as I handed him the child, and he began strapping him back onto his chest. I looked back down into the darkness, fighting against my agent instinct, which was telling me to leave. However, my family instinct kept me there. Then a huge grin crossed my face, as I heard the familiar gunfire from her pistol. As she came into view, I saw that she was firing down at someone coming up behind her. This time, as she came out of the chute, I grabbed her by the back of her pants and pulled her to me, so she landed on her feet next to me. It startled me when seconds later, the dead body of a Peon came flying out to land unceremoniously across the room. Then the hum of the engines went silent, and in the darkness of the chute, I heard a terrified scream. One of our pursuers was now falling to his death.

I didn't waste time and turned to look for an exit as Sam checked on the baby, who appeared to have fallen asleep, and was snuggled into Michael's chest.

I made my way over to the door, calling for them to follow. When Sam was sure that Duke was uninjured, they followed. I had no idea what to expect up here because, to be honest, I had no idea what was going on. Thoughts of Jenna and the others now came back to me. Were she and Hannah dead? I had no idea.

The door led out into a processing area, and as we came out, we startled a few of the maintenance techs, one of which came over to us. "Hey, you can't be in there," he said in the distinctive Martian dialect.

Sam stepped up to him. "I'm Officer Samantha Washington of the N.B.P.D."

He looked at her suspiciously. "Then let's see your badge."

"I don't have it on me."

"We don't have time for this," said Michael urgently.

I had to agree and swiftly punched the man right in the face. As he went down, Sam turned on me. "What are you doing? You can't just go around hitting civilians."

I shrugged. "Yeah, I can. I have diplomatic immunity. You can't arrest me."

She rolled her eyes at me as we headed to the next door with no one trying to interfere. We came out into a foyer, which I quickly recognized as the entrance to the building. People were coming and going as if nothing was happening. That was, of course, until they noticed me carrying a large and powerful shotgun.

That's when the running and screaming started.

This was when I realized that we had no plan, and no chance of getting back to Jenna. After all, that's what we needed to do – stroll down the road and get on the train.

"Can't we commandeer a car or something?" Michael suggested.

"And drive it where? Across the desert?" I snapped back.

The point became moot when several precinct cops approached us with raised weapons. I gently lowered the shotgun to the ground as Michael and Sam raised their hands. They looked confused as they approached us. "Sam? What the hell is going on?" One of the cops asked.

Sam sighed. "That is a very good question."

Chapter Eighteen

Return to New Philadelphia

L ess than ten minutes later, we were in Sam's precinct station. Once our credentials had been confirmed, we were no longer under arrest. Diplomatic immunity really rocks! However, it remained to be seen if we could grasp the situation. The sector chief had been called in, and Sam had disappeared into a long meeting where she was grilled about what'd happened. She was immediately suspended from service, but that was just the routine when any officer was involved in a shooting.

Michael and I tried to get more information on what had happened with Jenna, but they were as ignorant as we were. About two hours after the incident, we were sitting impatiently in a waiting room. I watched Michael bouncing Duke on his knee, cooing to him softly and making him giggle. I couldn't help but smile. I was surprised at how quickly the baby had taken to him.

"I find it hard to believe that you claim you're not good with kids," I said, eventually.

He looked up at me and pondered my words before smiling. "Oh, kids are perfectly fine at this age. It's when they hit puberty that I become uncomfortable."

"Why?"

"I've never been very good at confrontation, which I know is kind of ironic considering I'm working in the diplomatic profession now. I guess I'm a man of logic, and nothing in this universe is more illogical than the teenager."

I chuckled lightly. "I can understand that, but hey, you were a teenager yourself once."

"Yes, Ky, indeed I was. But I must admit, I was the quintessential nerd." I had no idea what quintessential meant, but I got the point. "I've never been very good at relationships in general. My marriage was a misery and didn't last long. I have never been able to maintain a relationship for longer than a few months."

At that, I was not as amused. "Well, it doesn't help if you cheat on your girlfriend."

At that, he stopped bouncing Duke and looked at me, flushing slightly. "That was a mistake. Everything at that time was so confusing. America surrendered, then Britain surrendered, and we were forming some sort of rebellion. I wasn't thinking straight."

I snorted. "That's just an excuse. But of all the people to cheat on, you decided to cheat on Jenna Plural, leader of the free Solar System."

"Excuse or not, it's the truth. I fell in love with both Jenna and Stacey at a time in my life when I had nothing. I was on board a foreign ship with military personnel. I was completely out of my comfort zone."

"So, what's the situation between them now?"

He sighed and started bouncing Duke again, as the child had started becoming fidgety. "Well, when I came back from Earth, Jenna didn't talk to me for a while, and then finally told me that from now on, our relationship would be a purely professional one. As for Stacey, she doesn't even want a professional relationship with me, let alone a parental one."

"If it's your child," I added.

At that, he actually looked sad. "Yes. If it's my child."

His reaction surprised me. "You want it to be your kid? Wouldn't it be easier for you if it wasn't?"

He said softly, "Yes, it would, but I guess there is an innate desire for a man to procreate, and to be quite honest, if it is my child, would you want Stacey to be the only person raising her? Don't get me wrong. Stacey is probably the most loyal and caring woman you could ever meet. Most of her wild behavior is a front. She's had possibly one of the shittiest lives you could imagine."

"Michael, I grew up in a community known to its inhabitants as Satan's Anus. I think I know what shitty is."

"Point taken. On the other hand, I was raised in a fairly affluent family, not rich per se, but comfortable. Stacey and I have nothing in common, and it would probably never have worked out anyway, but there is something endearing about that little Australian firebrand."

"Is there any chance the two of you could reconcile?"

"Oh no. Even if I could, it would be most uncomfortable."

"How so?"

"Jenna is her best friend, and there was something that will always be disquieting about the fact that I slept with both of them."

I laughed at this. "You certainly have the most complicated life, Mr. Phelkar."

"I certainly did create a confused one. But can I ask you a favor?"

"That really depends on what it is," I replied.

"Can we return to the convention of you calling me Michael? Literally, everyone calls me Mr. Phelkar, even Jenna."

I smiled softly at him. As I looked into those large brown eyes of his that appeared to be filled with the same innocence as little Duke's, I couldn't help but reflect on if I'd had him wrong all this time. "I think I can do that, Michael."

About an hour later, Sam and her sector chief came and joined us.

"I've arranged to get you back to New Philadelphia with a police escort," Was the first thing that the sector chief said, as he came through the door. "I assume you won't have a problem with Officer Washington here being amongst that detail. I'm aware of your familial relationship."

"Yeah, of course, that would be fantastic. But do you have any news about Jenna Plural?" I asked, as Sam relieved Michael of the baby.

The sector chief sat opposite me and said, as if he was giving us new information, "All we know is that a sniper shot Jenna Plural and Hannah Grant. I can't confirm if either lives, but they've both been taken to hospital as far as I understand." In other words, he didn't know anything, as it was obvious that she would be taken to the hospital, even if she was dead or alive.

However, I thanked him anyway and got up. "We need to get going."

"Do you mind waiting about thirty minutes?" Sam asked me. "My husband is coming to pick up Duke."

"I don't think that would be a problem," replied Michael. Time passed, and we were standing in the reception area, as a tall, dark-skinned man built like a wrestler arrived in a very dark mood. Sam immediately went over to him.

"What the hell is going on, Samantha?" he positively boomed. What drew my attention was the clearly Caucasian Duke was not the genetic child of this man who took the baby lovingly into his arms.

"Winston, please don't give me shit right now. There's too much going on to explain."

"Give you shit? I hear you're in a gunfight with my son, and you're worried about me giving you shit?"

"Please just come over here." She led him over to me. "This is my sister Ky. I've talked with you about her before."

His eyes widened slightly at the outstretched hand. "It's a pleasure to meet you, Ky. To be honest, from what Sam has told me, I had assumed you were dead."

"Nice to meet you, Winston, and yeah, the fog of war is a bitch."

He immediately turned his attention back to Sam. "So, what's going on, Samantha." His tone made it clear that he only ever called her Samantha when there was an issue between them.

"I'm escorting Ky back to New Philadelphia. I want you to take Duke but don't go home. Go to your sister's."

"Oh no, I'm gonna need a lot more information than that," he said coldly.

"Winnie, I don't have time now to go into it all, but it's all connected with that state visit from the Solar Confederation. I promise you that I'll explain everything when I return, which'll probably be tomorrow."

He looked at her angrily. "And when we do, we're going to have a very long talk."

Then to my surprise, his face softened. Looking down at her with the most loving expression I had ever seen, with the baby in between them, he leaned down and kissed her gently. "I love you, bubblegum." She looked back up at him with that same love in her eyes. "I love you too, my coffee cup." He looked a little embarrassed but smiled at me and Michael before saying goodbye and heading out with the baby. Sam watched them leave and didn't turn back to us until he was out of sight. "Come on," she said despondently.

We left via the back exit and met with two other plain-clothes officers. Sam led us to an unmarked car and jumped into the driver's seat. The other two cops got into separate unmarked cars. Michael and I climbed into the back seat, because there was no front passenger seat, just an array of equipment. We took the short drive to the train station, and when we arrived, Sam told us to stay in the car.

I saw the other officers get out to scope the situation. When they were sure it was safe to do so, she came back, and we followed her into the station. She took us to the front of the train's first-class carriage that had been sectioned off for us, with no other passengers allowed in. We climbed aboard, and Michael mildly asked for the large screen T.V. to be turned on to the news. I sat with Sam, as the two other officers sat at the front and the back of the carriage.

It was in the middle of a news report as the T.V. came on. "It has been confirmed that 'Mars for the Martians' has taken responsibility for the attack on the Solar Confederation head of state, Jenna Plural. This group, that was instrumental in gaining us our newfound independence, frequently stated that it would not support any alliance with the Solarians or the Europeans." That was the first time that I'd heard the term Solarian, and it was one that was going to stick. "It still hasn't been confirmed whether Admiral Plural lives or is in a critical condition. Also involved in the attack, was the C.E.O. of Grant Industries, Hannah Grant, causing an immediate fall in company stock." The news anchor then talked about the economic effects this would have on Mars, which I had no interest in listening to.

"We have to start planning what we'll do if Jenna is dead. This has a serious possibility of fracturing the Confederation," Michael said as he came and sat beside me on the opposite side of Sam.

I just stared at him and shrugged. "Hey, politics isn't my bag Michael. My responsibility is to ensure Jenna is okay, not to worry about if she's dead." I spent the rest of the journey talking to my sister and found out that her husband was once the best friend of Duke's biological father, who had run a mile when he learned he was to become a dad. I recalled the conversation I'd overheard between Michael and Stacey before we embarked on this adventure. I couldn't help but think she should be happy Michael wanted to take responsibility. However, all thoughts about everything except Jenna left my mind, as we pulled into the New Philadelphia terminus.

There were various officials and security there waiting for us. Our two police escorts remained on the train to return to their original district. At first, security wanted to separate me from Sam and excused her from further duty.

"She stays with us," Michael said firmly, as he stated that she was family to the official, who had rather rudely told her that her services were no longer required.

"That is, if you want to stay with us," I asked her, thinking she may be eager to get back to her family.

She pondered this a moment but shook her head. "No, I'll see this through. Make sure you're okay. I'll go back tomorrow."

I was pleased they kept us from the prying eyes of the media, as I was in a filthy state. I didn't feel comfortable being seen as a representative of the Solar Confederation.

As we were let out of the car, I did, however, receive quite a shock.

"Is Admiral Plural alive?" I asked the official.

"We don't know," he replied uneasily.

"What is that supposed to mean?" Michael asked.

"Your security detail refused to let her be taken aboard one of our ambulances. I believe her name was Dobson."

"Dodgson," I corrected, wondering why on Earth she had done that.

"They took her off in the limousine they arrived in." the official continued.

"And you have no idea where they went?" I replied incredulously.

"I hardly think it's appropriate for you to get annoyed with me," he said, almost venomously. "It was your Dodgson that drove the vehicle out of here and gave security the slip."

"Gave you the slip in a stretch limo?" said Michael, expressing my thoughts with equal incredulity.

"Clearly, this had been planned for, Mr. Phelkar. We were following them and only lost them for the briefest of moments, at which time they abandoned the vehicle. Which, I not only find duplicitous, but also very stupid."

"How so?" I asked.

"There was sufficient blood loss covering the vehicle's rear seat, clearly meaning only one thing. Plural is dead."

I couldn't hide my stress at this thought, but Michael took my hand reassuringly in his, and at the time, I thought nothing of it. I was so wrapped up in the events happening around me.

"Both Hannah and Jenna are GenMods. Trust me, Jenna has survived, what for us, would be a traumatic blood loss before, and she was up and moving within the hour."

I pulled out my communicator again. "Viper One, this is Viper Four. Do you read me? This is a party line." This last part was to let her know that we could be overheard, and it wasn't secure. There came no response, but then I heard a couple of clicks. That told me a lot. I returned the radio to my belt. I couldn't explain what was happening to Michael in the present company, for those two clicks had meant Dodgson had heard me. She was, however, either unable to or unwilling to respond. However, my entire world was about to turn upside down at the reply to Michael's next question.

"We need to contact the S.C.S. Freedom. Can that be arranged?"

"There's been no communication from the S.C.S. Freedom since this incident happened. We're not even detecting it on our scanners anymore. Would you care to explain that, Mr. Phelkar?"

CHAPTER NINETEEN

DISTRACTION

We were taken to the home of the First Governor, which was probably the most secure building on the entire planet. There was no getting out of it, and I prepared myself for my reunion with Terry Moulton. However, as it turned out, he wasn't present, and instead, we were met by his chief of staff, a tall officious man by the name of Renwick. We were also reunited with Abigail Thompson, who had also seen the events unfold via television. Learning that no-one had tried to take her out convinced me instantly that the target back in Brooklyn was, indeed, Michael Phelkar.

Renwick greeted us most pleasantly as he led us into his spacious office, but I could see in his eyes that he was irritated.

"You must surely understand, Mr. Phelkar, that we are not at all pleased about what is going on."

"With all due respect Mr. Renwick," Michael replied most indignantly. "It is us who should be angry at the incompetence of your security measures."

"Security is only effective, Mr. Phelkar, when the protected person cooperates with us. I must insist you tell us where Jenna Plural is."

"I can assure you of this. If I knew where my leader was, I would be with her now."

"Very well, Mr. Phelkar, if you want to play these games, so be it." He sat behind his desk, failing to offer us seats quite deliberately. "If it wasn't for the fact that we can't locate your ship, I would immediately expel you from the planet and end these negotiations."

"Something has happened to the S.C.S. Freedom?" Thompson asked with great concern, stepping toward him.

"Do you really think I'm an idiot, Ma'am?" Renwick replied. "You're clearly up to something, and that ship of yours has gone dark for a reason."

She stepped up to him angrily, and Michael placed a hand on her shoulder to restrain her. "If our ship has stopped communications, something is seriously wrong, and you want to blame us?!" He stated disbelievingly.

Thompson pulled away and slammed her fists on his desk. "I want to know what's going on, and I want to know it now!"

Renwick looked taken aback. Thompson had been so vehement, that his own security guards took a step forward towards me. He raised a hand to them, and they backed off. "Either you are an excellent actress, or you really don't know what's going on here."

She took a deep breath and forced herself to calm down. "I am begging you to find out what's going on with that ship, and if my daughter is safe. I will get down on my knees in front of the entire media and beg, if that's what it takes."

He stared at her for a long time and looked up at Michael, who shrugged and smiled. "Whilst I'll ask that you forgive my friend's outburst, she is speaking as a mother, not a representative of the Solar Confederation, of which she has no authority to do or promise anything." He said it in a cheerful laidback manner, rather than a reprimand of her actions.

"All the same, that was quite an outburst."

"Do you have children, Mr. Renwick?" Michael said.

He nodded, and Michael continued. "Then I ask you simply understand the concern we have about the safety of our daughter." Thompson glanced up at him with surprise as he said, 'Our.'

Renwick stared at us all expressionlessly for a long while before saying, "I will do what I can to find out what's going on, but I need your assurance you'll be open with me about everything."

"That goes without saying," Michael said with a smile.

Renwick looked us up and down as if finally noticing the filthy state of our attire. "Let me see if I can get some rooms arranged for you. Give you a chance to shower and a change of clothes."

"If it's all the same, I'd prefer it if we could stay together." Michael said, before nodding in my and Thompson's direction. "If, of course, that's acceptable to you." We both nodded, and as I turned to follow one of the governor's staff, I noticed Sam standing there looking at me curiously. I'd completely forgotten she was even there. As we headed towards the elevators, I asked her what was wrong, and she just shook her head as if to say, 'Not now, not here.'

Once again, we found ourselves in a luxurious suite, but as Michael was about to talk about the situation, I shook my head at him. "It's possible they are listening to us, so everyone, be careful what you say."

Michael chuckled. "They just heard you say that?"

I simply shrugged that off with a grin. "I'm sure they're aware that we would be using standard security procedures. If they take offense at that, then they really are oversensitive." I indicated the bathroom door. "Let's go in there."

The four of us entered, and I turned on the shower taps. With the water running hard, I said in a low voice, "Keep your voices low." I went to pull out my radio again, but Sam stopped me.

"I want some answers," she said sharply. "I wasn't happy about some of the things I heard the Chief of Staff saying."

"Like what?" I frowned.

"He seems to think that you're up to something." Sam scowled. "Be honest with me, are you?"

"Don't you trust me?"

Sam sighed and looked away before looking back at me. "Ky, you're my sister, and I love you, but you have to understand I haven't seen you for nine years, and you suddenly return to my life with a woman, who one side hails as the liberator of all humankind, and the other side brands her a fascist. You gotta understand that I have questions."

"She's neither," Thompson responded. "She's simply someone who's trying her best to ensure we don't live under Peon dominance."

Sam fixed her eyes upon her. "Just remember, I'm a Martian, not a Peon, and I'm not a member of your Solar Confederation."

I took offense at this. "I'm a Martian too, Sam, don't forget that. Trust me, I would never play any part that would bring harm to my home world."

"If I may interrupt you, there really is more important stuff we have to deal with here," Michael said in his politest tone.

I nodded and pulled out the communicator again. "Viper Four to Viper One. We have sanctuary."

"Affirmative, Viper Four. This is V...Viper one." The stammering voice of Emma Dodgson came back to me.

"Can you give me a sitrep? I asked.

"We've gone to g...ground. Clip-clop had prepared for such an incident." Clip-clop was the code name we had given Charlotte Kensett. Yeah, I know, not very imaginative, but it amused us at the time.

"What's the status of Jessica?" This time, I was using the code name for Jenna Plural, which we changed frequently.

"S...Seriously p...pissed off." And I grinned as I heard Jenna's voice. "What is your status, Viper Four?"

"We're at the governor's mansion. The Charmer is with me." Michael smiled at me when he realized that he was the Charmer, and I stuck my tongue out at him.

"That's good to know." Jenna came back. "I need you to get out of there as soon as possible. We believe the Freedom has been attacked by the Peons. We may have already lost it." Thompson tensed and looked most distressed. "I don't know if the Martians are in league with this," Jenna continued. "But either way, the stakes have just been raised. Get out of there and lose anybody following you, then make contact with us again, and we will tell you where to go."

"Give us a chance to take a shower, and we'll work a way out of here," Michael said.

"No hurry. Get some rest. I think I'm fairly confident that you haven't slept tonight. You can do this tomorrow."

"That would be truly appreciated. It wasn't exactly a walk in the park for us either," Michael said. "What's the status of Hannah?"

"Being a pain in the ass about announcing that she's still alive before her company stock drops to zero," Jenna replied curtly. "Maintain radio silence until you're in a position to meet up with us. Good luck, guys. Jenna out."

I returned the radio back to my belt. "I bag first shower," Michael said with a grin.

About an hour later, we were all showered and taken separate rooms. After lying there for a couple of hours, unable to sleep, I got up, pulled on a bathrobe, and headed out to Michael's room. Sam had got me thinking about Jenna's end game. She'd made it pretty clear that not gaining Mars would be tantamount to losing the war. Just how far would she go to gain victory? I needed to talk to somebody before my head exploded.

I was surprised to find him awake, and he turned the light on as I knocked gently at his door and entered. "Can't sleep either?" he said softly, climbing out of his bed.

"I can't stop thinking about what Sam said."

"And I can't stop thinking about Stacey and the baby." He sighed.

"Oh, I'm so sorry. I never even thought of that."

He sat on the edge of the bed and patted the area beside him. I sat and rested my elbows on my knees as the dark thoughts went through my head. "I hate this war...I hate what it turned me into."

"I remember Stacey once saying to me, 'If you don't hate war, you're a fucking psycho.'"

I managed to laugh at this. "You gotta love Australian wisdom." I looked up at him, and our eyes locked together. Don't ask me how it happened, or even why it happened, 'cause I can't give you a logical answer. His kiss was tender and reassuring, and my body tingled as he ran his hand up my thigh. Slowly the kiss grew more intense as I ran my hands up his chest, and he pushed aside the opening of the robe to run his fingers up the bare flesh of my waist. My hand slipped around his back, and the other ran my fingers through his hair as the kiss became harder and more passionate.

Slowly we fell back onto the bed, my robe now open, revealing my naked body to him. His fingers cupped my breast, whilst mine slipped down to his shorts and into them. I tensed at the feel of him.

"What's wrong?" He breathed.

"Nothing," I said, relaxing once more. "I've just never been with a non-Jewish guy before."

He was hard and ready for me, but I wasn't ready for him as we explored each other's bodies.

I slipped my arms out of the robe as he pulled off his shorts. At no time did I think what we were doing was wrong or inappropriate. I think my mind saw it as an escape from the intense stress that I was going through, but none of this was done consciously. I can't explain it. It simply happened.

I raised a hand and pushed his shoulder until he moved down slowly, kissing my breast, kissing my abdomen, and then finally kissing my...I let out a moan of pleasure. For someone who claimed he wasn't very good with relationships, he suddenly appeared to have a lot experience in making a girl happy. When I tugged at him to come up again, he did so willingly, and my hand reached down to circle his member and worked it gently, but vigorously, until he begged for me to stop, not wanting to end his experience prematurely. I closed my eyes as he entered me. It'd been literally years since I had been with a man. Just like when you drink alcohol after having abstained for a long time, the pleasure that coursed through me was extreme. With perfect rhythmic timing, we were one, and finally, we came together almost at the same time. His body tensed against mine and almost instantly relaxed. He rolled off and lay next to me. I curled up beside him as he held me tightly against his body. We lay there silently, and you would think at this point that I may have regretted it, but

I didn't. It was the first time I'd been intimate with a man that wasn't for the line of duty.

Chapter Twenty

Jenna Has a Plan

I woke before dawn. Michael was sound asleep next to me, and I slipped out of bed and went to take another shower. I then headed downstairs on the pretense of taking a walk. Telling us to get out without being observed was easy to say, and more difficult to do. No-one stopped me, although several members of staff did ask me if I needed anything. I went out onto the grounds and the artificial lawn, which made up the majority garden leading up to the surrounding wall of the estate. I made a mental note of where all the visible security cameras were. Not that there was any real point – places like this had nonvisible cameras too. The visible ones were more of a deterrent than actual security. After about fifteen minutes of walking around the grounds, Sam came out to join me.

She smiled at me, but there was concern in her eyes as she came over to me. "Did you manage to get any sleep at all?" she asked me.

"Eventually," I replied.

She sunk her hands deep into her pockets and eyed me carefully before speaking. "I gotta be honest with you,

233

Ky. I really don't know where I stand in this situation. Whether you're right or wrong in what your Jenna Plural wants to do, you're going against the authority of Mars."

I sighed, not wanting to rehash this. "Look, I get it. But someone just tried to take out the Confederation's head of state. We don't know who to trust. I understand where your loyalty lies, but perhaps you should go home to your husband."

"That's not really what I'm saying or at least trying to say," she said, sounding frustrated more with herself than with me. "You haven't been here for nine years, and those years weren't good ones. The Peons never officially took control. They did blockade us and control who came in and who went out. They manipulated our communities and had a heavy presence here, and roiled up a lot of animosity between the different communities that were ancestrally Pacific Alliance or European. We fought back. There was a resistance movement that started to attack the Peons, and we fought hard for this independence. We won. Many people think the First Governor is betraying that by negotiating with either side of a war that we no longer have a part in. For the Martians, the war was over."

"I don't get your point?"

"You're a Martian, Ky. You're one of us, not one of them. I really don't understand why you're not turning away from them now and coming back home."

"It's really quite simple, Sam. I don't know her end game regarding Mars, I really don't, but right now, Jenna Plural is the only one stopping the Peons from coming back. I'm doing this for Mars, and for the Solar Confederation. I will never work against Mars, as I have already told you...The one thing that I have learned about her, is that she is the greatest tactician you'll ever meet. If anyone's gonna get us out of this mess, it's Jenna Plural."

"So, nothing I can say will persuade you to give this up and come home with me?"

"Oh, I'll come back with you eventually. But only when I'm assured of the security and safety of everyone here."

Before anything else could be said, there was a bright flash of light, and I found myself flying through the air, amidst a shockwave that threw me against the estate's outer wall, winding me and causing excruciating pain to shoot through my head, as I was whacked against its surface. I fell to the ground, completely disoriented and trying to catch my breath. Instinctively, my training came back into action, and I looked up from the kneeling position on the grass to see the east wing of the governor's mansion aflame. I was on my feet in seconds, still dizzy. Panic started to well up within me as I saw Sam lying about thirty feet from me, not moving, and I raced across the yard towards her, feeling relief as she sat up. Within seconds, security was everywhere, checking on everyone. A young security officer in a suit and tie ran over to us.

"Any injuries?" He shouted. We both told him no, although I could feel a trickle of blood running through my hair and down the back of my neck. "Okay, stay where you are and stay down until we give the all-clear."

"There is a civilian in that house that's under my protection," Sam said, and when the agent looked at her questioningly, she answered, "I'm a police officer." She pulled her warrant card and badge from her back pocket.

He pondered for just a moment before saying, "Fine, come with me." We entered the house again, where smoke was billowing from every direction, although the fire had not yet reached this location. We headed straight for the stairwell, but before we even got there, it swung open, and still dressed in a bathrobe, Michael staggered out, followed by Thompson. We led him from the building.

"Any idea what happened?" Sam was asking the agent as we came back out. "I didn't even hear an explosion."

"It must've been some sort of subsonic device," he said, although he didn't sound too sure amongst the confusion.

"That's extremely high tech, and certainly no small-time terrorist group would be able to get their hands on such a device," I stated.

"Unless, of course, they were getting supplied by some government."

I turned around to see Renwick standing there with a detail of security. He was half dressed in pants and an unbuttoned shirt as he approached us. "I'm sorry about this, but I am placing you under arrest."

"I protest to the most extreme," Michael said, stepping in between me and him. "We have diplomatic immunity."

"You're free to go, Mr. Phelkar, but as I've come to understand it, Kyla Lieberman and Abigail Thompson are Martian citizens. And unless they've renounced that citizenship in favor of the Solar Confederation, diplomatic immunity can't possibly apply to them."

Michael looked at me. "Have you ever renounced your citizenship of Mars?"

"When I left, there was no such thing as Martian citizenship. So, I didn't honestly think I had anything to renounce. Not that I ever would."

Sam stepped up. "With all due respect, Mr. Renwick, you can't possibly think this is the work of the Solar Confederation. Unless you think they're totally psychopathic and would kill their own people."

"From what I've been hearing about Jenna Plural, I wouldn't put anything past her." He replied dismissively.

"And exactly what is it you've been hearing about her and more importantly, who from?" Michael said, sounding more aggressive than I'd ever heard him before.

"That isn't important. This is clearly an attack against the governor personally and, therefore, the Martian people. Probably in retaliation for what happened last night, even though we can't be held accountable for it."

"I beg to differ, Renwick," said Michael. "You are wholly responsible for the safety of your guests. You're either stupid or culpable."

The Chief of Staff looked infuriated at this. "Have a care, Mr. Phelkar. The governor can revoke your immunity and hold you in custody until arrangements can be made to return you to that damn fleet of yours."

Sam looked confused. "If you hold the Solar Confederation in such contempt, Sir, why on Earth are you negotiating with them?"

Renwick simply glared at her. "Unless you want to find yourself on foot patrol, I would keep your mouth shut, Officer Washington."

"She has a point, Renwick, and if you detain Lieberman and Thompson here, the Solar Confederation will consider it an act of war. Do you really want to take us on before you've finished discussing your options with the European Union?"

This caused him to hesitate. "You'll be escorted from here and taken to your yacht, where you'll remain until such a time as you can depart Mars safely."

"This whole thing is ridiculous. I have no clue what is going on here, but it all stinks," Sam said curtly.

"I gave you your last warning, Officer Washington. Consider yourself dismissed from your service." Renwick snapped.

"You don't have the authority to do that," Sam sneered. "I operate under the sector council."

"And who provides their budget?"

She was about to say something else, but I put my hand on her arm. There was no point.

Renwick turned to the agent that helped us out. "Drive them back to the starport," he said, and with that, he turned away.

"At least have the decency to allow us to get dressed first," Michael said.

"You have ten minutes." Renwick replied, and then to the agent, he said, "Go with them and let none of them out of your sight."

Fortunately, the fire had never reached our quarters, and we managed to get to the room without any incident. I was, however, surprised when the agent didn't stop me from going into my room alone to get dressed, and I also managed to retrieve the small three-shot pistol. Which I slipped into my pocket. The other two were already waiting for me as I came out. Sam was already dressed, and Michael was still tucking in his shirt. The agent looked at him, then looked at me, and then finally at Thompson and Sam. "I have a message for you," he said almost conspiratorially, and we all just looked at him. "Charlotte Kensett sends her love." My eyes widened, and I looked at Michael, then back at him. Sam just looked confused. "She contacted me after you made contact with Admiral Plural. I'm to assist you in getting out of here."

"You're working for Charlotte Kensett, but you're a Martian," I responded suspiciously.

He shrugged at that and looked at me quizzically. "So are you."

It was a good point, but it didn't put me at ease. "Do you have any more proof than that?"

"No, but think of it this way either I'm here to help you or I'm here to drive you back to your yacht. Either way, you don't really have an alternative."

That was another good point, and I was starting to become annoyed with good points. "What have you got in mind?" Michael asked.

"Ms. Kensett has given me a location to take you to, but first, we'll need to lose the cars that are tailing us. She has a plan for that, too, apparently, but I am not aware of the details, however. Needless to say, it's going to be an interesting ride." He grinned, and we followed him down to the unmarked car. Sam, Thompson, and I climbed into the back whilst Michael climbed into the front. As we pulled away, I looked around through the rear window. Two more cars pulled away, with us following closely.

Sam was unusually quiet and staring at our potential liberator. I knew she was having problems reconciling between helping me, and potentially helping someone that didn't have Mars's best interest at heart. At least from her perspective. "So, if you don't mind me asking you, Sir, how come you are assisting us?"

"I'm with the Pluralytes." He replied as if that was an answer.

"Pluralytes?" Thompson asked.

"It's a growing group that wants Mars to throw in with the Solar Confederation and become part of the anti-Peon war struggle. For the last three or four months, Ms. Kensett has been supplying us with weaponry and equipment through Grant Industries. We hope to convince the provisional government that being part of Jenna Plural's Confederation is in our best interests."

Sam responded coldly, "The First Governor has denounced the Pluralyte movement. He's one step away from declaring you as terrorists."

"Think about that for a moment, man. He happily condemns the Pluralytes, but not the Mars First Movement. An organization that he knows, as well as you and I do, cooperated with the Peons."

Sam sighed. "All I know is this bullshit is all confusing me. Why can't we just damn well have peace?" She turned and looked at me. "Do you understand any of this?"

"To be honest, I've given up trying. But I can confirm Moulton is part of Mars First," I replied. "We understand that someone tried to kill Jenna, and someone tried to blow up the First Governor's estate. Someone is up to some shenanigans to ensure everything fails."

"All I want to do is get back to the Freedom and find my daughter," Thompson muttered.

The sound of a loud crash behind us had us all turning and straining our necks to see. I saw some truck had rammed into one of the cars following us, taking it off the road and blocking the one behind it.

"That looks like my cue," said our driver and slammed his foot on the accelerator, peeling away and turning down a side street. He drove down it about a hundred yards and then slammed on the brakes. "Everybody out." We didn't hesitate as he followed us. I was closing the door behind me when a large station wagon pulled into the sideroad, and I instinctively reached down for my miniature weapon. The driver just simply waved at us as the passenger doors opened and indicated for us to jump in. We did, and there was enough room for the four of us in the back as the agent jumped into the front. The driver was a blonde-haired woman who said nothing but now started driving very slowly and carefully out of the side road and onto the main highway again. We sat in silence as I surveyed my surroundings and looked back to see if we were being followed, but we weren't.

The driver reached down and clicked on some device in the front of the car. "This is Silver Fox to Shadow Mistress. This line is secure. Do you read me?"

I can't describe my surprise when the well-articulated voice of Charlotte Kensett came back. "Go ahead, Silver Fox, I'm reading you loud and clear."

"Both packages are aboard, but there is an extra delivery." She looked up into the mirror at Sam.

"That is most unexpected. Is the extra package a problem for you?" Charlotte replied.

"She doesn't appear so. She fits well with the other packages."

"Very well. I look forward to delivery. Shadow Mistress out."

"Where are we going?" I asked.

The woman looked up in the mirror at me. "Sorry, ma'am, I'm not permitted to answer any questions," she said most politely, but her face remained grim. She glanced up at the agent sitting by her side. "How are you doing?"

"Well, I did expect my career wouldn't end here," he said softly.

"Don't worry," the driver said gently. "Charlotte promised to take care of us when we get back to the fleet."

"What's the problem?" Michael asked.

The young man sighed. "In doing this, we've blown our covers. If we're caught, we'll be arrested. It looks like we're going to be saying goodbye to Mars for some time."

Sam tensed beside me. I looked at her, but she stared straight ahead, clearly ignoring me. I decided not to pursue it at that point. We pulled into a garage of a commercial building, and it was only when we got out that I saw the Grant Industries logo. The agent led us into a side door, and we stepped into a veritable hive of activity. My mind was racing as it tried to work out what was going on. It was military, with the exception that no-one was in uniform. The two Pluralytes, as they called themselves, had been here before, for they led us past the banks of computer consoles where techs worked away feverishly, through to a suite of offices at the back.

The first person we encountered that I recognized was Hannah Grant. She was dressed in simple jeans and a t-shir,t and looked none the worse for wear for someone who had recently been assassinated. To be honest, at this point, my suspicions were running high.

"G'day, Ky," she smiled at me. "You look like shit."

Hannah may have been more upmarket than her sister, but she was still an Aussie through and through. I couldn't help but smile.

"Looking damn good yourself for someone who was assassinated a few hours ago," I replied, trying to sound humorous even though it was very odd. I was aware of the healing abilities of GenMods, but this seemed a little too good. My suspicions were further aroused when we were taken through to an office. The next person I saw was Dodgson, who looked quite bizarre in a short summer dress and sensible shoes, standing in the at-ease position in the corner. She smiled and nodded to me as I entered. I nodded back, but my attention was already turned to the woman seated at the table, deep in conversation with a couple of men, one of which I felt I had seen before but couldn't place.

Jenna looked up and smiled as she stood. "Good to see you all still alive."

She then looked at Sam. "Admiral Plural, I'd like to introduce you to my sister, Samantha Washington." I introduced her.

"Nice to meet you, Ms. Washington," she said to my sister.

"Likewise," Sam simply replied.

"Dodgson, would you see that our guest gets something to eat and drink?" Whilst it was said most politely, any dummy could see Jenna was removing the stranger from the forthcoming conversations. However, Sam went along with it and smiled politely, and followed Dodgson out of the room. Jenna's smile disappeared as soon as the door closed. She leveled her gaze at me. "Can you put your familial relationship aside and tell me honestly if you trust her?"

"I guess it all comes down to what you expect her to do or not, though. She is a Martian patriot and a member of law enforcement," I replied.

"What's her stance on the Solar Confederation?"

I shrugged. "She's uncertain of your intentions." Then I sighed. "To be honest, Admiral, we haven't really had time to reconnect, and it's been nine years since we last saw each other, and she was barely a teenager back then."

Jenna seemed to ponder this and then smiled at me. "Go get yourself something to eat. I need to talk to Mr. Phelkar alone. Get yourself acquainted with everything going on here. You have some catching up to do."

I nodded. Michael looked up at me. "I'll come find you in a bit."

Catching up? That was quite an understatement. I could see people I recognized from the Freedom, who certainly hadn't come down with us. At least, as it would turn out, not in a conventional sense.

I went into what looked like the operations room and saw Helen Tracker in her typical pink hoodie. She was talking to a couple of other technicians, looked up, and smiled as I approached. "Hey, good to see you safe."

"Likewise, Captain." I looked around at the people coming and going. And then back at her. "Care to tell me what the hell is going on here?"

She chuckled. "Welcome to Operation Marvin. Took us about three months to set up. Mostly Kensett's work, of course. She's built quite a network of operatives throughout the planet, mostly made up of those Pluralytes."

"But why? What does Jenna have planned?"

Helen raised an eyebrow. "We're planning to take full control of the planet."

Chapter Twenty-One

Operation Marvin

I stared at her, unable to accept what she'd just said. "By force?"

Helen looked surprised by my question and simply said, "Well, um, yeah...In every city, troops are being delivered by agents from your department."

"But how?" I asked, still unable to believe what I was hearing.

"Well, it's been quite a feat of technology, I can tell you." Helen was in her element, and her eyes appeared to light up. She was a total tech nerd. "We have successfully brought down around three hundred thousand troops."

I stared at her in disbelief.

"Without the Martian authorities knowing? That's impossible!"

Helen grinned. "Until recently, that was the case." She led me to another room, where I saw rack upon rack of small flat cylindrical objects, all apparently charging. She picked one up. "These are portable M.E.T devices that can hold three people each. Some boffins on Enceladus developed them, and one of the researchers improved upon them. It maintains the integrity of a human pattern for forty-eight hours."

I admit I stared wide-eyed, never having heard of such a thing. M.E.T. technology was still relatively new. "But even so, you said you've been bringing people down for months, not just forty-eight hours."

"We installed full-size charging racks on board every diplomatic vessel traveling here. And once Mars opened for trade and industry again, we started bringing them down on the Grant Industries' cargo vessels. We brought the disks down, and they had stacked up with a constant charge in every city on the planet."

My head was swimming, as I tried to wrap my head around all this. "So, Hannah Grant has been in on this all along?"

Helen nodded. "Turns out that Hannah Grant had been part of a resistance group long before the fall of the Pacific Alliance. She'd been using Grant Industries as a cover to supply arms and equipment to the Australian front. As I understand it, she was most willing to help."

"I see."

But I didn't. My mind was a whirl as I allowed all this to sink in. I found myself conflicted. I had no idea whether Jenna's intent was to liberate or occupy. I sighed. "Look, it's been a long night. Is there anywhere I can take a rest?" The reality was I just wanted to get away and be alone as I thought about things and, more importantly, avoid my sister, who I'd absolutely promised this would never happen.

Tracker handed me over to one of her people, who took me to a small bedroom. Once alone, I sat down on the side of the bed, trying to work out all the ramifications of this. I still didn't understand how this would work and what it would involve.

I then heard Thompson shouting outside. "Tracker told me all about the invasion plan! Well, at least enough to make me concerned!"

"I assure you it'll be done as peacefully as possible," Michael said to her gently as I opened the door and stepped out to find them in the corridor.

Thompson exploded. "You knew about this?!"

"Abby, I'm Jenna's Chief of Civil Affairs. An adviser on all matters relating to nonmilitary. I pretty much know everything she's thinking."

"You know Michael, I'm so conflicted right now. Until I arrived here today, my loyalty to Jenna Plural was without question. Hell, it still is! But you have to understand I don't like this. This is my home! I'm a Martian." She turned to me. "What do you think?" she asked.

"I feel the same as you. I'm very concerned," I replied.

"And we are doing this as much for the Martians as we are for us," Michael said intently. "They'll be better off under Jenna's rule than the Peons."

"Isn't it supposed to be our choice though?" I asked.

Michael sighed. "We are on the verge of extinction. Should we allow the Martians to make decisions that would lead to their destruction and ours? If the Europeans get an alliance with Mars, they will once more become unstoppable."

"But weren't they going to negotiate with us?" I frowned. "Form an Alliance?"

"Yes, and we will once again when the time is right." He paused and pondered for a moment or two. "Look, I really shouldn't tell you this, but you need to understand. Jenna was unsurprised that the Martians were bringing the Peons to the table. We found out about it a while back. They were playing games with us, and we found out. To get their agreement, we would have to virtually hand over veto power on everything that Jenna says, and we would've had to constantly supply them with equipment that we desperately need in other places. We would have our alliance, but also be cut off at the knees."

"Then why not simply withdraw?" Thompson asked.

"Because she can't risk the Peons getting control," I said, anticipating Michael's response.

"Exactly," Michael said.

"Who was it then that shot Hannah and Jenna?" Thompson asked suspiciously.

Michael let his hand fall down at his side. He looked down momentarily and spoke. "That was us," he said quietly. "Jenna was insistent on planning this operation on the ground herself. We needed a way to remove her and Hannah from the media spotlight. Jenna Plural can't just disappear. However, if she was dead, it fills two purposes. One, no-one will expect to see her anywhere, and two...."

His voice trailed off, and he looked away from me, and it hit me.

"The attempted assassination of the leader of the Solar Confederation would be grounds for war, if it could be blamed on the Martian authorities."

"Immediate retaliation," he said barely audibly. "They could deny it until they were blue in the face, but believe it or not, the only suspects would have been the Martians or the Peons."

Something else dawned on me. "That's the real reason Plural wanted me and Thompson absent, right? It's because we're Martians, and she doesn't trust us?" He nodded uneasily, unsure of how we would react.

Thompson didn't even go there. "And the Freedom disappearing, is this all part of the plan too? Is my daughter's life at risk, thanks to this 'Operation Marvin'?"

He looked at her squarely on. "No. Absolutely not! The ship really is under attack by the Peons."

"How do you know?" I asked. "I thought we'd lost all contact with the ship."

He had the expression of someone trying to find a way to tell us something that we didn't want to hear. "Someone has managed to make contact with us from the Freedom." He glanced at Thompson briefly, quickly looking away. "It's been hit by an E.M.P. and is completely dead. The Peons have boarded it and are in control of the vessel. Well, as far as they can be in control of a vessel that's been immobilized."

"Who was it that contacted you?" I asked.

"Does that really matter?" He asked.

"Well, it didn't until you just asked her that," Thompson said curtly. "Who was it, Michael?"

He sighed wearily and ran his hand through his hair, and it looked like he was looking for the courage to say it. "It was Bridgette."

"What?" Thompson's look of shock was extreme.

"Apparently, she's working in some guerrilla effort to fight back at the Peons," Michael advised.

"Are you serious?!" Thompson screamed. "I really hope that you told her to stop!"

He raised his hands defensively. "I was with Ky when the call came. She spoke directly to Jenna. I know that Jenna didn't tell her to stop. She didn't have time. However..." He didn't get to continue his sentence before Thompson was heading down the corridor toward Jenna's office, and I followed, leaving Michael just standing there looking worried.

Jenna was sitting at a table with two officers dressed in civilian clothes. She looked up, startled as the door flew open, and Thompson and I entered. "Ma'am, forgive the intrusion, but I need to speak to you."

She looked a little frustrated and said, "By the manner of your entry, I am guessing it can't wait?"

"No, I don't think so," Thompson replied in an icy tone that could be considered unprofessional. As she said it, Michael stepped in behind me.

Jenna looked at me, then with mild indignation, turned to the two officers and said, "Give me the room, gentlemen. I'll send for you when I'm done here."

They simply nodded, got up, and left. Michael stepped in, closing the door behind him. Jenna sat back and looked at us questioningly.

"I need to know what's happening on the Freedom, Ma'am." Thompson stated firmly.

Jenna shot Michael a look, and he looked back a little embarrassed, but then her face softened as she turned it back to Thompson. "As far as I know, Bridgette is fine. The Peons think they've rescued her from us, and she's playing along. Plans are in operation for us to retake the Freedom, and I assure you, Thompson, I'll make you part of that."

This had a calming effect on Thompson, and she appeared to breathe more steadily. "Thank you, ma'am. I appreciate that."

"Please take a seat." She indicated to the chairs opposite her. "While you're here, there's another matter I need to discuss with you both." As I sat down, she looked up at Michael. "Was there something you needed, Mr. Phelkar?" He started to reply, before it clicked that it was a dismissal. He simply nodded and withdrew, closing the door behind him. Jenna looked at me. "Whilst taking the Freedom is a priority, it's not the main priority. The whole future of our efforts relies on the successful completion of this operation down here. How much has Mr. Phelkar told you?"

"Well, I know about the M.E.T. troops and the intention, but that's about it," I stated. "I've got no clue how you intend to pull this off."

"At this very minute, Grant Industries is preparing the simultaneous activation of the M.E.T. devices in every community on the planet. We anticipate complete control within hours."

"Take a planet in hours?" I asked unbelievingly. "Such a thing has never happened before."

"We've never had the portable M.E.T.'s before. And as far as we're aware, the Martians know nothing about them and will be taken completely by surprise."

"And what happens afterward?" Thompson asked.

Jenna shrugged. "We'll assimilate Mars into the Solar Confederation."

"Admiral, I know these people. They will resist," I argued.

"That's Charlotte Kensett's problem. She has the names of the leaders of various groups that would oppose us and will be arresting them at the same time as our assault takes place. I'm not even going to attempt to suggest that this will be a bloodless coup. It certainly won't be. However, I have no intention of making this planet a battleground, I promise you."

I don't think there are words in the English language to describe the turmoil that was going on in my head. However, one thing kept me centered.

"I understand you're conflicted here. It's no different when I order us to attack Americans that are working with the Peons. We are doing this for the greater good, and I want to know that you trust me."

The question was double-edged. She wasn't really asking if I trusted her. She was asking if she could trust us. The main conflict I had was that I didn't trust her, never had, probably never would. She cared about her troops, and she did what she could to minimize casualties without jeopardizing her objective.

"I do trust you, Admiral," Thompson said. "I just find it hard to see the bigger picture."

She smiled. "I understand that, and if you don't want to participate, I'll allow that without prejudice against you. However, I really would like you at my side on this one."

"At your side? What're you planning to do?"

"The fastest way to ensure this goes as bloodlessly as possible is to take control of the government immediately. I intend to personally lead the assault against the First Governor's estate to remove him from office. I want you to be second in command of my unit."

"Are you sure that's wise, Ma'am?" Thompson said determinedly. "That's going to put you at direct risk."

Jenna rolled her eyes but grinned at her. "People with a lot higher ranking position than you have already argued that with me. I really don't want to go through it again. There's a certain amount of morale that comes with a leader who leads from the front, rather than the rear. Morale is a confidence booster, and confidence is a war-winner. Go on, Thompson. Go take some rest, get something to eat, and come back at 2100 tonight for a full briefing on the operation." She and I stood up, but Jenna looked at me. "Stay a moment, would you, Ky?" I nodded and sat back down as Thompson saluted and departed, glancing at me as she left, obviously wondering as much as I was at why the Admiral wanted me to stay.

As the door closed again, she looked at me, weighing me up. "I'm going to need you on the ground with Kensett during the assault on the Governor's estate. I know you are a civilian, but we believe your presence could help make the Governor more cooperative. Are you willing?"

I smirked at this. "I work for you, Admiral. I can hardly say no. Is it more you're yet again asking if you can trust me?"

Plural smiled ruefully. "See you at the 2100 briefing, Agent Lieberman."

Michael was outside in the corridor talking to the two officers that had left the room. I stepped past them, and as they went back in, Michael fell in step with me. "Is everything alright?"

"I need to go see Sam and talk about what's going on."

"Can I come by and see you later?" he asked as I stepped away from him.

I glanced over my shoulder and gave him a smile. "Come by my quarters in about an hour," and he grinned back at me.

However, I looked around for Sam, but she was nowhere to be found. I started to grow concerned. I then ran into Dodgson and asked her about her.

"She d..decided to go home. Ms. Kensett has arranged transport for her." I thought this strange, but truly, I didn't know my sister that well, and I was pissed that she didn't even say goodbye. I assumed it was probably because she couldn't get behind what was happening here and probably didn't want to face me. I headed back to my room and lay on my bed, pondering everything.

When there came a knock at the door, I had forgotten all about inviting Michael. I sat up as he came in. "Was it really an hour?"

"Well, I am a tad early, but I can go and come back if you want."

I laughed. "Shut the door, you ass."

As he came over to me, he asked, "How are you doing?"

I smiled up at him saucily. "Well, I'll probably feel better if I get some more of what I got last night."

He looked at me questioningly with some confusion in his eyes. I frowned softly and rolled my eyes at him. "Get your clothes off, Michael."

He didn't need to be asked twice.

CHAPTER TWENTY-TWO

SURGICAL STRIKE

"Okay, boys and girls. If all goes according to plan, we should only encounter civilian security."

We all stood in the large garage dressed in all-black camos. Our faces were smeared with blacking. Yet, as Jenna Plural addressed us, the genetically modified goddess looked more amazing than I had when I had been dressed up for my bat mitzvah.

"We've been through the plan, and you know what will happen. Our primary target is the First Governor. We will go in with extreme prejudice, but check your targets. A single unarmed civilian goes down, and we may win the military battle, but we lose the P.R. battle war. The entire operation will be done with radio silence, except for when the target is located. It must be reported immediately directly to me. Is everything understood?"

"Yes, Ma'am." We all replied in unison. Jenna pulled out her radio.

"We're ready, Ms. Grant."

"Striker One is inbound." Came back the cultured Australian tones of the Grant Industries C.E.O. "Opening up the hanger."

Slowly the roof above us began to open silently.It was quite a feat of engineering for it to have been installed secretly. However, that was nothing next to what was high in the sky above it. I could barely see the black craft hanging silently against the night sky, completely unlit. In total silence, it lowered itself. It was known officially as a dark energy transport, but was euphemistically known as Black Death. It could deliver troops anywhere planet-side in total silence and could usually only be spotted on a starry night as they twinkled out of sight, as it passed in front of them. It lowered to the ground but didn't touchdown.

The ramp at the back dropped open, and Charlotte and I watched the troops run aboard before we followed them, and Plural brought up the rear. Striker One had been kitted out for a short-range trip and had no seats. We gripped the looped handles hanging down from the ceiling.

We shook slightly until the inertial dampeners came online, and it literally felt like we were standing in a small motionless room on the ground. There were no windows, so there was no sensation of motion whatsoever.

"This is going to be a cakewalk, boys, and girls!" Plural said, pepping up the troops. She knew what they wanted to hear and what they didn't. It was allegedly almost impossible to go into battle with her, without feeling invincible. "Just a bunch of pansy-ass secret servicemen who are more concerned about how their ties look." This elicited a round of laughter.

"Fifteen seconds until we're over the drop zone, Admiral." Hannah's voice came over the speaker, and I actually thought she was piloting the craft. Yeah, yeah, I know, dumb, right?

"Okay, boys and girls, activate your D.E. belts and check your partners."

Jenna stepped over to Thompson, who was to be her partner. She double-checked Thompson's belt, then Thompson did the same for her. As she lifted her head back up, their eyes met. Jenna smiled at her.

"Bridgette will be proud of you when you tell her about this tomorrow." She turned to me and Charlotte. "Get up front, ladies!"

We both went to the cockpit, where Hannah Grant sat beside the pilot, and Helen Tracker was seated immediately behind her. She turned back to us and handed us headsets.

"You can watch through their helmet cams if you like," she said, and I slipped it on. It turned out I was tuned in to Thompson's camera. It was like some V.R. game, as I looked out through her lens. I had to steady myself as I saw the floor drop open beneath them, and I was disorientated as she dropped fast, down to the lawn of the Governor's estate.

With less than four feet to go, they suddenly slowed as the belts were programmed to do. The house was lit up, and even before they touched down, they opened fire on the various lights to give them the cover of darkness. Thompson and Plural landed together, dropping down to one knee. Everything went quiet for a moment once the lights were out, and then we heard shouts that I knew to be the enemy, as none of our team would make themselves so obvious. They had planned this down to the last detail, having studied the estate plans provided by Charlotte.

Plural checked in on where her team members were and made sure that they were on course, and nothing had gone awry. She then pulled down her night vision goggles, and Thompson did the same, and then they were up and running towards the front of the house. Others would be doing the same at all entrances and ground-level windows. Plural's front door assault was the most dangerous, because that was where most of the people inside would be coming out from. When the front door opened, they dropped again to one knee and opened fire on the security men coming out. They went down amid the hail of rapid-fire armor-piercing bullets. They shredded their opponents and the door behind them, which someone was now desperately trying to close to no avail.

Thompson took aim at him but checked herself when she saw the person wasn't armed.

"Get down on the ground!" Jenna shouted to him as they got up again and continued running. Keeping up with a GenMod was difficult, and I'm certain that Plural slowed her pace for Thompson's benefit.

They entered the building, and as they stepped over the man covering his head on the floor, Thompson shouted to him, "Don't get up until one of us tells you to!" I don't know if he heard her, as Jenna was opening fire on more security coming down the hallway.

They made it to the ornate stairwell that curved around as it went up. Going up in a normal manner would make them an easy target for someone on the next level. So, Plural turned and slowly went up backward while pointing her gun upwards, as Thompson guarded them from behind, and soon they were safely on the second floor. There was a long corridor that went left and right. Thompson gave a hand signal to acknowledge a team that had come up another stairway from the east wing. So far, so good. They began making entry to each room, ordering out anyone they found unarmed and shooting anyone who was. I was startled when Plural's radio barked into life. "Mother Hen, we have the target. Location in the basement."

"That's a roger. On my way." She replied. Just as gingerly, they headed back down to the ground floor. There were now prisoners in the foyer kneeling with their hands behind their heads. Everyone from cooks and cleaners to officials in suits. Thompson quickly checked behind the ears of the suits for radios. Whenever she found one, she yanked it out. She then made them move out to the front yard with the other security personnel that had been taken without violence. She then caught up with Jenna, who was already heading down the stairs to the basement.

"He made it in there before we even got into the house," one of the troopers was saying to her.

"Oh, it's not going to be a problem, Trooper Travis," she said, just as they reached the bottom of the stairs and saw what the problem was. The First Governor and his family had sealed themselves inside a panic room. Through the window was what looked like a very comfortable living room, almost like one of the suites we had been provided, but much smaller. Moulton stood there looking angry, and at his side was a nervous looking woman. Sitting on the couch were three children, aged from two to six. "Captain Tracker will be arriving soon, and I'm sure she'll make short work of this. And even if she doesn't, he's not going anywhere." She turned away and called for a sitrep from all teams. The building was secured. "Plural to Grant."

"Go ahead, Jenna," Hannah responded.

"Go ahead and land."

At that point, I pulled off the headset, as did Charlotte and Tracker, and I looked back to see the floor in the main area had closed. We were on the ground in less than a minute and making our way to join Plural in the basement.

"Is there a communication device?" Jenna was asking, and Travis indicated the small device next to the window. She stepped up to it with Thompson next to her and hit the button.

"Good morning, First Governor. A pleasure to see you again, albeit under rather strange circumstances."

"What the hell are you playing at, Plural? What do you hope to achieve? The entire military of Mars will be heading here right now. All you have achieved is starting a war with us and forcing us to do a deal with the Europeans."

Jenna sighed. "That was your biggest mistake, Governor. You treated me like an idiot, and you still think that I'm stupid."

"I certainly think you're an idiot now, Plural! In a couple of hours, you're going to be dead, and I'm going to be dancing on your grave." He sneered.

"I assume, amid all the luxury in there – that you don't afford your people – that you have a television. I suggest you turn it on."

He appeared to pale somewhat as he reached down to a small table and picked up a remote control. We couldn't see the T.V., but we could hear the broadcast coming out over the radio. "All over the planet, Solarian troops have been appearing out of nowhere," the news reporter was saying. "They've been taking out defensive posts and de-livering surgical strikes to our weapons and ammunition supplies. Many cities have already gone offline, and we have no knowledge of what's going on within them. The heavi-est fighting has been in the outskirts of New Philadelphia, but for the most part, they've taken out our bases before we even knew they were here. There have been multiple explosions coming from government centers and military offices. There is no resistance as far as we can tell, and it is utter chaos out there." With that, the broadcast suddenly went dead, indicating that we had successfully taken out planetwide communications.

Moulton turned back to Jenna. "What do you want from me?" he said in the tone of a defeated man.

"A public announcement of your surrender would save a lot of lives."

"And what exactly would happen to me after that?" He sneered.

"Well, of course, there will be a trial for your crimes against the Martian people and the attempted murder of myself and a prominent member of the Australian com-munity," Jenna shrugged.

"You expect me to agree to that?" He snorted at her. She just smiled again. She looked at his wife and let her eyes linger there before moving to each of his children in turn, before looking back at him. "Yes. I do. You will go on record publicly stating that you support an alliance with the Solar Confederation. You will sound convincing, and state quite clearly, that for the safety and security of the Martian people, you're turning over authority to me in this state of emergency."

He looked at Jenna incredulously. "You're out of your fucking mind, Plural! You have no idea what I've sacrificed to gain Martian independence. I'm sorry, but no matter what you do, there is no way I'm giving that up to you or the Peons."

Charlotte Kensett took a step up to stand beside Jenna, smiling sweetly at him. "Well, there is an alternative, First Governor," and at that, she took me by the arm and pulled me forward. "I believe you are acquainted with this young lady?"

He looked at me confused, but slowly the dawn of recognition crossed his face, and he actually smiled.

"Jennifer?" By his reaction, I realized he had no clue that it was me who had set him up all those years ago. "We all believed you were dead."

"Hi, Terry. Yeah, that happens to me a lot." I said softly.

He then looked a little confused. He looked back at Charlotte, and then at Plural. "What's going on here?"

"I don't think you've been formally introduced," Charlotte said with her sweetest smile. "This is Agent Kyla

Lieberman, formerly of the Department of Outland Security."

His eyes started to widen as all the dots started to connect for him. "It was you?! It was believed that you'd died in interrogation! We proclaimed you a hero of the resistance." I said nothing, and he looked back at Charlotte. "I still don't get what the point of this is. Are you just trying to rub it in my face that I was stupid enough to trust this little bitch?"

Charlotte smiled softly. "Well, not exactly, Terry.... Do you mind me calling you Terry?"

"Yes!" He snapped.

Charlotte looked disappointed. "Well, First Governor. Do you deny that you had intimate relations with this young woman?"

He looked at me, then back at Charlotte. "What's your point, apart from making me realize my poor choices in my partners?"

"The whole interaction was recorded, First Governor. My young friend here was wired for sound."

"So?" he said, bewildered at where this was going. I must admit I was pretty confused too. "Since when is it a crime to have sex with someone?" He snorted.

"When that person is only seventeen years old. We call it statutory rape, I believe."

His face dropped, and you could almost see his mind working overtime for an answer to that. "So, you intend to blackmail me, despite the fact it was you who aimed an underage girl at me? This is no more embarrassing for you than it is for me."

"Not really. The Department of Outland Security operated on earth dates. To us, she was eighteen and well able to consent."

"Oh, there you go." He smiled smugly. "Case closed."

"Well... not exactly," Charlotte said again, clearly enjoying herself tremendously. "For you to use that defense, you have to openly admit that you recognized that American law superseded that of Martian law. You see, under Martian law, it was still statutory rape. It's quite clearly the case, that were the United States still in control here, you wouldn't have an issue. However, you can hardly go on record with the defense that you didn't recognize American authority for years, yet now, suddenly, you want to claim a defense under American law. No, even if the Martians don't try you for it, the court of public opinion will. They really don't like sexual predators holding office. So...you have a choice. You cooperate with Admiral Plural, or I'll distribute the recordings of you and my colleague here to every media outlet on the planet. History will report you as a child molester."

He didn't reply and just continued to stare at her. In the role of 'good cop, bad cop', Jenna stepped up to him. "Look, if it helps you out, I'm doing this as much for Mars, as I am for Earth. I promise you once this is over, Mars will gain its independence. These are desperate times, and we have to take desperate measures."

Terry looked at her with utter contempt. "It doesn't look like I have much of a choice, does it, Admiral? Come on, let's get this over with." As he came out and the pair of them walked away, I spun on Charlotte. "Did you really record everything in the bedroom with Terry?"

"Of course we did." Charlotte smiled. "Do you really think we would've turned off the possibility of compromising the young man?"

"Where are those recordings now?" I asked.

"Oh my dear, I'm not even sure they still exist. It wasn't on my highest priority to take them with me when I evacuated this planet." And with that, I realized Charlotte Kensett had just made a successful bluff that was about to change the course of interplanetary history.

Less than 30 minutes later, Moulton was standing out on the lawn in front of the cameras, making a statement that I later found out Michael had written.

"My fellow Martians. It has come to my attention that all cities are now in control of the Solar Confederation. I ask you, for the sake of the lives of everyone the people, to stand down and cooperate with the Solarian forces. Admiral Plural has assured me that their presence here will be temporary, and only for the security of both the Solar Confederation and the people of Mars. I hereby tend to my resignation and transfer all authority to Admiral Plural or her appointed official. May your God or gods go with you."

He stepped back, and Jenna stepped up, no longer dressed in her camo gear with a black face, but with a designer business outfit, no doubt supplied by Hannah. She rarely appeared without a uniform, but Michael had suggested that when appealing to people to not fear the military, appearing as the military was probably not a good idea. She was dressed in a tailored white suit jacket and matching skirt, with heels that almost rivaled that of Charlotte Kensett's. She stepped up to the podium and paused dramatically. With a somber expression, she looked down the lens of the camera.

"People of Mars. I ask that you be calm. Some of you will be pleased we are here. Some of you want to maintain your independence, and sadly, some of you want to subjugate yourselves to the European imperium. But I say to those who stand for Mars's independence, I promise you that you will still have that. It is only the work of the Europeans and your corrupt government that has me standing here today. We came as allies. As friends, to unite in a common cause of freedom, but I was met with lies, corruption, and attempts on my life. The days ahead may be hard. There are many enemies out there who wish to do us harm and sell us out, to what is both a Solarian enemy and a Martian one. I intend to honor the agreements of the alliance that we sought. We will work closely with the new government to ensure a smooth transition to the new order of things. We will be compelled to hunt out the traitors and see how far the First Governor's conspiracy goes. But I understand his crimes are not your crimes, and I ask you to bear with me as we bring Mars into a new dawn of prosperity. Clear skies to you all!"

She stepped away, and as the cameras went off, the First Governor was handcuffed and led away. We returned to the house, as Jenna took over the First Governor's office. Michael soon joined us. "Excellent speech Admiral."

She grinned up at him. "I'm sure you think so, Mr. Phelkar, considering that you wrote it." He sat down in a chair, and I remained standing near the door. She turned on the terminal in front of her and tuned it into a Solar Confederation frequency. She tapped in some personal codes and started reading the reports that came in. "This is better than I predicted." She eventually said. "Every city has capitulated except for two. A French one and the Danish one. I expected many more of the European communities to fight back."

"What do you propose to do about those two?" Michael asked.

"I'll give them twenty-four hours, during which time we'll make it known that all the civilians can evacuate. Military personnel can turn themselves over for processing, and we'll level the city regardless of who remains in it after that time."

Some people have questioned me about why I didn't object to that proposal. The honest truth was, I didn't really give a shit. Do you think the Europeans would have given them 24 hours?

I don't.

Chapter Twenty-Three

Last Train to Brooklyn

L ess than an hour later, we were back at the base of operations, and we were barely off the shuttle when Jenna began giving us a rundown of her next move.

"I had intended to stay and see this through, but we have to think about the Freedom now. Let Paul Bunker know, but I'm making him the new governor of the planet a couple of weeks earlier than I had planned." I had no idea who he was, but then, the instruction wasn't aimed at me. She then turned to Thompson, "Let's not waste time. We don't know the location of the Freedom at this moment, but Tracker has worked out where it's likely to be, based on its orbit speed when it lost power. The bad news is, she predicts that the ship will have started to spiral down toward the planet. We must not only get on board and take out the Peons, but we also have to get the ship active. I have some things to finish up here, so I'm relying on you to pull a team together in thirty minutes. I want to be heading out to the yacht to get us back on my ship."

They would be taking around forty men and women in a ship designed for just eighteen people. Tracker went ahead to prep the M.E.T., and it was done with military precision. With the advances Dr. Mahoney had made to the storage devices, no-one needed to undress or even disarm anymore. As a result, the troops ran in one after the other, and Tracker uploaded them in seconds, and it took less than five minutes to load everybody.

"Are we all set, Lieutenant Thompson?" The Admiral asked as she came up the ramp.

"We're all set, Admiral," Thompson replied as Hannah and Donovan headed up the ramp, followed by Dodgson.

As per usual, Charlotte and I were bringing up the rear, and we watched everyone board until there was just myself, Charlotte, and Jenna left. Charlotte took a couple of paces forward but stopped when I didn't move and turned back to me. Both she and Jenna leveled their gazes in my direction. I shrugged slightly. "I'm not going," I said quite simply but with determination, for I expected an objection.

However, to my surprise, Jenna simply grinned at me and gave me a simple nod. "Good luck, Kyla." She then turned and headed into the shuttle.

I turned to Charlotte, who was looking at me with curiosity. "You know this planet is going to shit in the next few days, don't you?" She said casually, folding her arms.

I shrugged again. "Yeah, I do. And my sister's out there in it, and this time, I'm not leaving my family behind to face the music."

She raised her carefully cultivated eyebrow quizzically. "That implies you're going to leave eventually."

I shrugged yet again. "Maybe, maybe not. But either way, it'll only be if my sister leaves too. Mars is my home, Boss. It always will be, and I just played a part in seriously fucking everything up. Whether that's for good or bad, only times going to tell, but I can't just walk out now and leave Samantha behind to clean up my mess."

"Well, I'll certainly miss you," she said casually.

This surprised me, and I raised my own less well-sculpted eyebrows. The concept of Charlotte Kensett missing anyone was quite the oxymoron if used in the same sentence. "Seriously?" I asked disbelievingly.

She almost looked offended at the implication of my question. "Of course. You are one of my best agents."

Oh, now that was more believable! I grinned, and to her complete and utter astonishment, I threw my arms around her and hugged her close to me. "I'll miss you too, Charlotte."

I felt her entire body stiffen in obvious discomfort. "Oh, we are doing this, are we?" she said and patted me on the back, as if touching a copperhead snake.

"You know something, Boss?" I said cheerfully as I released her, and she looked back at me questioningly. "You really need to get laid occasionally. It might loosen you up a bit."

I think for the first time in her life, Charlotte Kensett flushed slightly. "Oh, I'm probably sure it would, but there aren't many men willing to cater to my personal proclivities."

Oh hell, that turned the tables on me, and it was now me who was embarrassed, as I pondered what particular perversions she was probably into. This caused her to grin. "Take care of yourself, Ky. There will always be a place for you in the Solar Confederation, and in my organization. Don't get yourself killed."

"Same to you, Boss. There are plenty of people out there that probably now want you dead."

She simply smiled. "Oh, that goes with the territory, Ky." She then did something that, if you'd ever told me she was going to do, there was no way I would have believed you. She stepped forward to place a hand around the back of my neck and pulled me to her, kissing me gently on the forehead. "Until we meet again."

I just stood there speechless as she grinned at me, then turned away and headed up the ramp, which began to rise behind her.

The last thing I saw was Jenna Plural in the doorway, giving me a smile and a smart salute. I moved out of the way and watched the shuttle lift off, disappearing up into the sky through the force field that kept our environment intact. Slowly I turned away and headed out of the docking bay.

To say Mars was in chaos would be an understatement. Unlike the slow infiltration of the Peons, the Solar Confederation had performed a blitzkrieg all over the planet. Confed troops were taking control of key installations, and the Peons were fighting back. However, this time it didn't appear my fellow Martians were staying out of it. On the one hand, the anti-Confederation people, who it would turn out were actually small in number and would be quickly suppressed, took the side of the Peons. On the

other hand, there were those that sided with the Confederation, known as the Pluralytes. On the third hand – yes,
I know this is a weird analogy, but just go with it – were the
stalwart Martian independentists. That, of course, didn't
include the people that were gonna take advantage of the
situation to loot and rob as the authority of the cities
collapsed around them.

Fortunately for me, with the Confederation mostly in
the upper hand, it meant my passage through the city was
relatively unencumbered. My credentials as a member of
the Ministry of Internal Affairs got me through checkpoints without question.

The hard part came when getting transport from New
Philadelphia to New Brooklyn. The Confed forces had
stopped movement from the cities in order to maintain
control, and whilst I was permitted to travel anywhere I
wanted to, there wasn't any actual transit operating.

"I'm sorry, Miss Lieberman," a rather officious Lieutenant said to me as I arrived at the terminal to catch the
train back to my hometown. "We have strict orders that
nothing comes in or goes out of this city. I can't make any
exceptions."

I didn't have the patience for this, and I took a page from
Charlotte Kensett's playbook. "I completely understand
that, Sir, but I would like you to completely understand
me. I'm operating under the direct authority of Jenna
Plural. You do know who that is?" Sure, it was a lie, but
considering Plural should now be aboard the S.C.S. Spirit
of Freedom in a firefight, it wasn't like they could call for
confirmation.

He glared at me contemptuously, for what was an obviously patronizing question. "What's your point, Ma'am?"

"Only that there will be serious repercussions if you hinder my transit."

It didn't have the desired effect of intimidating him that I'd hoped for, but he merely smirked at me. "Fine, show me your orders and confirm this."

Shit! Well, he hadn't got me yet. "I'm from the Ministry of Internal Affairs, Sir," I said in the most incredulous tone that I could muster. "Do you really think that we operate with a printout of what we're supposed to do?"

He shrugged, and that annoying smirk didn't diminish. "If you'll excuse the vernacular, Miss Lieberman, I honestly don't give a fuck how you operate. I operate on the system of obeying my orders, and that means no-one goes out of this city. You can report me as much as you like to Jenna Plural, but as a former United States Marine, I'm quite sure she'll understand the chain of command, and be well aware of our operating procedures. If you can't confirm that you have the authority to override my superiors, then this conversation is pretty much over."

Game over!

He wasn't going to comply no matter what I did. I think as I walked away, I muttered 'motherfucker' audibly enough for him to hear, but he was clearly too smug to be bothered by the offensive name. I headed outside of the terminus and found a small cafe that was still trying to operate, despite everything going on. But I couldn't provide a ration book, and they refused to take my Solarian dollars and serve me any food, but the operator was a kindly woman who provided me with coffee and some toast. I pulled out my phone, hoping that I could still log into the computer systems back at our secret hideout. It turned out I could, and I downloaded the schematics of the terminal. If I was going to get through, I was going to have to find a way myself. I've stated several times in this memoir that I have no particular loyalty to the Confederation, but what I did during the next few hours still haunts me. Although I would receive a presidential pardon later, the guilt of it still weighs heavily on me.

I would have to steal a train, simple as that. Well, for most people, it would've been a rather complicated matter unless they knew how to drive one of those devices. I didn't, but that was only until I downloaded detailed instructions on how to.

My next problem was getting through the terminus without being stopped again. And with a quick study of the plans, I found the maintenance entrance where staff could enter. There was a chance that this would also have guards at it, and I would have to take them out. However, my only concern was that of my sister and my nephew. I recorded the directions through the terminus in my head, thanks to my eidetic memory chip, that would follow a course that, hopefully, only the maintenance people used. After all, the Confederation forces were trying to stop the general public from coming in.

With my makeshift plan on hand, I finished my coffee and toast, and thanking the woman kindly, I headed out and back to the terminus. I pulled out my decoder as I approached the small rear door. It was down the back of an alley, hoping they had adjusted the door codes to something the Confederation would recognize. To my considerable annoyance, they hadn't.

I had to find another way, and that wasn't quite as simple. I had to wait until someone came through the door. I hung around for more than an hour until it finally opened, and an older man started to come out. I made my move quickly because if he stepped out of the door and it shut behind him, I would be in quite a fix. He was most startled when I pushed him back in through the door.

"You can't come in here!"

I quickly took in my surroundings. I was in what looked like a staff room with various tables around and lockers matching what I had seen on the floor plans. Now, I'm no military trooper, and although I've been trained in various arts of self-defense, that training fell short of outright murder. However, my youth, compared to his frailty of age, gave me the upper hand, and I brought up my elbow to slam it into his face. He staggered back, clutching at it, with blood starting to appear on his lip. He managed to grab some objects that I can't recall now to defend himself, but I stepped up quickly, grabbed his hair with both hands, and slammed his head down onto the nearby table. He fell to the ground, clutching his head and crying out.

Fuck! Someone was gonna hear him.

I had hoped that I was gonna be able to do this without killing someone, but he now gave me no choice. Not that I'm blaming him. It's not like he asked for some bitch to come in and ruin his day. I pulled out my snap pistol and placed it under his jowls, and fired, jumping back as the top of his head exploded with viscera all over the floor. I had done it this way for only one reason. I needed that uniform, and I didn't want it covered in his brain matter. That was also why I hadn't simply shot him with the almost silent weapon in the first place. I had often seen what people did when they wanted to change into a dead man's outfit in movies, but it usually involved a cut scene, from where they went from the killing to suddenly wearing the outfit, and I can now see why.

I'm not exactly a muscular girl, and even though he wasn't overly large, it was still a struggle to remove the dead man's uniform. It took me nearly thirty minutes, and my plan to avoid getting my disguise not messed up was honestly ludicrous, for it was absolutely blood-soaked by the time I was finished. To make matters worse, the damn thing didn't actually fit me, even if I wanted to put on an outfit now covered with the liquid contents of his body.

I'd wasted so much time, and I was still putting myself at risk, and I felt like an utter amateur. I'd heavily relied on being supplied with everything I needed from the Department of Outland Security. In the two years I operated, I'd always considered I was operating solo, but I now realize the Department made everything easy for me.

To make matters worse, my own clothes were now covered in blood too, and it had been a complete waste of my time. I covered the body in the overalls, in order to maintain his dignity in death and headed for the door with my snap pistol gripped in my hand. I made it through a storage room, relieved that no one was there. I was now hoping that this would be a fortune that continued. Of course, it wasn't. However, one thing you can count on is the typical military grunt being rarely quiet unless ordered to be so, and I could hear the conversations of men and women long before I encountered them as I made my way through the corridors. This gave me time to hide in rooms as they passed, and eventually, I managed to make it to a platform where one of the trains was parked. I quickly looked for one that was on the line that went through to New Brooklyn and found it on Platform Twenty-seven.

No-one ever expects anyone to steal a train, which is why the front cabin was unlocked. I stepped inside. There's one bizarre aspect of the eidetic memory chip – well, actually, there are a lot of bizarre aspects – but there's only one that I'm gonna talk about now. Everything around me was incredibly familiar, despite having never seen it before, and it always gives you a weird sensation when you become aware that it's a false memory in your actual brain.

I started up the D.E. engine and felt the vehicle lift slightly. Fortunately, it was a small train with only three carriages, as there was very little passenger traffic that went through to Brooklyn, and I started to relax a little, knowing that I had made it this far. Suddenly the door to the cabin opened again, I spun around to face a young trooper.

"Hey, you can't be in here. Get out!"

Unfortunately, my response was simple. I picked up my snap pistol from where I had laid it on the console, and I shot him squarely in the chest, hoping to inflict a non-mortal wound. I don't know if I did, for as he fell back, I pushed the lever that thrust the vehicle forward. I kept it held at maximum acceleration. I was clear of the terminus before he even hit the ground. To this day, I don't know whether he survived or not, but I truly hope he did. The sheer force of the momentum caused the door of the cabin to slam back shut, and with that, I was on my way to my hometown.

I'd never seen Mars from the position of looking out straight ahead before. When I'd traveled as a passenger, you could only see it by looking out the side. However, I was too disturbed by my actions back in the terminus to really enjoy it, and it would only be a couple of minutes before I had another problem. I virtually jumped out of my skin when a voice came out of the speaker near my head.

"I strongly advise that you stop what you are doing." Came the current voice of a woman who clearly had that military air about her as she gave me the instruction. "I'm only giving you one chance to stop. We are not going to let you reach your destination, and I've already informed the New Brooklyn Confed security forces to apprehend you."

"My name is Kyla Lieberman of the Ministry of Internal Affairs. Operating number 53198." This hadn't worked with the guy back at the terminus, but I hoped that since I would already be in Brooklyn, I was offering them a fait accompli. At least I shouldn't go down in a hail of bullets...I hoped. "I'm here on the official authority of Admiral Jenna Plural." I then waited for the response.

There was a long silence, during which time I made no attempt to slow down. "Identity confirmed Agent Lieberman, but this doesn't change the fact that you're breaching the regulation imposed by martial law. I must ask you to desist."

"Are you honestly asking me to stop in the middle of the Martian wilderness in a transit tube?" I said reproachfully. "It'll take you several hours to walk down the emergency access platform in full E.M.U. gear in order to arrest me. And since this can't go in reverse and would require me to access the cabin at the rear of the train in order to drive it back, which I can't get to for the same reasons... wouldn't it just be wiser that you wait for me in Brooklyn?"

Again, there was another pause, and this time, it was for several minutes. By the time she responded, I could see the dome of Brooklyn ahead of me.

"Agent Lieberman, you are putting me in a very difficult position. Are you aware that new Brooklyn is not contained, and fighting is still going on there?"

I had absolutely no idea but replied, "I'm well aware of the situation, but I'd appreciate it if you updated me with any more information you may have." Fortunately, she didn't call my bluff.

When she next spoke, she sounded clearly like she wasn't sure that she should be doing so. "You clearly aren't aware of the true situation, Agent Lieberman, because I just lied to you. The situation is very much different. However, my superiors have just told me to cooperate with you, as you may be able to help." Now this made me very nervous indeed. "Fighting broke out between Confed supporters and Martian terrorists." I really didn't like her term for the Martian independence contingent, but I made no comment. "We managed to take control of the situation and eliminate most of the insurrectionists. However, a small contingent are taking control of the Grant Industries air processing plant, and are threatening to blow it up."

"But that would be suicide," I replied in disbelief. "They'd be killing the entire city."

"What can I say? They're fanatics."

I wanted to argue with her on that point but realized that blowing up the air recycling plant would pretty much be the end of New Brooklyn forever. A pretty fanatical move, to say the least. "What do you expect me to do about it?"

"Well, as an agent of Internal Security, we understand that you have certain resources that can get us in there covertly, instead of just blowing open the doors and immediately alerting them that we're coming."

Shit, and fuck!

I just wanted to get my sister and not involve myself in what was going on. However, this was New Brooklyn, and even if I'm starting to sound repetitive, it was my home.

Chapter Twenty-Four

Farewell to Mars

"Okay, fine," I said reluctantly. "I'll help you, but I need you to do something for me. I need you to go to Broadway house and get Samantha Lieberman and her family out of there and to the terminus."

Again, a pause before she replied. "So that's why you're here. To get your sister." She had clearly checked the records on who Samantha Lieberman was.

"Look, are we gonna talk about this, or are you gonna do it? I'm getting closer to the terminus, and if I don't see my sister there, you can frankly go fuck yourselves."

There was another long pause which was starting to irritate me. Finally and quite aggressively, she replied, "She is on her way."

It didn't sound believable that they could have picked her up in just a couple of minutes. "Are you shitting me?"

"Lieutenant Washington is a police officer and was on duty. We have simply put in a call to her to report to the terminus."

"What about her husband and son?"

"We've sent someone to pick them up. Samantha Washington will meet you at the terminus."

I began to slow the train as it reached the city. There was a group of troopers waiting on the platform as I brought it to a halt. I was uneasy as I jumped out, and they surrounded me, thinking they were about to clap me in chains and arrest me.

"Welcome to a new hell, Agent Lieberman." A young officer approached me.

"This is my home, Lieutenant," I said aggressively. "I'd appreciate it if you treat it with some respect." It was one thing for a resident to talk shit about Brooklyn, but a foreigner was a different matter.

"Apologies, ma'am," he said quite casually. "If you come with me, I'll give you a sitrep on the situation." The troopers around me parted to let us through, and followed behind as we headed out of the terminus.

"The sitrep can wait until I see my sister, Lieutenant," I said quite curtly.

"Relax, Agent. I'm taking you to her now." He replied with equal curtness.

As we exited at the main doors of the terminus, there was a squad car from the N.B.P.D. sitting on the side of the road. I smiled as I saw my sister standing beside it in her police uniform, talking to her very confused-looking husband, who was clutching Duke close to him. As the officer and I approached them, she turned to look at me, but her look was one of concern and confusion, rather than a pleasant surprise. "Kyla! What the fuck is going on?"

"I'm getting you out of here," I replied.

"I think I made it very clear to you when we last saw each other, that I have no intention of leaving Mars." Sam protested.

"For Duke's sake, I don't think we have any choice, sweetheart," her husband said softly. "If Kyla can get us out of here, then we better."

Samantha sighed and shook her head but said, "Fine. But we're coming back here, Winston." She turned back to me. "So, what's your plan?"

I didn't answer her directly but turned back to the officer. "I need you to get them to New Philadelphia and on a transport out of here."

Before he could even respond to that, Samantha stepped up to me. "You're not coming with us?"

I shook my head. "No, I need to do something here first, but I won't be far behind you."

This did not seem to appease her, and she looked at the officer. "What's going on?"

He quickly explained to her the situation at the air treatment plant, and she looked at me, then back at him. "Fine. I'm coming with you."

It was Winston's turn to take exception with the conversation. "For Christ's sake, Samantha, it's like you want to get killed."

She turned on him. "It's my job, and it's my duty. These are our people here, and if some nut jobs are gonna bloody kill them all, I'm gonna do what I damn well can to stop them."

Winston sighed at the determination in his wife's voice. He just shook his head slowly but didn't say anything. I knew there was no point in arguing with her, and I turned to the officer, indicating Winston and the baby. "Get them to New Philadelphia and out of here."

"Oh no!" said Winston forcibly. "We're not going without you."

"Winston..." Sam started to protest, but he cut her off.

"I'm not arguing with you. I'm your husband." Then he grinned. "It's my job and my duty to see that you're all right."

Anger filled Samantha's face, but it suddenly dissipated, and she smiled at him. "I love you, you asshole." She reached up and kissed him.

Ten minutes later, we were in the back of a troop truck, and as Samantha waved goodbye to her husband and son, we headed off toward the plant.

"Study this." The officer said to me, handing me a tablet with a floor plan of the environmental plant.

I shook my head. "Oh no, there's a much simpler way than this." I tapped out a few commands on the tablet, and once more, there was a queasy feeling as the plan uploaded into my head. "Okay, got it."

He looked at me a little confused, but made no comment on it. "Okay, so this isn't gonna be easy," I said casually. "Pretty much these plants are vast warehouses filled with machinery, but it's just getting around them based on a grid pattern. You're gonna need to literally know where everybody is, because if one of your men gets spotted, we're talking game over. I take it you have access to the internal cameras?"

"Unfortunately not. They require an access code from the Security Division of Grant Industries, and they pretty much bugged out as soon as the fighting started. We've put in a request with the head office, but since that's now on Enceladus, it's gonna take a couple of hours to get a response."

"Oh, I think I can do that a lot quicker," I chuckled lightly. "Do you have the facilities here to put in an off-world call?"

He looked down the line of his troops. "Bennett, get your ass over here and bring your gear." A short, but stocky young woman got up and moved over to us. A man who was sitting next to me got up to give her his place, and he went down and took hers. "Get me an off-world line, would you?" The officer instructed.

Without a word, she pulled out a chunky device which she quickly powered up. It wasn't like I had the frequencies of the person I wanted to call, but I knew someone who could probably find her pretty quickly. I could only hope that Jenna and the gang had been successful in finding and retaking the ship.

"This is Lieberman to S.C.S. Spirit of Freedom calling on the emergency frequency of the Ministry of Internal Security. This is a Code Red emergency, and I need Charlotte Kensett on the line fast."

The voice that came back to me was a complete surprise, because I was hardly expecting her to be acting as the communications officer. "Well, I didn't expect to hear from you so quickly, Ky. To tell you the truth, I didn't expect to hear from you at all."

"Well, hello there, Admiral Plural. How's it going up there? Seems like a little bit of a demotion to be answering the phone."

Jenna laughed. "Well, let's just say we're not at a full crew complement just yet. Anyway, let's get to the point. We've still got some mopping up to do around here."

I quickly explained the situation and my need for the Grant Industries' codes.

"Let's see what we can do." She replied.

Within a minute, her voice was replaced, with that of the affluent Australian. "Hannah Grant here. What can I do for you, Ky?"

I once more explained the situation, and I heard her call out to Stepanchikov. There was a long wait, which I assumed was the looking up of the magic codes. I couldn't hear the South African's reply, but Hannah repeated the codes.

I then heard someone saying, "Hey, give me the radio hand." The distinct husky voice of Bronwyn, Donovan came online. "Hey, Ky, do me a favor and try not to do too much damage to that place? That's about $980 million worth of corporate assets."

I laughed at that. "To be totally honest with you, Miss Donovan, that's not our first priority. However, I can readily assure you we are gonna do everything we can to minimize damage to the equipment that provides us the ability to breathe."

I could hear Hannah chuckling at her friend in the background. "Oh, good point," Donavan said meekly.

"Take care of yourselves. Lieberman out."

The officer had already had someone input the codes, and cameras from around the plant had come up on screens that surrounded the walls of the truck. One of his techs was switching between cameras looking for the terrorists.

"So, you know Jenna Plural and Hannah Grant?" he asked me, actually sounding quite impressed.

"Oh, yeah," I said, trying to sound casual. "We're like that." I crossed my middle and index finger. However, our attention was quickly drawn when one of the troopers said, "We got them." We looked up at the screen and saw a small group of about four people standing around the recreation area, apparently arguing with each other. Two of them were armed with rifles. Three men and one woman. There was something familiar about the woman.

"Hey, can you zoom in on the girl with green hair there," I asked. The officer nodded to the tech in control of the visuals. The camera quickly zoomed in. "I can't place her, but I know that woman from somewhere."

At my side, Sam, who had changed into civilian clothes before we'd departed, had been quiet for the entire journey so far, deep in thought about something or other, probably her husband and kid. However, now she suddenly said, as if I was stupid, "That's Sally Maynor. She was one of your buddies back in the day."

Sally? Fuck! Time had not been good to her. She looked a lot older than me, even though we were the same age, and her face was pitted with small scars. The once radiant beauty of Mars looked like she'd been through hell.

"Focus in on the others. Maybe I know them too." One by one, they focused on the faces of each of the occupants of the room, but I didn't know them. Sally and I had been frenemies back in the day, but that was a long time ago. We'd been well-known to each other, and I pondered over the seed of an idea. "It might be possible for me to talk them down. We really want to avoid a firefight in this place, if possible. After all, we don't want to damage Hannah Grant's expensive equipment." I said the last bit rather tongue in cheek, and the officer grinned at me.

"Well, they're clearly not professional. We've been through that building, and no one's keeping a lookout for anything. Provided you can get us in there silently, we could take them out with a flash bang and four shots."

"You can still do that if it comes to it, but just give me a chance. Sally Maynor might've been a bitch, but she was still sort of my friend."

He looked quite doubtful and slowly shook his head. "It's far too risky, Agent Lieberman. For all we know, it'd only take one push of a button to blow that place sky high."

I pondered this for a moment, but there was no way I could let them just walk in there and kill Sally. "Fine, drop us off here. We'll make our own way back to the terminal."

Obviously, that didn't please the officer. "Are you seriously gonna walk away without helping me, just to save one person and put the entire city at risk?"

No, I really wasn't, and if he had called my bluff, I would agree to do it his way. However, I simply said, "Every Martian life is sacred. I'm not gonna go in there and have them killed, if we can end this quietly, and I'm very confident that we can end this safely. Let me go in alone."

"You're not going alone," Sam said softly as she checked her police-issued sidearm. I knew it was pointless to argue.

"Fine, let's compromise. We're gonna come in with you, but you approach the targets, and we'll wait outside the room."

I agreed. When we arrived at the site, we all jumped out, and I literally led them up to the front door, which was quite a surprise to them. "They don't have access to the cameras, because I'm fairly certain none of them are Grant Industries Security," I explained as I slapped my small device on the front door and transmitted the codes provided by Hannah. The door slid open, and Samantha and I walked ahead. The soldiers came in behind us cautiously, with their weapons raised. Sam and I were not so cautious and simply walked through the building.

It was exactly the same layout as the water treatment plant that I'd worked in nine years previously, so it didn't take me long to find the metal stairs that led up to the recreation room, silently followed by the armed contingent, who held back a few steps from the top. The door to the recreation area was closed, and I simply opened it and let it swing back, and raised my hands into the air as two rifles were suddenly pointed in my direction, and the other two whipped out handguns from their waists. "Easy, easy, I'm not the bad guy."

The fear and aggression on Sally's face suddenly diminished as she recognized me, and she gave me that stupid grin that I was so familiar with.

"Well, well, well, look what the dust storm dragged in." She started to lower her handgun but raised it again swiftly, as Samantha walked in behind me.

"What's going on, Sal?" Said a burly man, looking incredibly nervous with an itchy trigger finger.

"This is Ky, and as far as I'm aware, she's kosher, but her sister there is a shit-eating motherfucking collaborator, who worked as a cop for the Peons."

Sam scowled. "I worked, and still do, for the Brooklyn PD. I didn't work for the Peons," she said quite defensively.

"You really think there's a difference?" Said the burly man leveling his rifle at her. "You answered to the administration, and the administration was the Peons."

Samantha reached round to her back where she'd stashed her firearm, but I nudged her to stop.

"Okay, let's calm this down a little bit, shall we?" I said, trying to sound friendly. "The Peons are gone, but they can come back because that's what this fighting is about, after all. The important thing here is that we do what's best for Mars, and let's be honest, blowing the fuck out of the air recycling processors really isn't in the best interests of Mars."

"Isn't it?" Sally said grimly. "The Alliance Remnant is taking over. Do you really think they're gonna be any better than the Peons?"

"Confed is not an Alliance remnant." I replied. "It's made up of all nationalities. Only recently, they announced the new citizenship arrangements, and the first citizen is some French girl."

"How do you know so much about it?" Sally asked quite aggressively. "And where the fuck have you been for the last ten years? You literally disappeared overnight. We thought you'd been arrested, especially considering what your parents had been doing."

This completely confused me. "What my parents were doing? What the hell are you talking about?"

Sally's face turned to that of complete surprise. "You had no idea that your parents were the leaders of the New Brooklyn Mars independence movement?"

My brain went into a spin as I tried to assimilate this information. I looked up at Samantha and realized from her expression that she'd known this to be true, but now was not the time to debate it. "Look, Sally, I'm not going to debate the politics of the situation. I'm just gonna ask you very nicely not to blow up this plant and basically destroy New Brooklyn. This is our home."

"That's up to the Confederation forces," said the large man aggressively. "If they leave, everything's gonna be fine, but as the old saying goes, 'It's better red and dead.'" That was based on an old saying when red meant some political spectrum, but in this case, it referred to the Red Planet. Better to die a Martian, than live as a Peon or an Alliance flunky.

"It's not gonna be like it was under the Peons. I promise you that." I said, surprising myself that I was actually arguing for the Jenna Plural agenda. "We actually have a chance to end the conflict without surrender, and without being subject to their rule."

"Kyla, you sound like you're fucking working for them!" Sally said sharply.

"Look, Sally, I'm not gonna deny that. I have been working with both the Pacific Alliance and the new Solar Confederation, but..." I never got the chance to continue because gunshots suddenly rang out, and I saw a faint wisp of smoke leaving the muzzle of Sally's firearm. Then there was a second gunshot, and in my peripheral vision, I saw my sister's gun was out, and there was a neat bullet hole just below Sally's right eye. Then a whole hell of pain hit me, and I clutched at my chest, feeling a wet sticky substance soaking into my shirt. "Fuck!" was all I said, as I flopped down onto the ground. At the same time, Sally also hit the floor. Another shot rang out, aimed at Samantha, but fortunately, they missed, but by this time, the Confed troopers were in the room, and in seconds all the occupants lay dead. I lay on the floor staring up at the ceiling, finding it difficult to breathe, as Samantha dropped to her knees beside me and started ripping open my shirt. "You're gonna be okay, Ky," she said as the unit's medic dropped down beside her and started tending to my wound. All around me seemed like chaos, but everything was clearly under the control of the officer.

I don't know how long I lay there, unable to speak. I was barely able to breathe, because apparently, one of my nice new lungs had been punctured, and was now filling with blood. Samantha gripped my hand as I was lifted up onto a dark energy stretcher which floated up and automatically followed the medic without any assistance. He placed a small device over my face covering my mouth. I don't know how it worked, but my breathing became easier, and I was finally able to talk. As the medic then led me out of the room, I could see the officer on one side and Samantha on the other. She refused to let go of my hand and was rubbing it gently with her other.

The officer looked down at me, smiling quite warmly. "Nice try, Agent Lieberman, but maybe you'll learn a lesson from this one. You can't negotiate with fanatics."

"What's your name?" I asked, barely able to rise above a whisper.

"Emerson Grainger." He said softly with a smile, and I couldn't help but notice that sparkle in his eye.

"Are you Jewish, Lieutenant Granger?" I asked. I heard Samantha chuckle, for, unlike the officer, she realized the question was a typical Brooklyn pick up line.

He frowned at the question but answered it all the same. "No, ma'am, I was raised Presbyterian."

"Oh, what a pity." I sighed but smiled softly. The painkillers the medic had given me were now causing me to seriously trip out.

"Oh, I don't know," said Samantha chuckling at my side. "You can always get them to convert, you know."

"Really?" I responded, thinking it was quite stupid that I'd never considered that option before, and it momentarily crossed my mind to wonder whether Mr. Phelkar would do that or not.

"Winston did," Samantha continued. "Just don't mention circumcision before you get them to commit." She grinned at me.

An ambulance was waiting for me outside, and that's where I would temporarily part company with Samantha. This caused me some considerable distress, because I didn't know if she would actually come with me to ... well ...wherever I was going.

She'd had to forcibly remove my hand from hers, promising faithfully that she and Winston were going to follow.

I was transported directly down to the terminus, where this time, I was taken onto the train on the floating gurney. I actually fell asleep, which I think was due to the soporific effects of the painkillers. When I woke up, I was back in New Philadelphia, unloaded from the train, and appeared to be in some docking port. I was very relieved to see Samantha and Winston there. They were going through some discussions with a port security officer. It turned out they weren't on some list authorizing them to leave the planet. I looked around and saw Emerson talking to a couple of his troops. I managed to catch his eye, waving him over to me.

"Do me a favor and tell that dickhead over there that if he holds up my sister, I'll have him fucking court-martialed." Emerson grinned and walked over. They exchanged a quiet word, and two minutes later, I was loaded onto the shuttle with my sister and her family.

When I'd left Jenna and co, I hadn't intended to leave Mars, but right now, I didn't really give a fuck. I'd realized now that I'd been away too long, and Mars wasn't really my home anymore. They parked me next to a window, and as we took off and I looked out at the stars, I realized that this was my home now.

The void of space and the beauty of the Solar System.

I wanted to find Petrov and go back to the Kamchatka as Ksenia Bortnik. But I never saw him again.

Chapter Twenty-Five

Harper and Harper

I spent several weeks in the Medical Center onboard the Spirit of Freedom. I found myself reunited with Doctor Cooper, who had taken care of me after the Battle of Deep Space. He neither recognized me nor my name, and I saw no reason to remind him. I'd had to undergo surgery to remove the bullet from my chest and repair my lung, but it was nowhere near as severe as my previous incapacitation. It would probably have gone a lot smoother, had I updated my medical nanobots, but they weren't exactly a priority on Mars, and I hadn't had them renewed since I was a child. As a result, most had died off and been dumped in the usual biological way that crap leaves your body...literally. However, thanks to my new ties to Jenna Plural, I received the latest and greatest nanobots from Grant Medical Services, who it turned out the doctor apparently worked for. So after a couple of weeks, I was ready to get up and go. I was just waiting for the overly cautious doctor to sign me off for release, and it was during that time that everything went to shit for Jenna Plural.

As I lay in my bed trying to sleep, I was disturbed when Dr. Cooper came in with a young woman who was carrying a baby in her arms. They seemed oblivious to me watching them as she placed the child into a cot.

"Got a name for her yet?" The doctor asked.

"Sure have, mate." Australian, falsely confident, working class.

"Well, don't keep me in suspense, Stace." Cooper laughed. Stace? Possibly Stacey Grant, best friend of the Admiral and the legendary pilot.

The woman stood upright proudly, hands on her hips. "Doctor Deacon Cooper, allow me to formally introduce you to Miss Harper Jennacia Bridgette Grant."

He chuckled. "That's quite a mouthful."

"Yeah, well, I'm just gonna call her Harp." She grinned at him.

"I do have to tell you that I've got the results of the DNA tests on her parentage."

The tension in the room rose quickly. "Okay then. Let's hear it." She replied uneasily.

"There is absolutely no doubt that Michael Phelkar is the father."

"Fuck!" she muttered. Clearly, this was news she didn't want to hear.

"Do you wish me to inform him, or would you rather I left that to you?" The doctor asked.

"Coop, no-one's gonna to tell him."

He looked startled. "But I'm legally obligated. We can't refuse to deny a parent's right to know."

"I don't give a shit about what the legality is, Coop. Michael Phelkar isn't gonna have any part in my child's life if I can help it. You don't have to lie to him. You just gave me the choice of telling him, and if it ever comes out, you can say you thought I did so."

The doctor hesitated, looking unsure before his shoulders drooped in resignation. "Have it your way, Stacey." He replied reluctantly.

"Thanks, mate." She smiled at him, holding his hand. So, they were romantically involved, early stages but intense. "Shit. I'm late for a meeting. I gotta go." As she headed out, he went into his office, leaving me alone in the room once more.

Emma Dodgson arrived shortly after Stacey left. She had her long hair tied up in a ponytail, clearly indicating she was off duty, so why she was still in her uniform, I had no idea. The doctor had left the baby and returned to the small office off the side of the Medical Center, and I could see him through the window sitting at a desk, working on his computer.

Dodgson looked around and over towards the office, looking in the window while standing in a position to make it less likely she was going to be seen. This immediately put me on the alert, as it was highly unlikely that she was up to any good. She looked in my direction, and I half closed my eyes, pretending to be asleep. She turned away and looked toward the baby. As she made to reach down towards it, Dr. Cooper came out of the office. "Well, g'day there." He said to her, and her head spun around fast, startled at his arrival.

"Hello," she said, standing upright and facing him squarely on.

"Are you related, or just a friend of the family?" he asked pleasantly.

"N...n...either," she said, and I couldn't help but notice, for the first time, the pronounced stammer in her voice.

He looked a little confused by this and glanced down at the child, before looking up at her again. He offered her his hand. "Deacon Cooper. Nice to meet you, ma'am."

"Emma Dodgson " she replied, but as she took his hand, to my complete and utter shock, she suddenly pulled him towards her, stepped in, and slammed her forehead into his face. He cried out in pain as she spun him around and placed an arm around his throat, pulling it tightly. By this time, I was already scrambling out of my bed to go to the doctor's aid. I quickly came up behind her. I'm no trained Marine, and within seconds of my placing my hand on her shoulder, she released the doctor and spun around backhanded me across the face. Before I even had time to even consider a response to this, she followed it up with a punch to my gut, and I went down. I was completely winded, and by the time I recovered and looked up, she was gone. I quickly rushed over to the doctor, who I discovered was unconscious, but still very much alive. I turned and looked around the room, trying to work out what the hell was going on, as I wiped the blood from my nose. When I looked down at the cart, I saw that the baby was gone too.

I raced over to the commlink, wondering who the hell to call. I went back to old faithful. "Lieberman to Kensett. Charlotte Kensett, do you read me?!"

Moments later, the clipped voice returned. "Go ahead, Ky."

"Emma Dodgson just came in here and tried to kill me and the doc! She's taken Stacey's baby, and I don't know what the fuck is going on."

"Interesting," she said quite calmly. "Let's see what I can pick up on the monitors. I'll call you back."

"What the actual fuck is going on?!" I turned to see Stacey coming back into the room, and she ran to the doctor to check on him. He was groggy but starting to revive. She then looked up at me questioningly.

"Dodgson came in here to try to kill me and the doc. She took your baby." I found myself repeating. Abject fear then crossed her face, and she jumped up and ran to the cart bassinet as if she didn't believe me. In sheer terror, she turned back and looked at me.

Without another word to me, she ran to the intercom. She opened the ship-wide communication. "Dodgson, you absolute fucking cunt! What the hell are you doing with my kid? Anything happens to her, and I'm gonna fuck you up so bad, no surgeon in the fucking universe will be able to fix you!"

The response didn't come from Emma Dodgson. Instead, Charlotte Kensett replied. "I've picked her up on monitors, Captain Grant. She appears to be heading to the docking bay. I've alerted security, but there's no-one in that area at present."

Then Jenna Plural came online. "Stacey! What's going on?" But the Australian captain had already headed out of the room, so I quickly stepped up.

"Admiral Plural, this is Kyla Lieberman. Captain Grant has gone. I believe she's in pursuit of the woman that took her child."

"I'm on my way."

The line went dead, and I headed out after Stacey and ran to catch up with her. She glanced over her shoulder at me.

"Anything I can do to help, I've got your back, Captain."

"Thanks," she said grimly.

We stepped into an elevator and went down several levels, breaking into a run as we left. As we passed the bodies of two Peons, she stopped and bent down, relieving the corpses of their firearms. "Do you know how to use one of these?"

"Of course," I said, taking the weapon from her and checking its load.

Breaking into a run once more, she said to me, "I don't know what the fuck Dodgson thinks she's doing, mate. She's just this dumb fucking kid who can't speak properly."

Whilst I was more intent on caution, Stacey just burst into the docking bay without a care for her safety and having little else to do, I followed. In front of us was a large shuttle, and it was clearly powered up and ready to leave. We saw two women standing by the entrance. Both redheads, one dark and one light, the darker one being the aforementioned Emma Dodgson, who held the oblivious child tightly in her arms, and the other was the technician Helen Tracker.

What they were arguing about, I didn't know. The moment we entered, they both spun around to face us. Helen Tracker immediately raised a firearm and pointed it toward us.

"I don't know what's going on here, Helen, but that bitch better give me my kid back," Stacey growled at her.

For her part, Helen looked utterly confused. "I have no clue Stacey, but please stay back. I don't wanna shoot you, but I will if I have to."

Helen wasn't the only one that looked confused as Stacey stared at her in utter bewilderment. Her own weapon was now pointed at the technician. "Helen, what the fuck? We're mates. I know she's your wife, but whatever she's doing, she's fucking batshit."

Tracker glanced at Dodgson. "I don't understand this. Emma, what are you doing? Give Stacey her baby back."

Determination in her eyes, Emma Dodgson shook her head. "No, Helen, it's n..n...not her baby. It's mine. Mine and Jenna's."

"Are you fucking insane?!" Stacey screamed at her.

Helen started to lower her weapon. She was staring at Dodgson, completely unable to comprehend what she was talking about. However, the gun swiftly came up again as footsteps came in behind us. I turned to see Jenna and Charlotte racing in. I looked back at Dodgson to see that she was smiling at the Admiral with a delight and adoration in her eyes that only confused everyone even more.

"What's going on, Dodgson?" Jenna asked quite calmly as she stopped at Stacey's side, but before she let her answer, her eyes alighted upon Tracker. "Put the gun down,

Helen. You're not going anywhere. It's game over, and you've lost."

"Fuck me sideways! Will someone tell me what's going on before I start shooting people?!" Stacey shouted.

"It would appear that Lieutenant Tracker is the traitor I've been looking for," said Charlotte quite calmly. "And she's led me on quite a merry chase, I can tell you. My first ever failure, to be honest. Bravo, Helen."

"I'm not the traitor here," Helen said softly, clear regret in her voice. Her eyes fixed upon Jenna. "I followed you. I believed in you. And here we are, living in some regime where anyone who disagrees with you just disappears. You've taken absolute control, like some sort of fascist dictator! I may have betrayed you, but you've betrayed humanity."

"We're fighting for our very survival, Helen," Jenna responded coldly. "I admit that I've taken extreme measures to ensure that survival, and to give us a chance to free our people back on Earth, but I didn't do anything that wasn't necessary."

"Tell that to the poor bastards you massacred on Phobos. Civilian communication workers. Tell that to the thousands that are dead in the Battle of Deep Space."

"Oh, my dear Helen, that's a bit rich coming from you," Charlotte said with a snort. "It was you that provided the European Union with the location of our fleet, which resulted in the Battle of Deep Space. Those deaths are on your hands, as are the deaths of the crew of this ship, that died when you disabled it with your E.M.P. Don't be a hypocrite, dear. There are more allied deaths on your hands than there will ever be on the Admiral's."

"I didn't want anyone to get hurt. I just wanted to stop her." She wiggled her gun toward Jenna.

"You did what you had to, didn't you, Helen?" Jenna said softly with the sound of regret in her voice. "You made sacrifices for the cause you believe in."

"Don't compare me to you!" A flash of anger crossed Helen's face. "I did what I had to do to ensure the survival..." her voice trailed off, realizing she was repeating what Jenna had said.

"I don't give a fuck about any of this!" Stacey snapped. Her gun was still trained on Dodgson. "I just want my kid back, and I want her back now. Trust me on this, Helen, if your psycho wife harms a single hair on my kid's head, I'll fucking kill both of you. I mean it."

"Trust me, Stacey, I have no idea what's going on here with Emma. This is as much a surprise to me as it is to you." Helen calmed herself down as she looked at the young Australian. "I didn't mean for any of this to happen. We're friends, and I don't want anyone getting hurt here."

"Your wife is standing there with my kid, and Kensett is telling me that you've betrayed Jenna, and you wanna call us friends?"

Helen frowned and shook her head. "Stacey, Jenna is no friend of yours. She never has been."

Stacey looked confused once more. "What the fuck are you talking about?"

"Do you remember the Starbourne mission?"

"Get to your point real fast, Helen," Stacey growled. "I have no patience right now."

"You think Harper died, don't you?"

"Harper did die. I was there." But now Stacey's voice faltered, and the look of confusion grew.

Helen sighed and looked at Jenna before looking back at Stacey and, speaking in a very soft voice, said, "No, Stacey. Harper is very much alive, at least as far as I know. The Starbourne was a highly advanced ship. At the moment of impact, the section Harper was in was ejected. We didn't know about it until I did a full inspection of the vessel, but Jenna ordered me to stay silent. She knew you'd go looking for her, and she wanted you to be a part of her team. Tell me, is that something a friend will do?"

With her gun still pointing at Dodgson, albeit now shaking in her hand, Stacey looked at Jenna, whose eyes were still fixed upon Tracker. A wave of cold, violent anger emanated from those eyes. There was silence, and I saw a tear run down Stacey's cheek.

"She's not lying, is she?" she asked barely audibly, but Jenna made no answer, keeping her steely gaze on the technician.

I noticed Doctor Cooper coming into the room, but he remained in the doorway when he saw what was happening.

Stacey turned her eyes back to Helen, then back to Dodgson. "Just give me back my baby," she said softly.

"It's not your b...baby!" Dodgson replied vehemently, fixing a look of, what can only be described, as pure hatred at Stacey.

"What are you talking about, Emma?" Helen asked desperately. "Give Stacey her child back. Or they're just gonna damn well shoot you."

At that, Dodgson smiled. "She won't shoot me while I'm holding my son."

Jenna finally spoke. "That's not your son, Dodgson. It's not even a boy."

Dodgson looked a little confused now, but it dissipated very quickly. She smiled again. "It's our child Jenna, you know that. Yours, mine, and Michael's."

"I have no idea what you're talking about, Dodgson," Jenna said calmly. "But give Stacey the child, and let's go talk about it."

"That's not the plan, Jenna," Dodgson laughed. "You told me to do this."

Stacey looked up at Jenna, but the Admiral shook her head this time. Stacey turned back to Dodgson, but when she spoke, it was to the Admiral. "I trust your genetically enhanced reflexes are still at their peak?"

"They are Stacey. Trust me on that." Jenna replied, leaving me unsure of what they were talking about, but in a few moments, I would have my answer.

"Yeah, well, we can talk about trust when this situation is dealt with," Stacey growled. Everything that happened next is almost a blur to me even now.

Stacey fired her gun directly at Dodgson's head, but before the bullet even reached her, Jenna Plural was running toward her. Dodgson just stood there, looking dazed with a neat hole just above her left eye where blood was running down. Jenna dove the last few feet as Dodgson started to fall, and she snatched the baby out of the lieutenant's arms. She then spun around to land on her back with the baby neatly clutched to her breast, landing next to the body of Lieutenant Emma Dodgson. More gunshots rang out, and I dove to the ground with Charlotte beside me, as Helen Tracker screamed and began firing at Stacey. She was no marksman, and all but one of her shots missed, hitting her in the side of the arm. Stacey returned fire, but she was too busy looking at Jenna and the baby, and no bullets found their purchase.

Helen was sobbing and looking at Emma, as she turned and ran up the ramp of the shuttle. I fired several shots. She stumbled as I hit her in the leg. I dove onto her back, bringing her down and pinning her there with my knee.

Looking back toward Jenna, I saw Stacey taking the baby carefully from her. She didn't say a word, other than to speak softly to the child and give her a kiss on the cheek, and she walked over to where Doctor Cooper was waiting. As she handed the baby to him, she said quietly, "Take her back to my quarters, would you Coop? Stay with her until I come back."

He didn't say a word but simply nodded. Then leaning forward, he kissed her gently on the forehead and turned and left the room. Stacey turned back toward Jenna, who was now standing again, dusting herself down as she looked down at the body of Dodgson and shook her head slowly. When she turned back to face us, she was startled as Stacey slammed her fist into her face. GenMods can usually take quite a punch, but as I saw Jenna knocked back a couple of steps, I understood the force with which

Stacey had just hit her. Jenna didn't retaliate and stood there rubbing her cheek.

"Is she still alive?" Stacey asked as tears silently streamed down her cheeks.

Jenna stared at her unapologetically. "We were at war, Stacey, and I needed you. What use would it be to get yourself killed looking for your friend?"

"You didn't answer my question..." the soft venom in her voice was more intimidating than when she was screaming.

Jenna sighed softly and, with obvious reluctance, said, "Yes. She was picked up by the Peons and taken back to Pallas."

"Where is she now?"

"She's in a prisoner of war camp, but we don't know which one." It was Charlotte who answered her question.

There was a pause as Stacey turned around and just stared at her. Her expression was blank, as if she was overwhelmed with all this information. "Did everyone know except for me?"

"No. Helen reported her findings to me once she examined the Starbourne," Jenna said. "I asked Kensett to find out what she could do, to see if retrieval was possible. It wasn't."

"I see." Stacey looked deflated, and she looked as if she was about to turn away but at the last, she swung back around towards Jenna and threw her fist once more, but this time the Admiral deflected it with a sweep of her arm. Tears continued to stream down Stacey's face as she looked despairingly up at her.

"Do you have any idea how much I've grieved for my best friend? Do you even remotely understand how much guilt I've felt these past five years, thinking I led Harp to her death?"

"What would you have done if I had told you?" Jenna looked almost patronizingly at Stacey. "You would've gone looking for her, you would've just gotten yourself killed, and that would have been a waste. You couldn't help Davis, but you could help me."

"That's all I was to you, wasn't it? Another fucking war asset." She stepped away from Jenna, disgust and betrayal written all over her face, and then turned back. "I trusted you. I trusted you almost as much as I trusted Harper. I sat with you. I got drunk with you. You heartless cunt...you watched as I cried over her, and you fucking comforted me the whole time, knowing that she wasn't fucking dead!" Her voice began to rise.

"Put yourself in my position, Stacey. What would you have done?"

"Well, I wouldn't have spun you around, slammed your face down on the table, and shoved a twelve-inch dildo up your arse, mate!" Stacey screamed, and spittle flew from her mouth. "Fuck! That would've hurt a lot less than what you've done."

"I'm sorry you feel that way, Stacey. I truly am."

Stacey laughed mercilessly. "And there's the rub, mate, because that's really all you're sorry for, isn't it?"

There was a silence before Jenna said, "What would you have me do, Stacey? I did what I did, and I can't take that back. If I can make this up to you, tell me how."

Stacey shook her head slowly, and with a slightly patronizing laugh, she responded in a low menacing voice. "Oh, there's nothing that you can do to make up for this. You betrayed me, you shafted me, and you fucked me over big time. We are done, Jenna. We are so fucking done." She poked a finger into Jenna's collarbone. I noticed two guards step up. They must have come in while I was watching Stacey and Jenna. They made as if they were going to stop Stacey, but Jenna shook her head at them and nodded toward me. I'd almost forgotten that I was holding down Helen Tracker. She just lay face down, her head to one side, staring at the lifeless body of her wife. She didn't resist. The men cuffed her and led her out. The whole time, Stacey continued her tirade.

"Fuck you, Jenna Plural! You and your fleet can go suck a bag of fucking dicks! And your Solar Confederation can fuck right off! I don't ever wanna see that fucking perfect cunty face of yours again. I'm fucking out of here." And with that, she turned and started heading towards the door.

"You can't just quit on me, Stacey!" Jenna called after her. "We're in the middle of a war. No-one's allowed to resign their commissions."

Stacey didn't turn back or even pause in her stride, as she flipped two middle fingers into the air back at her. "Just try and fucking stop me, Jenna."

Charlotte stepped in front of her, blocking the doorway. A huge grin crossed Stacey's tear-streaked face, as she wiped the snot from her nose with her sleeve and an angry chuckle escaped her. "Oh, just give me a fucking reason,

Charlie. I will fuck you up." Charlotte stepped aside, and the Australian pilot headed out.

Jenna just stared at the opening, and Charlotte took a step towards her. "Do you want me to have her stopped, Admiral?"

Jenna just glanced at her and then back at the doorway. "Just shut the fuck up, Charlotte." She said, and she too strode from the room.

"Of course, Ma'am," Charlotte replied, remaining the picture of serenity and completely unfazed by the Admiral's reaction.

"Have a chat with Helen. I want to know how far this goes and who helped her." Jenna called back.

"It will be my pleasure, Ma'am," Charlotte replied.

I let out a long sigh. "Wow! It's certainly exciting around here, even if I don't know what the hell that was all about."

Charlotte smiled at me impassively and said, "Welcome to the Solar Confederation and Jenna Plural's 'inner circle'."

"What's going to happen to Tracker?"

A positively cruel smile crossed her face, and it made my hair stand on end. "Oh, trust me, Ky. I intend to go positively medieval on her arse. No-one makes me look a fool the way she has without living to regret it. I'll then give what's left of her to Jenna for execution." She then turned toward the door and, with the clip-clop of her heels, strode out of the room.

I turned and looked back at the body of Dodgson. "Hey, is anyone supposed to clear this mess up?" I called out to no one in particular. I was now alone in the room, and I stepped over to the body and looked down at her. Emma Dodgson stared up at me lifelessly, blood pooled into one of her eyes. "I barely have any idea who you were, honey, or why you did what you did, but that was fucking intense."

I turned away and followed everyone else out of the docking bay, wondering what other interesting situations Charlotte was going to put me in.

CHAPTER TWENTY-SIX

EPILOGUE

This is pretty much where this story ends. I moved into an apartment with Samantha and Winston on the Twilight Wanderer. We weren't the sort of people that could afford apartments aboard the cruise ship, but thanks to my association with Hannah Grant, we got a substantial discount.

Samantha even got a job working for Grant Industries Security, and quite a high-up one as she only answered to Stepanchikov, the head of the division. Winston did what he did best, and became a chef for one of the upmarket restaurants that the luxury liner offered.

Me? Oh, that's a whole new story.

It was barely a week after the Dodgson and Tracker incident, and I was home alone babysitting Duke, while my sister and husband were at work, when I received very unexpected visitors.

"G'day," Stacey Grant said as she stood in the doorway. "Can you spare us a minute? We've got something we wanna talk to you about." Standing with her was Abigail Thompson. No doubt you can understand that my curiosity was in overdrive, as I invited them to come in. Fortunately, it was Duke's nap time, so we were undisturbed. I offered them a drink.

"No thanks, mate, I'm trying to quit," Stacey said as she sat down on the couch with Thompson, who also declined my offer. I poured myself a whiskey and then joined them, sitting on an armchair adjacent.

"So, what do I owe the honor of this visit?" I asked, too eager to find out what was going on to engage in idle chat.

Stacey looked at Thompson, who rolled her eyes as she realized it was she who was going to have to bring up the subject of their visit.

"You know about my daughter Bridgette?" She started. "Well, during the attack on the Spirit of Freedom, I was forced to evacuate her when we thought the ship was going to spiral into the planet. She launched into a life pod heading for Mars. I lost contact with her." Her voice became choked, and it was very unusual to see the usually stoic United States Army officer so emotional.

Stacey picked up the story. "We don't know where she is. To be honest, we don't even know if she survived. Sorry, Abby, but I've gotta say it." Thompson simply nodded. "I'm leaving the fleet. I intend to go out to the outer planets and look for my mate, Harper, but I promised Thompson here that we'd go to Mars first and look for Bridge." She stopped and patted Thompson on the knee. "We'd like you to come with us. You know the planet, you know the way everything works there. Even more so than Abby. And you'd be an invaluable help in finding her."

Whatever they could've possibly wanted, this was the last thing I'd imagined, and I sat there silently for almost a minute as they stared hopefully at me. "How long will we be gone?" I asked.

Stacey then looked shifty. "Well, here's the problem. I won't be coming back to the fleet. It'll be a diversion of several months, were I to do so, 'cause it's literally the opposite direction I'm heading for. You and Thompson'll have to find your own way back."

I stared at her incredulously. "That's an extremely big ask," I said, finding the idea positively ludicrous.

Thompson sat forward. "We absolutely realize that, Kyla. But just hear me out. Bridgette is just fifteen years old, and she's French. She's landed on a planet that's in a state of war. Neither side is going to want to help her. Being European, she faces the possibility of either being shot or incarcerated by our own side. She has a high public profile for being the first citizen of the Solar Confederation and won't find a safe harbor with the Peons either, who now see her as a traitor. She's just a sweet kid who's lost on a planet that she knows nothing about. She's my daughter, and if I can do anything for you in return for my help, you just have to say what it is. I don't have much money. They don't exactly pay a fortune to low-ranking officers in the army, but I have some savings, and you can have it all."

I stared at her, and again, a silence drew tension into the room. Until then, I prided myself on my ability not to get emotional about situations, but if you had seen the look in that mother's eye, I don't think anyone could have said no.

"I'm not interested in your money," I said softly. "But, yeah, I'll come."

And I did, but that's another story, and one that my friend Stacey will tell you all about.

THE ADVENTURE CONTINUES IN
THE HAND OF JENNA

PART ONE THE PACIFIC ALLIANCE

By Charlotte Kensett

The British called her unstable.
The Americans called her an asset.
Jenna called her her right hand.

Set up for the murder of a prominent British political figure the Honourable Lady Allegra Hargreaves is on the run.

Escaping into the United States, Allegra finds herself recruited into the dark world of covert intelligence that will send her on a collision course with the woman who will become the most powerful individual in the solar system.

Turning her back of her privileged aristocratic life. It is time for Allegra to reinvent herself.

It is time for the rise of Charlotte Kensett, The Hand of Jenna.

www.ingramcontent.com/pod-product-compliance
Lightning Source LLC
Chambersburg PA
CBHW030924260626
47169CB00002B/370